A SINGULAR WOMAN

A Tabitha & Wolf Mystery: Book 2

Sarah F. Noel

To my father, Jeff.

CONTENTS

FOREWORD

This book is written using British English spelling. e.g. dishonour instead of dishonor, realise instead of realize.

British spelling aside, while every effort has been made to proofread this thoroughly, typos do creep in. If you find any, I'd greatly appreciate a quick email to report them at sarahfnoelauthor@gmail.com

PROLOGUE

The stabbing was sudden and deadly; the knife aimed for the heart with almost surgical precision. The victim barely had time to gasp in shock at her attacker. There was no time to struggle; there was scarcely any time to scream. The attack was swift, sure, and resulted in immediate death.

The killer looked at the corpse, the blood blooming on the bodice of her dress like a glorious scarlet rose and whispered, "What a shame. A dreadful waste of youth and beauty."

CHAPTER 1

London 1897

Wolf and Tabitha sat together, eating breakfast but barely speaking or even eating. Neither had much appetite. Despite the silence, the meal was companionable. The new earl and the late earl's young wife, respectively, had been housemates for not even two months. Initially, Tabitha had considered it a temporary arrangement while she helped the new earl adjust to his unexpected inheritance of the title and the large household that came with it. However, they had recently agreed on a more permanent arrangement.

For the most part, this arrangement pleased Tabitha, but sometimes she questioned the wisdom of her decision. She wasn't sure what was more disconcerting, the thought of one day being supplanted as the lady of the household when Wolf married or her growing feelings towards him. Because while she had tried to deny it for many weeks, she could no longer ignore the butterflies in her stomach whenever she was in his company.

This wasn't how she had felt when she was first courted by her deceased husband, Jonathan, Wolf's cousin. She had been barely out then and in the middle of her season, a young, guileless innocent. Jonathan's attentions had flattered her and delighted her parents, more to the point. Jonathan had been an earl and extremely wealthy, a highly eligible match in every way. A naive young debutante, Tabitha had been caught up in the romance of it all and her parents' pride, so rarely directed towards her previously.

But with Wolf, it was different. He treated her as an equal, and he respected her intelligence. Perhaps more importantly, he was kind; she could never imagine him raising his fists at her like Jonathan had done many times. And despite having a slightly disreputable roguish air about him, thanks to his frequent beard stubble and refusal to keep his hair to a fashionable length, he was an undeniably very attractive man. That beard stubble somehow only highlighted a rugged jawline, and his heavily lashed, brilliant blue eyes, shaped like a cat's and high cheekbones, made for a very handsome face.

Wolf was tall, with broad shoulders. He refused to wear a jacket in the house and usually compounded that sin by rolling up his shirtsleeves. Tabitha had many opportunities to appreciate his well-muscled arms.

Tabitha and Wolf had successfully solved a murder investigation together a little more than a week before. Rather than settle back into a normal household routine, they'd almost immediately been catapulted into another investigation by Tabitha's erstwhile mother-in-law, the Dowager Countess of Pembroke. Truthfully, Tabitha hadn't been included in the dowager's demands for help; only Wolf, "dear Jeremy," had been. But Tabitha was sure Wolf was under no illusions that she would be left out.

In all honesty, Wolf wasn't sure he could have solved the murder of the Duke of Somerset without Tabitha's help. Of course, his old thief-taking partner, now putative valet, Bear had helped. As had Tabitha's maid, Ginny. And rounding out their investigative team was eight-year-old ragamuffin orphan Matt, or Rat as he insisted on being called.

Much against Wolf's better judgement, Tabitha had brought Rat and his four-year-old sister Melody, known as Melly, into the household. Rat was living in the carriage house and helping the coachman and the gardener, but Melly was ensconced in the nursery and, in a very short time, had charmed the entire household. Wolf refused to acknowledge that he was amongst those under the little girl's spell.

Wolf glanced at the newspaper before him, finished his

second cup of coffee, put his napkin on his plate to acknowledge that he was no longer trying to eat breakfast, and said, "I'm sure we're both worrying about the same thing. The dowager's visit yesterday has put us both off our food."

Tabitha mirrored his actions, draining her cup of coffee and removing her napkin from her lap. "I'm not sure what there is to say. You agreed to help the dowager countess prove her butler's innocence. Of course, we don't know if he is innocent of murder," Tabitha pointed to the newspaper with its lurid front-page headline about the murder. "Her insistence that he must be because she can't run her house without him is hardly solid evidence. Indeed, the newspapers have proclaimed him guilty already."

"Moreover, I had been under the impression the investigation into the late duke's murder was a unique event because a Whitechapel gang leader had something he was threatening you with. Is the thief-taking not behind you? Do you not have many other issues demanding of your time?"

Wolf sighed. Tabitha had perfectly articulated the issue. He had never expected to inherit the earldom from Tabitha's late husband, his cousin, Jonathan. But now that he had, he hoped to be able to use his new title, wealth and power to improve the lot of the many tenants, farmers, and factory workers whose lives he now held sway over.

His two predecessors had been greedy, immoral men who had, at the very least, mistreated their employees and tenants and possibly treated them criminally. Wolf had been busy with his man of business, his solicitor and his steward, trying to understand the full extent of his holdings and business ventures. And once he understood them, he intended to rectify any unfairness or worse.

But understanding and managing a large estate, multiple businesses and a fortune were time-consuming. Wolf hadn't considered when he would take up his seat in the House of Lords. Before he did, he wanted to ensure he was knowledgeable enough about legislative issues. Not only had Wolf never expected the earldom, he had never desired it. But, now that he had inherited, he took his enormous power and ability to enact change very seriously.

"You are entirely correct. But, in the moment, I found myself unable to deny her request."

The dowager countess, while barely five feet tall, was a force to be reckoned with. She strongly disapproved of Tabitha, her short mourning period for her husband and her continued residence in Chesterton House with Wolf, an unmarried man, only tenuously related to her.

The dowager also held Tabitha at fault for Jonathan's sudden death. He had fallen down the stairs during a particularly unpleasant drunken fight with Tabitha, ending with a black eye for Tabitha and a broken neck for her husband. Tabitha had been briefly under suspicion for the death but had finally been cleared of all charges. But this was irrelevant to the dowager who continued to hold Tabitha responsible, if only because she was insufficiently docile in her marriage and incensed her husband, bringing his wrath and fists upon her. Aristocratic society had followed the dowager's lead, and Tabitha had been a social pariah for more than nine months. Something she increasingly found she didn't mind.

With a nod, Tabitha acknowledged the difficult position Wolf had found himself in when confronted with the dowager's demand that he prove Manning, her butler, innocent.

"However, be that as it may," Wolf said hesitantly, "my involvement does not necessitate your involvement." He could see her hackles rise, and held up a hand, saying, "Hear me out. There is absolutely no disputing how valuable your involvement was in solving the duke's murder. But that doesn't mean you now have to participate in this investigation, which I alone agreed to. You have many other demands on your time; there's Melly, and there's the education of most of your household staff which you've somehow taken upon yourself. To say nothing of the house in Dulwich. I'm assuming your involvement with it will not end now that the girls are settled there."

As part of their last investigation, Tabitha and Wolf rescued a group of young girls sold into prostitution in a brothel owned by the murdered duke. The duke's heir, Anthony, the Duke of Somerset, had been appropriately horrified by his late father's actions and had sworn to do whatever was necessary to rectify the situation. Everyone involved in the rescue had decided that the best course of action was to sell the building in Holborn housing the brothel and purchase a new home for the girls in Dulwich. The girls had moved there, under the no-nonsense but kindly care of Bear's mother, Mrs Caruthers, known as Mother Lizzy. The intention was to care for and educate them for as long as needed.

"Well, Anthony has asked me to continue to be involved in the girls' education," Tabitha acknowledged.

"There you go then. You have many worthy demands on your time and should feel no pressure to engage in whatever activities I must undertake to fulfil my promise to Lady Pembroke."

Tabitha found herself in a difficult position; while she disapproved of Wolf's agreeing to investigate on behalf of the dowager's butler, she didn't want to be left out. In truth, the investigation had been the most interesting and thought-provoking thing she had ever done. A good student as a child with an inquisitive mind and a thirst for knowledge, her marriage had put paid to any opportunities she had to engage her intellect. As Jonathan's wife, her only jobs were to ensure the household ran smoothly and to be the perfect ornament on his arm at social events.

The investigation had awakened her love of puzzles. It reminded her of her ability to organise and analyse complex information. She knew she had been an integral part of solving the murder. She had realised who the murderer was, likely long before Wolf would ever have realised it alone. She might disapprove of him undertaking the investigation but would be damned if she'd be excluded.

"Well," she said hesitantly. But the smirk on Wolf's face made clear that he fully understood her dilemma. "You know what the issue is, don't you?" she demanded tartly.

"I know you enjoyed participating in the investigation and do not wish to be left out of this one. Am I correct?"

"Fine! Yes, you're correct. I disapprove of your taking on the assignment, but given that you have, I insist on participating."

Wolf stood from the breakfast table and said, "Then let us not hesitate any longer and begin our investigations."

Tabitha couldn't deny the excitement she felt at his words. "Where do we start?"

CHAPTER 2

Tabitha and Wolf agreed that the first step was to better understand the crime with which Manning was charged. "Much as I loathe to admit it, Bruiser is likely my best source of information," Wolf acknowledged.

Bruiser was a detective inspector who had grown up in Whitechapel and now policed the area with a somewhat fluid sense of morality. Known to be good with his fists as a young man, he now patrolled his old neighbourhood using many of the same bully-boy tactics. But he also had genuine compassion for the people in the neighbourhood living in such abject poverty and misery. But, as Wolf knew all too well, Bruiser wasn't above supplementing his income by occasionally helping on the criminal side of the fence, particularly when the work came from the local gang leader, Mickey D.

Bruiser and Wolf had a wary respect for each other. They had worked together in the past, but neither expected loyalty from the other. Bruiser was one of the few people from Wolf's past aware of his new status as an earl. As far as Wolf knew, Bruiser kept this information close to his chest, at least for now. Wolf had no doubt Bruiser would use his silence as currency in the future if necessary.

Wolf knew Tabitha would want to participate in his meeting with Bruiser. In their previous investigation, he had pushed back successfully on occasion with such demands but had also been forced to give in quite a few times, much against his better judgement. He had the utmost respect for Tabitha's intellect and courage. Still, there were some places in London he couldn't expose her to, and The Cock, the notorious Whitechapel public house frequented by Bruiser, was one of those places.

Tabitha railed against such attempts to protect her or keep her in a gilded cage as she saw it. Her determination to be involved in every aspect of Wolf's investigative activities had even led her to wear some of his clothes and attempt to pass as a young man when they visited Mickey D's home. But while even Wolf had admitted her disguise was better than he might have expected, he also knew it hadn't fooled Mickey D for a moment.

"I agree," Tabitha said, "Mr Bruiser would be a good place for us to start."

Wolf sighed, "Tabitha, do we have to have this same battle repeatedly? You know why I can't take you with me. Why I won't take you with me." He held up a hand to forestall her inevitable argument, "And no, this has nothing to do with seeing your contributions as less valuable because you're a woman. Quite the contrary, you have a feminine insight that has proven invaluable. You know what this is about. Whitechapel is no place for you, and The Cock certainly isn't."

Tabitha started to interrupt, but Wolf continued, "And no, coming disguised as a man is not an option."

"I think my disguise was very effective last time," Tabitha pouted.

"Do you? Do you really? Mickey saw through it immediately, and I'm sure Angie did too, and that was at night. I'm planning to go this morning. You cannot pass for a young man in broad daylight. Nothing you can say will convince me otherwise."

"Fine," Tabitha said, pouting again. But, realising how childish she sounded, she immediately rearranged her face. "Then what can I do?"

"Honestly, nothing at this point. Go to the nursery and play with Melly. We both know that once this investigation is in full flight, you won't have much time to devote to anything else. And I know you felt guilty about that before. So, spend time with her now. When I return, we will discuss everything Bruiser has to say to me, and there will be plenty you can be part of. I promise."

Tabitha knew Wolf was right about it all. She might rail against her exclusion from trips to Whitechapel, but even in disguise, the neighbourhood had scared her. It felt as if the very air itself was darker, heavier, and more weighted with danger than Mayfair. She had both been appalled at the extreme poverty she had witnessed and afraid of what those paupers might do if they realised she was a countess living a charmed life in a Mayfair mansion.

Even though Wolf was born the grandson of an earl and educated at Eton and Oxford, he spent many years living and working in and around Whitechapel. He may have always been different from the citizens of Whitechapel, but he also knew how to blend into the neighbourhood well enough. No disguise was good enough to enable Tabitha to blend in. So, she acknowledged his argument, realising this was not the hill she wished to die on.

Happy she had accepted his word on this subject but fully aware this would not be the last time they had such a conversation, Wolf went to his room to change into his old thief-taking attire. He had no intention of going to Whitechapel as the Earl of Pembroke. When he had visited in the past, he had taken a hackney cab to the outskirts of the neighbourhood and then walked. Such was his intention this morning as well.

When he had cast off his thief-taking life, or thought he had at least, Wolf had spread a story that he had left town. Luckily, no one other than Bruiser had thought to question that story or why Wolf had occasionally appeared again over the last few weeks. Most people in Whitechapel were too concerned with where they would get enough food to feed their families to mind his business.

Walking through Whitechapel, Wolf was reminded what a depressing place it was. He hadn't lived in Mayfair for two months yet had become used to its clean streets and sweet-smelling air.

The Cock was a notorious public house located in the heart of Whitechapel. Its hand-painted sign featuring a rooster swung outside the door, creaking in the wind. Dimly lit, it smelled of stale beer and tobacco smoke mixed with the scent of burning coal.

Despite its rough reputation, The Cock remained a popular spot among the working-class men of Whitechapel, who found solace in its cheap drinks and rowdy atmosphere. But, it attracted certain criminal elements in the area, making it a place to avoid for the more timid or law-abiding citizens.

The decor had not changed much over the years. Faded paintings and photographs adorned the walls, and the furnishings were basic and worn. The fireplace remained, providing warmth and light on cold winter nights. The publican, Bill, known as Old One-Eye, had been in charge for as long as most people could remember. His gruff demeanour and short temper were infamous among the regulars.

In his thief-taking days, Wolf had often used The Cock as an informal office. He once did Old One-Eye a favour, which the publican had always remembered. Much as people had always known they could find Wolf and Bear in The Cock, or someone there would know where they were, Wolf now went there in search of Bruiser.

The Cock made a delicious meat pie. Even though Wolf now had most of his meals cooked by the very talented Mrs Smith, he still found himself craving one of these meat pies on occasion, washed down by their equally excellent ale. He knew Bruiser was also very fond of the pie and ale, and indeed, as soon as he entered The Cock, he spotted the policeman enjoying that very meal. Wolf ordered the same for himself and joined Bruiser at his table.

Bruiser was finishing up the last mouthful of his pie, and a small stream of gravy ran down his chin. As Wolf approached, the policeman nodded a greeting and wiped his chin with a handkerchief he pulled from his pocket. "Didn't expect to see you around here anytime soon," Bruiser said, raising his eyebrows as he spoke.

"From what I've heard, the investigation into the theft of the Somerset Diamonds suddenly stopped, and even the family seemed to lose interest in discovering who murdered the duke.

The general feeling in the force is that it was Mickey D's nephew, Seamus, who was responsible for both. And he seems to have disappeared. The word is, he may have hopped a boat to America."

"Is that so?" Wolf asked, trying to convey a casual disinterest.

"I think you know that's so," the other man claimed. "The most interesting part of the whole thing is that even Mickey D seems suddenly to not care about proving Seamus' innocence. Now, why do you think that would be?"

Wolf did not doubt that the policeman, even if he didn't know all the details, had some strong suspicions about what had happened. Despite Bruiser's sometimes conflicted loyalties, Wolf knew he couldn't come out and confess the truth that Her Grace, the Dowager Duchess of Somerset, had killed her paedophile of a son before he had a chance to assault his eight-year-old daughter the same way he had his sister. Nor that Mickey D had been persuaded to let the matter go by being assured that the diamond search would end and that Seamus would be well taken care of.

Wolf knew better than to take Bruiser for a fool, "Let's just say the matter was concluded to everyone's satisfaction, and justice was served."

"Justice was served, was it? I guess I'll have to take your word for that. So, what brings you back to Whitechapel if that case is closed?"

"Against my better judgement, I've been dragged into another case. The Dowager Countess of Pembroke's butler, Mr Manning, has been arrested for murder. I don't know any more details than those. But she has demanded that I exonerate the man. I assume you either know the case details or can find them out. It would also be very helpful to find out who performed the autopsy."

Bruiser took another sip of his ale and looked over his glass at Wolf, "Maybe I do, and maybe I don't. But why would I share that information with you?"

"I also know you have criminal connections, not the least, our mutual friend, but also some powerful connections high-up in the police force. Maybe even in government. You're a smart man who knows how to play both sides of the law to his advantage."

"Maybe that's true, and maybe it isn't. What does any of that have to do with you?"

Wolf hated to use his newly acquired title, but he recognised it had its uses, "Bruiser, let me be blunt. You know who I am. I am now one of those high-up people on whose right side you want to be."

Bruiser chuckled, "I think I liked Wolf the thief-taker better than Wolf, the Earl of Pembroke. However, your point is well taken. I'll see what I can find out today. Send the lad tonight, and I'll give him what details I can find out. Mind, I'm not promising anything. But I can at least find out what I can about the evidence against this butler. I assume you read the newspaper this morning, like everyone else. So you know the victim was a high-end prostitute? She must have done well to have owned a nice house in Chelsea." Bruiser winked at Wolf, "Of course, Chelsea isn't as swanky as your new neighbourhood, Mayfair, but it's not bad for a lass who makes her money opening her legs."

"No need to be crude." Wolf remarked, "But you're right; the victim must have been servicing a higher-end clientele than Old Ma Hutchins." He pondered, more to himself than to the policeman, "A girl doing that well could have had just one very wealthy patron."

"Well, that's not what the rags are saying," Bruiser pointed out.

Unlike most other peers, Wolf didn't only have The Times delivered each morning. He kept abreast of less salubrious newsworthy items by reading many of the same 'rags' he suspected Bruiser did. So he knew what the other man was referring to. According to the more sensationalist dailies, Manning had been one of Collette's clients who had become obsessed with her and killed her in a jealous rage.

Wolf answered, "I think we both know that, whether or not Mr Manning killed her, it wasn't because he was a client. A butler doesn't make the money necessary to frequent a high-end prostitute. He would have been lucky to afford one of Old Ma Hutchins's girls." Bruiser nodded his agreement.

CHAPTER 3

Wolf had decided to walk back to Mayfair from Whitechapel. Before ascending to the earldom and having a comfortable, well-sprung carriage at his disposal, he and Bear had walked a lot. Now, between much less daily exercise and regular, excellent food courtesy of Mrs Smith, his cook, he was starting to feel his waistband get a little tight. Wolf was determined not to become one of those portly lords with a bulbous red nose and gout.

Walking also allowed him to think about where to take the investigation next. It also gave him time to consider what he would say to Tabitha about involving Rat again. When he'd agreed to allow Rat and his sister Melody to be part of his household, the agreement had been that Rat would be part of the household staff and run errands for Wolf. But, when he and Tabitha had made that arrangement, she had only just found out about Wolf's previous life as a thief-taker and that he had sometimes used Rat as an errand boy.

Later, she discovered those errands sometimes included picking locks and housebreaking. Tabitha had been extremely unhappy that Rat had continued some of these activities at Wolf's request as part of their investigation into the duke's murder. She was encouraging Rat to learn to read and to bathe regularly. Generally, to have a fresh start in life. She didn't want him sucked back into any part of his old life.

Privately, Wolf had been sceptical that an eight-year-old Whitechapel street urchin, who had led a rough and tumble life even before his parents had died, leaving him in charge of his four-year-old sister, could assimilate into a Mayfair household. Of course, he mused, the same might be said of Wolf himself.

And to his surprise, the boy had done an excellent job fitting into the household staff.

The situation was complicated because his sister, Melody, lived in the nursery and was treated as a surrogate daughter by Tabitha. Rat was granted certain privileges because of this, such as taking meals in the nursery with his sister. But, he navigated the household politics well and had ingratiated himself with everyone. He was an intelligent boy and a hard worker. Wolf knew that Tabitha would argue it was precisely because he was doing such a good job of fitting in that they shouldn't drag him back into any aspects of his old life. Wolf consoled himself with the thought that all he was having the boy do was collect a message. But he knew that rationale wouldn't convince Tabitha that the errand was benign.

Wolf was so absorbed in his thoughts that he didn't realise a carriage had slowed beside him. He recognised the same Pembroke insignia that adorned his carriage.

If there had been any doubt about what that meant, the commanding voice directed at him put paid to that, "Jeremy! What on earth are you doing walking the streets of London? And in such an outfit." The Dowager Countess of Pembroke had taken quite a shine to her son's heir. Sometimes Wolf was a little worried that it was more than a shine. There was something uncomfortably flirtatious about the older woman's behaviour towards him.

By this point, both Wolf and the carriage had come to a standstill, and the dowager was leaning out of the carriage window, her steel grey eyes squinting in consternation. The dowager had some vague sense of Wolf's career before becoming an earl, but even so, seeing him in his old clothes and wandering the streets of London caught her by surprise. Given she was the one who had propelled him back into an investigation, he wasn't sure why she was as confused as she seemed to be, and he told her as much.

"Jeremy, I asked you to help Manning, not debase yourself and the earldom by rambling around dressed as a pauper."

Wolf couldn't help raising his eyebrows. The clothes from his previous life were hardly of the quality he now wore as the Earl of Pembroke. However, they were clean, and his boots weren't scuffed. Even in his thief-taking days, he'd taken some care with his clothes, and the ones he'd chosen to keep were those in the best condition. However, he let the dowager's melodramatic judgements slide and said, "Lady Pembroke, you are looking particularly well today."

Even though this was blatant flattery, the dowager blushed like a debutante at her first ball and batted her eyelids, "Jeremy, you naughty boy, you know how to charm a lady. However, I cannot let the Earl of Pembroke continue to walk the streets, and in such attire. What will people say?"

The dowager was a force to be reckoned with; she considered herself the doyenne of society and was more skilled than any battlefield general in manipulating people and situations to keep herself at the pinnacle of aristocratic circles. Wolf knew that "What will people say?" meant "What will they say about me?" For the dowager, any event was refracted through the lens of how it might reflect on her. He wasn't sure why his outfit and mode of transport were connected to her, but Wolf knew better than to say such a thing.

"Why are you walking when you have a carriage? What will be next? Is it the Earl of Pembroke on one of those omnibuses or underground train contraptions? Heaven forbid!" Before becoming an earl, Wolf occasionally travelled by omnibus, tram, and underground trains. But he had found the omnibuses and trams slow, given the traffic congestion in London, and the underground train made him claustrophobic. He had always enjoyed walking and found it conducive to problem-solving.

The dowager continued her tirade, "Now, please get in the carriage. I will accompany you back to Chesterton House, and you can update me on how soon you will prove Manning's innocence."

Wolf sighed. It had been barely twenty-four hours since the dowager had demanded he investigates the case, yet she was already impatiently demanding results. Furthermore, despite his questions about whether a butler could afford to be the customer of a high-end prostitute, he still had no reason to believe the man was innocent. But he knew there was no point in mentioning this to the dowager, at least not yet. Resigned to his fate, he climbed into the carriage and allowed her to accompany him home.

On entering his palatial Mayfair residence with the dowager countess in tow, Wolf made eye contact with his butler Talbot. "Milady, milord," the inscrutable butler said, "shall I serve tea in the drawing room?"

"Lady Pembroke, if you don't mind, I will change out of these clothes into something more appropriate and will return shortly," Wolf explained. He intended to find Tabitha. The last thing she would want is to stumble across the dowager without warning.

"Well, don't be long, Jeremy dear. But I do agree that you need to change your clothes. I can only pray that nosy, old gossip, Lady Davenport, wasn't looking out of her windows and saw me accompany you in that outfit." Wolf did agree with this sentiment. He usually slipped in and out of the back door while wearing his old clothes. Wolf left the dowager countess to Talbot's ministrations and rushed to his room. He changed quickly and headed to the nursery, hoping to find Tabitha there.

Tabitha was in the nursery. He stopped in the doorway, watching her sit at the child-size table and chairs practising letters with the adorable little girl she had become so attached to. Melody had red-gold ringlets and a spray of freckles across her nose. Tabitha had been unable to bring a baby to term during her marriage to Jonathan, and Wolf knew she had latched onto Melody as the daughter she had been unable to have. Melody was a delightful little girl who had acclimated to her new and very different life surprisingly quickly. While he wouldn't want to call such a young child manipulative, Melody was smart enough to have the good sense to charm all the adults she came into contact with. Particularly Tabitha. If Wolf were honest, she had charmed him as well, despite his attempts to resist.

Wolf continued to worry about the potential long-term dilemmas and even heartbreak involved with bringing this child into the household. Tabitha had persuaded Rat to let Melody live in the nursery and to stay near her as part of the household staff. Wolf had questioned what Tabitha might do if and when Rat decided to leave Wolf's employ. Would she let him take Melody with him? At the time, Tabitha had said yes, but Wolf couldn't imagine her being able to let the child go if that time should ever come. And, of course, with every passing week that went by, it became harder and harder to imagine how this young child, who had completely adapted to life as the ward of a countess in the home of an earl, could ever be expected to return to a dramatically lesser lifestyle. Wolf could only pray none of them ever had to face that possibility.

Tabitha looked up, and Melody immediately ran over and embraced his knees, "Wolfie, Wolfie, come and play!" Despite his better judgement, the child had started calling him Wolfie, which he found charming. He knew Tabitha loved to hear the nickname, if only because she hoped Wolf would fall as in love with Melody as she had, thereby helping to ensure the girl's continued welcome at Chesterton House. Of course, Tabitha had made it abundantly clear on multiple occasions that if Melody and Rat were not welcome, she would move out and set up her own household. Besides the fact that he had no idea how to manage a household the size of Chesterton House, Wolf didn't want her to leave. He was beginning to realise he didn't want her to ever leave.

Wolf crouched down and accepted Melody's embrace, "Are you being a good student, Miss Melly, and learning your letters?"

"Oh yes, Tabby Cat said I'm doing very well."

Wolf smiled at the child's nickname for Tabitha. In deference to her title, Rat called her m'lady Tabby Cat.

"Well, I'm delighted to hear it. But Mary must keep helping you because I need to talk to Tabby Cat."

"But, I want you to read to me!" the child said, pouting.

"I promise I will come and read to you before bed tonight if you're a good girl for Mary now." On multiple occasions, since she had come to live with them, Wolf had found himself in an armchair with Melody ensconced on his lap while he read to her. He honestly was unsure where the innocent guilelessness of a small child stopped and the calculated manipulations of a little girl who knew how to wrap adults around her little finger began.

He managed to disentangle himself from Melody and sent her back to sit at the table with her nursery maid, Mary. Tabitha stood up and followed him out of the room. In the hallway, away from sharp little ears, she asked, "What is the matter?"

"The dowager is here."

"Now? Why? I'm sure I didn't receive a note from her this morning," Tabitha was flustered. She looked down at her simple day dress, perfect for a morning in the nursery but hardly appropriate for receiving guests, let alone receiving the dowager countess. Having only gone into half-mourning shortly before Wolf arrived at Chesterton House, she had recently made the scandalous decision not to even bother with its greys and lavenders.

If that wasn't bad enough, she had started updating her wardrobe to be less conservative than the rather prim and austere clothes favoured for her by her deceased husband. Despite her own recent shift out of mourning attire, the dowager had made clear her disapproval of Tabitha's casting off of full mourning after less than a year. The dowager's excuse for doing so was that if his wife couldn't be bothered to mourn him properly, why should his mother? Tabitha hadn't bothered to point out the irrationality of such a statement.

Trying to decide on the greater crime, receiving the dowager underdressed or making her wait for company, Tabitha decided the dowager would complain about any dress that wasn't black bombazine, so she might as well stay dressed as she was.

Tabitha was unclear as to the reason for the dowager's visit. Of course, the older woman had made unannounced calls in the past. In fact, she'd made one only the previous morning to demand Wolf take on their current investigation. But that very recent visit made her current one even more surprising. Wolf quickly clarified the situation, "I was walking back from my meeting with Bruiser in Whitechapel when the dowager countess came upon me. Apparently, if I am seen walking the streets of London rather than taking my carriage, it will reflect poorly on her. I'm not sure why it will. But I didn't argue and instead, let her drive me home. At which point, she insisted on coming in to get an update on the investigation."

"But it's been little more than twenty-four hours; how much progress can she expect?" In reply, Wolf merely shrugged his shoulders.

CHAPTER 4

The dowager's drawing room had been furnished for her diminutive frame rather than anyone else's comfort. Tabitha had never been sure whether this was a power play or selfishness. Perhaps both. There was no doubt that the dowager used her guests' inevitable discomfort to her advantage whenever possible. During recent visits by the dowager, Tabitha had taken a leaf from her mother-in-law's battle tactics and claimed the higher chair, leaving her guest looking up at her from the lower settee. But on this visit, with the first-mover advantage, the dowager stole the loftier perch. When Tabitha entered the room, the smirk on the other woman's face made clear this was no accidental arrangement.

As Tabitha had anticipated, the dowager looked her mint-green day dress up and down, disapproval clear on her face. Unusually, she kept her opinion to herself. Tabitha considered the surprising lack of criticism and realised that any battle-hardened general knew when to hold their firepower. The dowager wanted their help. Well, she wanted Wolf's help. But she also likely realised that however much she disapproved, Tabitha and Wolf were a packaged deal.

"Mama, what a lovely surprise visit," Tabitha said archly as her opening manoeuvre, seating herself on the settee but holding herself as straight as possible to reduce the other woman's advantage. Tabitha oscillated between the informality of "Mama" and the formality of "Lady Pembroke," depending on her former mother-in-law's attitude towards her and the tone she wished to set.

Under normal circumstances, Tabitha might have expected such a greeting to be repaid with an opening salvo of cutting remarks. But, yet again, the dowager held her fire. Tabitha thought she might enjoy having the older woman beholden to her or at least needing something from her. She filed away this observation for future pondering.

Just as the visit was getting underway, they heard a sound from the hallway; a high, childish voice was singing a nursery rhyme. "Oh, heavens," thought Tabitha, "Mary must be taking Melly for a walk. I forgot to mention the dowager's visit."

There were many things the dowager found to criticise Tabitha over. Her lack of appropriate mourning, her continued residence in the house with Wolf, her inability to provide Jonathan with a son and heir, and more than anything, her past unwillingness to be an utterly docile wife and submit to her husband's temper. But the one thing she hadn't had a chance to weigh in on was Melody. That omission was because she didn't yet know about the little girl. Tabitha wasn't sure when she would have got around to enlightening the dowager. Still, in all the turmoil of solving the duke's murder and the almost immediate arrival of a new case, it was a genuine oversight.

"Is that a child I hear singing?" the dowager asked. Tabitha might have imagined it, but she could have sworn she heard a slight crack in the dowager's voice. Even before Jonathan's death, their relationship had been so continuously antagonistic that Tabitha had never stopped to consider the pain the lack of a grandchild might be causing. Of course, the dowager did have grandchildren by her two daughters. But they hardly spent time in London, and Tabitha was sure the dowager had longed for the day there were grandchildren in Chesterton House. Hearing a young child's voice ringing through the house must have brought back all that pain and longing.

"There is someone you should meet," Tabitha said as she rose and went to the door. Mary and Melody were preparing to leave, but Tabitha indicated they should accompany her into the drawing room. Taking Melody's little hand, she led the girl into the room and up to the dowager. "Melody, I want you to meet the Dowager Countess of Pembroke."

The normally exuberant child seemed overawed by the situation and hid behind Tabitha's skirt. The dowager, with a kind, if somewhat confused, look on her face, reached out a hand towards Melody and said, "Come child, I will not bite." Melody was not a naturally shy child, and it didn't take much encouragement for her to come out from behind Tabitha's skirts and walk towards the dowager.

Melody took the gnarled, blue-veined lined hand held out to her and moved closer to the dowager. She seemed particularly enthralled by the large diamond engagement ring the dowager still wore. Noticing what had caught the child's attention, the dowager said, "Would you like to try it on, Melody?" The child nodded, and the dowager somehow got the ring over her arthritic, swollen knuckles.

With the child mesmerised by the diamond, the dowager faced Tabitha, who had retaken her seat, and said, "She is a charming child. To whom does she belong?"

Tabitha took a deep breath and said, "Well, for now, she is living here with us."

The dowager raised her eyebrows and asked, "Is that a fact? Where are the child's parents?"

At least this was a question Tabitha could answer honestly enough, "They both died over a year ago. Melody, Melly, and her brother were orphaned and lived with a neighbour. But the neighbour's family had a change of circumstance, and the children had nowhere to go." This was a highly edited version of the story, leaving some very salient points out. Tabitha hoped they didn't have to discuss Rat, at least not yet.

"So, you took the child in, or at least the earl did?" Tabitha could hear the dowager's critical tone starting to seep back.

"I took her in," Tabitha said very clearly. "His lordship has very kindly agreed to let Melody stay here for now. But I have assured him I will seek my own house if and when this becomes inconvenient for him."

Wolf jumped in, "And I have assured Tabitha that she and Melody are welcome to stay for as long as necessary."

The dowager harrumphed, "Have you indeed? I believe you both fully understand my views on your living situation. And, indeed, the views of society. But, clearly, my opinion counts for nothing, nor how this unconventional situation reflects poorly on me."

Neither Tabitha nor Wolf wished to follow the dowager down this well-trod rabbit hole, so they ignored this statement. Realising her grievances would be denied oxygen, the dowager gave them up for now. Instead, she returned to the matter at hand, reaching for the little beaded bag on her lap, "Melody, would you like a sweetie?"

Tabitha felt she could barely keep up with the dowager's sentiments as she ricocheted between a censorious battleaxe and a delightful old lady. When Melody solemnly nodded, the dowager reached into the bag and retrieved a small paper-wrapped cube. Unwrapping it, she presented a piece of fudge to the little girl. Seeing the look on Tabitha's face, the dowager explained, "I find the afternoon teas offered in London's drawing rooms often shockingly low in quality. So much so that I carry some treats for sustenance. My cook is particularly adept with fudge."

Melody's delight in the piece of fudge was wonderful to behold. Tabitha was sure the child rarely had experienced such sweets before. "Melody, give her ladyship back the ring and say thank you for the sweetie."

"Thank you, Miss Dowager Countess," the little girl said.

"Tabitha, there's no need to force such grandiose formalities on Melody. She may call me," the dowager paused, "Melody, you may call me Grandmama." On hearing this, Tabitha almost fell out of her chair. She could honestly say she had never been more surprised at hearing anything than she was at that sentence. She had been prepared to battle with the dowager to defend Melody's residence at Chesterton House. She had expected statements along the lines of, "How do you think it will reflect on me to have an orphan living in the same nursery once inhabited by multiple generations of earls?"

The best reaction Tabitha had hoped for was benign disinterest. But the one thing she had never expected and would never have predicted in a hundred years was the dowager's suggestion that Melly call her Grandmama. She tried to school her features but couldn't help glancing over at Wolf, who raised his eyebrows just enough to indicate his amazement.

"Grandmama," Melody practised. Then she paused, went and put her little hand on the dowager's not much larger one and said, "No! I'm going to call you Granny."

That will do it, Tabitha thought. She's going to be incensed at the child's nerve.

"Granny? Is this what you're telling me you'll call me? What a little madam you are." There was another pause, and Tabitha held her breath, "Then Granny, it shall be!" If Tabitha had been surprised before, she was speechless now. "Give Granny a hug, and then you can go out for your walk. But next time I come, we will spend some time together, and I will begin to teach you how to be a young lady."

By this point, Tabitha was so stunned that it took her a moment to realise the slight against her parenting skills implied by the dowager's statement. Once she realised it, she decided that, for once, she didn't care.

Melody hugged the dowager, and Mary led her out of the room. A few moments later, they heard the front door shut.

"On reflection, Tabitha, the child should come to me rather than vice versa. I'll expect her for lunch Tuesdays and Thursdays and will take her out on Saturday afternoons." With that command, the dowager stood up and turned towards the door. "Oh, and don't think I've forgotten the matter of the investigation. But I do not have time to spend now, so I expect a full accounting of your progress the day after tomorrow. You will attend me with Melody for afternoon tea." And with that, she swept out of the room.

Tabitha leaned back on the settee and said, "That was the most unbelievable quarter of an hour I believe I've ever spent. Of all her possible reactions to Melly, the one I could have never predicted was what happened. I'm so shocked that I haven't fully processed her outrageous demands about Melody's visits."

"Has the dowager countess ever made a demand that isn't outrageous?" Wolf mused, as much to himself as to Tabitha.

"It is starting to feel that way, isn't it?"

"May I make a suggestion?" Wolf asked tentatively. Tabitha nodded. "Rather than seeing this as an outrageous demand, embrace it as an opportunity."

"An opportunity?" Tabitha asked incredulously.

"Well, for one thing, it can only be to Melody's advantage to be championed by someone of the dowager's social standing. Even more so as she gets older. I know we haven't talked about her status long-term, but if she is to be your ward and raised as a lady, being on the right side of the doyenne of high society can't be a bad thing."

"Especially when I'm on the wrong side of society?" Tabitha added wryly.

"There is that. In addition, as wonderful as Mary is with Melody, you cannot deny the cultural and educational doors that could open for Melody by spending time with the dowager."

"More so than could be opened by spending time with me?" Tabitha asked, suddenly on the defensive.

"Of course not. But you are busy, and the dowager is, well, perhaps the dowager is lonely, which is my final point in this plan's favour. As much as this was phrased as a demand, we both know she can no more compel you to allow this than she can compel you to continue to wear mourning clothes." Tabitha smiled at this point, and Wolf continued. "In her own, inimitable way, she asked you to allow this." Seeing Tabitha ready to argue this point, Wolf raised his hand and said, "I know she has a less-than-ideal way of phrasing such requests. But if you allow this, she will be in your debt. And we both know nobody appreciates the value of having people indebted more than she does. She is a better friend than she is an enemy."

Tabitha laughed out loud at this, "You can't possibly be naive enough to believe that all it will take for me to win the dowager over is to facilitate a few afternoons with Melly?"

"Not at all. But it may soften her towards you, at least somewhat. And as she softens, so will society." Again, he held up his hand to forestall a protest, "I know you don't care about society, but you've made it clear that I need to care about it and socialise with these people. And I'll be damned if I continue doing so while leaving you at home, a social pariah. So, let Melody spend time with Granny. That does take a bit of getting used to, doesn't it? I promise that at the first indication that the child is not enjoying their time together, or if you ever feel this is no longer a good idea, I will personally inform the dowager of its termination."

Tabitha sighed, knowing Wolf was right. Maybe this would be a good thing for them all.

CHAPTER 5

Wolf left the drawing room and went in search of Rat. He hadn't said anything to Tabitha about sending the boy to Whitechapel, and on reflection, he thought it better not to broach the subject. Part of their agreement had been that Rat would occasionally run errands for Wolf, and this was all it was, an errand. Nevertheless, creeping around his house to find the boy rather than asking Talbot to send him spoke to a guilty conscience.

He finally tracked the lad down in the gardens, "Rat, I need you to do something."

"Wot, m'lord Wolf. Bit more breaking and entering?" The boy chuckled.

Wolf didn't find this comment amusing. He knew Tabitha had barely forgiven him for having Rat break into a house on their last investigation. "Nothing like that, lad. I just need you to go to The Cock early this evening and get a message from Bruiser. And ask him where the prisoner is being held." Wolf knew enough about the prisons in London to hope the man wasn't being held in Newgate Prison. Newgate had long been known for its harsh and inhumane conditions. Another possible option was Pentonville Prison, a newer facility built in the middle of the century. Or maybe it was Wandsworth, not known for being much better than Newgate.

Wolf turned to go and then turned back, "Oh and Rat, no need to mention this errand to her ladyship."

"Aye, aye, governor!" Rat said.

Feeling even guiltier, Wolf hurried to his study moments before Tabitha entered. "You never had a chance to tell me what Mr Bruiser had to say," she commented, dropping into one of the armchairs.

"Uh, well, that is not much. He's going to see what he can find out for me," Wolf stuttered.

Tabitha narrowed her eyes, immediately made suspicious by the usually very articulate earl suddenly fumbling over his words. But she decided not to pursue it. "And so what do you believe should be our next steps?" she inquired.

"I believe the next logical step is to speak to the accused murderer. Bruiser will let me know which prison Manning is being held at. But even when I know that, I can't imagine how to get access."

Tabitha laughed, "Wolf, you're the Earl of Pembroke now. The rules are different than they were when you were just Jeremy Chesterton. Even so, talking to Anthony is the easiest way to gain access. The old Duke of Somerset was an extremely well-connected man." Tabitha paused and added, "Albeit not always for the right reasons." The murdered duke had been blackmailing various well-connected men with photos taken while indulging themselves at the duke's underage brothel. His heir, Anthony Rowley, had given the photos and the story to a newspaper, exposing the men, and his father, to public censure, if nothing else.

Picking up Tabitha's train of thought, Wolf mused, "I wonder how much ill-will Anthony has engendered? I doubt the great and good of London society normally take kindly to having their dirty laundry aired in the London journals."

Tabitha agreed with him but added, "While that's usually true, and perhaps even true in this case, amongst some circles, I would hope that even the most self-absorbed aristocrat would have been appalled at the behaviour Anthony exposed. Regardless, he is our best option for gaining speedy access to Manning in prison. Anthony is now the Duke of Somerset. Most people find it very hard to say no to a duke."

Wolf noticed but didn't comment on her use of the word 'our'. He had no doubt Tabitha imagined herself accompanying him to the prison. But only because she had no idea what the conditions were like in prison, even in a more modern one. He swore to himself that there was no way he would allow her to convince him to take her. While she often managed to wear him down in such debates, this would not be one of those times.

However, her idea of asking the new Duke of Somerset for assistance was sound. "I'll send a note to Rowley House requesting an audience with Somerset. I know the man feels he is in our debt for our sensitive handling of his grandmother's murder of his father. Lord knows the woman might have followed through on her threat and shot herself in the library had we not assured her we would not expose her crime."

A short while later, Wolf received an immediate assurance that Antony, the Duke of Somerset, would be honoured to meet with the Earl of Pembroke at his earliest convenience that afternoon. By the time the note arrived, it was already three o'clock. Tabitha had changed out of her day dress in anticipation of the visit, and within fifteen minutes, they were settled in the carriage. Rowley House was also in Mayfair, and it was no more than a five-minute walk to the stately ducal mansion. The dowager's admonishments about earls strolling the streets of London aside, Wolf would have walked if he'd been alone.

Shown into the recently refurbished drawing room reminded Tabitha that she had yet to ask Cassandra, the Duchess of Somerset and Anthony's mother, for decorating tips. The last time they had all been together in this room had hardly been the time or place for such things.

They had been sitting for just a few minutes when the duchess entered, followed by the butler with tea and cake. "Lord and Lady Pembroke, how lovely to see you." The duchess was not beautiful, but intelligence and gentleness shone in her eyes and made her handsome.

Tabitha noted that the other woman had a peacefulness about her that she had not had on their previous visits. Of course, that was hardly surprising; Cassandra had lived with Martin Rowley, a cruel man, for over two decades. She had suffered eight years of anticipating if and when her husband would try to assault their daughter, as he had his sister, Fannie, more than twenty years before. And then, with that particular suffering removed when her mother-in-law killed Martin, there had been the ongoing fear of the crime's discovery. But, thanks to Wolf and Tabitha, that worry had also been removed, and the duchess had a lightness about her being that was lovely to see.

It was evident in the genuine warmth with which the Duchess of Somerset greeted them that she was well aware of the debt she and her family owed them. The social pleasantries were just over when the door opened, and they were joined in the drawing room by Anthony, the young Duke of Somerset, and the pleasantries repeated. Anthony and Tabitha had been childhood friends, and there was a friendliness to his greeting beyond merely the debt he knew he and his family owed her.

Finally, they were all seated, drinking tea and nibbling on a fine Madeira cake. "How may I be of assistance?" the duke asked. Wolf explained about the case the dowager had thrust on them and the need for him to visit Manning in prison. At his use of the singular term, he could see Tabitha glaring at him out of the corner of his eye. She was far too decorous to argue with him in public, but he was fully aware of the argument they would be having in the carriage on the way home.

The duke listened carefully and said, "My father was on good terms with Sir Matthew White Ridley, the Secretary of State in charge of the prison system. Seeing the looks on their faces, he added, "No, he was not someone my father was blackmailing." He added, "At least as far as I know. I believe they merely knew each other socially. I will seek him out immediately and get you admittance. Do you know where Mr Manning is being held?"

Wolf admitted they didn't but hoped to find out from a source. "No matter," the duke continued, "I'm sure Sir Matthew can find out. I believe this is the murder splashed across the front page of the journals yesterday, so he will know immediately who this Mr Manning is."

"Thank you, Your Grace," Wolf said respectfully. This slight, delicately featured young man, who had an almost feminine grace and gentleness, had proved to have an inner core of steel forged in a crucible of familial scandal, dishonour and malfeasance. Wolf continued to have the highest regard and respect for the man. He could have exposed the men involved in the abuse of young girls while shielding his father's pivotal role in that abuse. Yet, he didn't hesitate to choose the more honourable yet far more challenging path that brought public shame on his family and his title. Luckily, and due in part to the influence of the Dowager Countess of Pembroke, the general view, at least in aristocratic circles, had been sympathy towards the degenerate late duke's family rather than censure.

Towards the end of their visit, the dead duke's sister, Lady Fanny, joined them unexpectedly. The first of the cruel duke's victims when she was only 8, the abuse's trauma had sent the previously lively young girl into a shell from which she had never fully emerged. One disastrous season had been sufficient for her mother, the dowager duchess, to realise her daughter would never take. Lady Fannie had led a secluded life ever since as her mother's companion.

Tabitha was surprised to find Lady Fannie far more talkative and animated than she had been when they had met previously. Tabitha glanced over at the duchess, who smiled and inclined her head slightly towards her sister-in-law. The implication was clear enough; the previously cowed woman had been brought back to life with the death of her abuser. Yet again, Tabitha felt justice had been served when she and Wolf decided not to reveal the dowager duchess's murder of her son. It was hard to condone murder. Yet, if it was ever justifiable, it was in the case of Martin Rowley, the Duke of Somerset. There was little doubt the world would be a better place without him.

The visit lasted more than an hour, much longer than societal norms allowed for such things. However, the entire party, each in their way, had already fallen afoul of society's expectations, and none of them was concerned by its strictures anymore.

As Wolf had suspected, no sooner were he and Tabitha settled in the carriage to return to Chesterton House than she turned accusatory eyes on him and demanded, "Do you plan to visit Manning in prison without me, Wolf?"

Wolf sighed and paused for a moment before answering. Throughout the previous investigation, he learned concerns over her safety would not sway Tabitha. Indeed, previously she had been infuriated by what she had seen as attempts to cosset her. She had justifiably accused him of, on the one hand, accusing her of living a sheltered life, unaware of the brutal realities of the world, but on the other hand, refusing to expose her to any of those realities. But Wolf had also learned that when presented with rational arguments for why her involvement might hinder the case, Tabitha usually saw reason and was accommodating.

However, if he was honest, the truth was murky; his primary intention was to shelter her. A visit to a London prison was more exposure to the brutal realities of life than he would wish on anyone. But he knew that would be an insufficient reason in Tabitha's eyes. So, he tried to think of a way to frame his refusal to allow her to accompany him that would meet Tabitha's threshold of reasonableness.

"Yes, not only is that my plan, that is what will happen!" As soon as those words came out of Wolf's mouth, he knew they sounded imperious and would be received poorly. He tried again, "I realise I cannot command you nor have any agency over your actions." Wolf saw that these words had immediately taken the edge off Tabitha's growing anger.

Wolf continued, "However, wherever Manning is held, it is no place for a woman. Everyone we encounter there, from the warden to the guards, is unused to having a woman in that environment and likely will not take kindly to it. Even with a letter of introduction from Sir Matthew, we will be at the mercy of the good humour of the men running the prison. They could permit us entry if they are charged to do so by Sir Matthew and yet make it impossible to achieve our objective."

"And how could they do that?" Tabitha demanded. The determined look on her face showed her willingness to continue to fight for her case, but her voice indicated that her state of high dudgeon had diminished.

"Tabitha, people can follow the letter of an order but not the spirit of one. Surely you realise that. Perhaps they let us in but allow insufficient time to talk with Manning. I don't know what they might do, but I know it will not improve the situation if you are there. Hopefully, I will be turning up with a letter from their higher-ups; this will cause resentment from the get-go. I need to ensure that nothing else ratchets up that resentment.

Tabitha slumped against the carriage seat and crossed her arms irritably, but Wolf knew he had won this battle.

CHAPTER 6

As they ate breakfast the following morning, Talbot entered the room with a note from the Duke of Somerset. He had secured a letter from Sir Matthew introducing them to the warden at Pentonville Prison.

Thanks to his information from Bruiser, retrieved by Rat the night before, Wolf already knew where Manning was being held. Bruiser had also given him some interesting details about the case against the butler. The newspapers had all reported that Manning was found kneeling over the victim and covered in her blood. What they hadn't reported was who had found him this way. The victim, Collette DuBois, had given her staff the night off. Apparently, she did it every Sunday, encouraging them to go out for the evening. However, her butler had returned earlier than expected and discovered the body and Manning kneeling over it.

Finally, Bruiser informed Wolf that a Dr Blackwell had performed the autopsy. This was great news as far as Wolf was concerned. His thief-taking activities had sometimes bled into murder investigations, and he had formed, if not a friendship, then at least a professional relationship based on mutual respect with the doctor at St Thomas' Hospital. Dr Marcus Blackwell had been a client of Wolf's at one time when some letters of a sensitive nature had been stolen and used to blackmail him. Wolf had returned the letters, earning the doctor's gratitude and respect.

Wolf hoped he could share Bruiser's information with Tabitha over breakfast without revealing he'd sent Rat for it. Indeed, he managed to intrigue her with the news to such an extent that she didn't stop to wonder how the information had been retrieved.

Tabitha finished her cup of coffee, deep in thought about the new information. Having drained her cup, she sat back in her chair and mused, "While giving servants time off on a Sunday to go to church and visit their families is usual, it is rather unusual to give them the evening off. You'd particularly think that, given Miss DuBois' line of work, her evenings would be when she would need her staff. So, what happened every Sunday such that she didn't just give them time off, she encouraged them to leave the house?"

"Perhaps she had a patron whose identity she wished to keep secret," Wolf conjectured. "That seems the most likely reason."

"True. However, you'd think anyone in her line of work would only employ extremely loyal, discreet, and liberal-minded staff. I'm sure she paid them well to mind their tongues."

"Indeed, even the deceased duke managed to find a staff who could be paid to run a brothel of underaged girls for him. I'm sure it's possible to find staff who will turn a blind eye to anything."

"But, if that's the case," Tabitha pointed out, taking another slice of toast and buttering it, "then why was Manning visiting her that evening? If our assumption, well really everyone's assumption at this point, is that he somehow found the money to frequent a high-end prostitute, then why was he there at the same time as a patron so important that his identity needed to be kept a secret, even from her staff?"

"I think we can discount the possibility that Manning was the important client whose identity she needed to shield."

Tabitha agreed, "I'm still not sure he makes enough money to be a customer at a brothel such as that. But it's beyond the bounds of credibility to imagine he pays enough to justify giving the entire staff the evening off. Or indeed, that his identity needs to be hidden."

"Well, that isn't so hard to imagine. After all, as we know, servants know each other, and they talk. We have benefited from that knowledge and their gossiping. It does seem that if Manning regularly frequented brothels, he likely would not want word of it spreading back to the dowager countess. However, I agree that he could not afford to pay for such discretion. This is something we should talk with the dowager about.

"This brings me to something you can do today while I visit Manning." Wolf was loathe to wade back into the matter of his visiting the accused butler alone. But, he also knew Tabitha would be mollified somewhat if she had important tasks to accomplish. "You should talk with the dowager's staff and find out what they know. Someone either knew something or at least suspected something."

"I agree, but first, I will talk with my staff," Tabitha replied. Wolf's face showed his confusion. Tabitha continued, "Manning was the dowager's butler when she lived at Chesterton House. Indeed, I believe he started in service here as a young man. When I married Jonathan, Manning was the butler. Manning chose to go with her when the dowager established her residence, and Jonathan hired Talbot."

"Is that usual?" Wolf enquired.

"Well, it isn't unheard of for family retainers to be extremely loyal and committed even under changed family circumstances. However, there's also no doubt that working in the household of a dowager countess is less prestigious, in general, than working for an earl. And while perhaps the pay is equal, it's unlikely to be more. I imagine Manning is in his mid to late fifties, so he has some years of service ahead of him. One might wonder whether the best career move was to leave the household of a relatively young earl to join one belonging to an elderly dowager. Anyway, my larger point is that the staff in my household, sorry, your household, have known Manning for far longer than those in the dowager's household." Wolf concurred with her logic.

They continued eating, and Wolf scanned the newspapers, "The inquest into Collette DuBois' murder is set for next week. It would be good if we had more information by then. Perhaps, we can even prevent Manning from having to go to trial. I want to try and get my hands on the coroner's findings before they're presented at the inquest."

"Well, I'm sure such reports are usually confidential, but, again, Anthony may be able to pull a few strings," Tabitha suggested.

"I don't want to exploit Somerset's gratitude and generosity. In this case, I may not need his help." Wolf didn't want to say too much then, and Tabitha didn't press. They drained their coffee cups and parted ways, each making plans for their part of the investigation.

While Wolf felt Sir Matthew's letter assured him entry to the prison, as he'd told Tabitha, he wasn't sure what his reception would be. He thought it prudent to take Bear with him. While everyone who knew him well realised his innate gentleness, Bear lived up to his nickname. He was a mountain of a man, not merely so tall that he needed to stoop through doorways but broad-shouldered with a thick, muscular neck. Thick dark hair covered the back of his hands and crept out of his neck collar to meet a full beard that reached up his cheeks to almost his eyes. The hair and size gave the impression of a vast, almost mythical-looking beast. Bear's mere presence usually deterred trouble.

For household order and hierarchy, Wolf referred to Bear as his valet. Apart from anything else, whenever a member of his staff fussed around him, trying to perform tasks he felt were absurd and unnecessary, he could usually placate them by assuring them his valet would take care of what they felt needed doing. As it happens, Bear did perform some of the usual tasks a valet might, at least to the extent a man as unconcerned about maintaining a fashionable appearance as Wolf might need them performed. Talbot quickly located Bear in Wolf's room and sent him to the study.

With Bear apprised of the task ahead, the two men set off for Pentonville Prison. In the north of London, in the borough of Islington, Pentonville was one of the largest and most modern prisons. Even if the accommodations were slightly better than a prison such as Newgate, Pentonville was well known for its harsh conditions.

A local prison, Pentonville was mainly used to house prisoners for short periods. The prison practised separate confinement, hard labour, sparse living conditions, and a minimal diet. As most local prisoners only served short periods, often a month or less, the first stage of the sentence was the most severe. Only after this would prisoners slowly receive a little extra food or some minor improvements. Wolf had been around criminals long enough in his thief-taking career to be under no illusions about what state they would find Manning in.

The neighbourhood around Pentonville was densely populated, filled with narrow streets and crowded tenements. It was a working-class area with a high population of immigrants. The prison was in the middle of the neighbourhood, and Wolf's carriage had to navigate the busy streets and alleys to reach the prison gates.

On finally reaching the prison, Wolf presented his letter from Sir Matthew. The guard to whom he had presented it let them in and escorted them to a small waiting area. A few minutes later, a man, whom Wolf assumed was the warden, hurried in. He was a small, wiry man with barely a handful of grey hairs left on his head. His demeanour seemed more fitting for a law clerk than a prison director, and his speech amplified that impression.

Wolf's concerns about his reception turned out to be wholly unwarranted. He introduced himself, and rather than engendering hostility, Wolf's rank and the letter seemed to have reduced the warden to a stuttering, nervous wreck. "Your lordship," he began. "My name is Featherstone, Warden Featherstone. I must tell you what an honour it is to have our lowly prison graced by someone of your rank. I can only imagine you are here as a member of the House of Lords to report on prison conditions. It will be my honour to give you a tour and answer any questions you might have. I am sure you will only find positive things to report back to Sir Matthew on."

There was barely a pause in this snivelling obsequiousness in which to correct Warden Featherstone's assumption. Finally, the man stopped to breathe, and Wolf said, "Warden Featherstone, I have no doubt you run an exemplary establishment. Indeed, I would be happy to make such a report back to the Lords and Sir Matthew if I were asked. However, that is not the reason for my visit this morning. I wish to see a prisoner you've been holding for a few days, Mr Gerald Manning."

"Oh!" was all the warden could say, clearly disappointed he wouldn't get a chance to ensure a glowing report of his prison was announced on the floor of the House of Lords. However, Mr Featherstone was not a man to be kept down. He still had a chance to impress a peer of the realm and would not let that opportunity pass him by.

"Of course, Lord Pembroke, I would not expect you to mingle in the area normally used for visits. I will happily extend the use of my office. I will ensure there is a guard in the room for you. Manning is a murderer, after all."

"Only accused, not convicted, Warden Featherstone," Wolf pointed out.

"Well, be that as it may, he is an accused murderer. And quite a violent murder by all accounts. I would not like to leave you unprotected."

Wolf gestured to Bear, "As you can see, Warden Featherstone, I am hardly unguarded. I can assure you that my associate is as capable of protecting me as any of your guards might be."

"Yes, well, such an arrangement would be quite unorthodox and against the usual protocols." The warden paused, clearly torn between obsequious pandering to an earl and his commitment to following the rules at all costs. The pandering won out, "But in this case, I may rest assured that you are, of course, more than capable of determining your own protection."

Wolf was grateful for the man's speedy capitulation. He would have tolerated the presence of a guard if he'd had no choice, but his preference was to speak to Manning in private.

Warden Featherstone called a guard and ordered him to collect Manning from his cell and deliver him to the warden's office. Featherstone then led Wolf and Bear through a series of corridors until they reached a solid oak door with a well-polished brass nameplate attached to it bearing the warden's name. Wolf found it hard to imagine how many people were randomly roaming the prison's corridor, unsure who the warden was and where to find him. He considered it more likely that the man before him had a puffed-up ego and needed to ensure he had all the pomp and ceremony he believed due his position.

The warden steered Wolf to his comfortable-looking, leather-upholstered chair behind an imposing mahogany desk. "May I get you any refreshments, your lordship? Perhaps a glass of sherry?"

Wolf was about to refuse but then considered the quality and quantity of the food Manning must have received in prison and said, "Tea would be most welcome. Might your kitchen be able to supplement that with some light refreshments? I missed breakfast this morning and would be grateful for anything they might be able to offer."

"Of course, of course. I'd be delighted to instruct our cook to prepare some tasty morsels for you. Perhaps some finger sandwiches and some sweet treats." With that, the warden left the office, backing out with an inept attempt to bow as he walked.

Bear closed the door behind him and took the far less comfortable chair facing the desk, "Well, if you were worried about a surly reception, I suppose that concern has been well and truly put to rest," he observed.

"Indeed, though this level of unctuous servility is only just preferable." Wolf then conceded, "Though perhaps more productive than antagonism."

They waited just a few more minutes before there was a knock on the door. At Wolf's command, the door opened, and a guard entered with an extremely tall, rail-thin man, whom Wolf barely recognised as Manning. On the occasions Wolf had interacted with Manning on his visit to the dowager's home, he had exhibited all the inscrutability and ability to mask his thoughts and emotions that members of society expected from their butlers. Only his extreme lankiness made him stand out from the many almost identically dressed, equally inscrutable, highly efficient men who opened the front door in all the best homes in London.

However, the man who entered the warden's office was almost unrecognisable. Manning, the butler, had always been impeccably dressed and groomed, as befitted someone in his position in the house of a dowager countess. Much like every other butler in London, Manning had always dressed in a black, well-made suit with tails, a white dress shirt with a stiff collar, a black bow tie, and black dress shoes. In stark contrast, his prison uniform consisted of a shirt and trousers made of coarse, rough material. The shirt was a plain, white button-up shirt, and the trousers were loose-fitting and made of a heavier material than the shirt. The outfit had not been made for a man of Manning's proportions, and the trousers stopped at his ankles, and both they and the shirt hung off his frame, which looked even thinner than usual.

Manning's normally perfectly smoothed hair was lank, and he had dark circles under his eyes. The man looked as if he had aged ten years in the few days he had been imprisoned. Bear stood up, and Wolf indicated that the prisoner should take the vacated seat. Wolf then told the guard he could leave. As the man began to protest, Bear stepped closer to him and repeated Wolf's request. The guard quickly left the room, and Bear closed the door behind him.

It seemed the imprisoned butler was observing rank and waiting for Wolf to speak first; the formalities of a servant towards an earl were to be maintained even in these dire circumstances. "Mr Manning, I would ask if you are well, but it is obvious you are not. I hope the conditions you are being kept in are not too awful."

Manning inclined his head and said, "It is very kind of you to ask your lordship. The conditions are much as you might imagine. If I can be so bold as to ask, what do I owe the honour of a visit?"

"Mr Manning, Lady Pembroke, the dowager countess, is very concerned for your welfare and staunchly believes in your innocence which she has asked me to prove."

To his initial surprise, Manning didn't ask why the dowager would make such a request of him, of all people. But then he considered Tabitha's wise statement in their previous investigation that servants know everything happening in a house. No one paid attention to servants gliding in and out of rooms as if wearing an invisibility cloak. Between listening at doors and overhearing conversations when serving tea, butlers probably knew more than most.

Then, there was the inter-house servant hall gossip that he and Tabitha had taken advantage of in the past few weeks. Wolf was sure Manning had a very good idea of his previous profession and a good sense of how he and Tabitha had helped solve the duke's murder. If he didn't know the full details of who they had determined the murderer to be, it was only because, despite her grumbling about the fact, they had kept that information from the dowager. Nevertheless, she knew enough about how they uncovered the duke's perversions, his brothel, and blackmail scheme, and Wolf had no doubt Manning knew almost as much as the dowager.

CHAPTER 7

Before they could talk any further, there was a knock at the door and a guard entered with a tea tray holding a cake stand laden with sandwiches, scones, and little iced cakes. It was clear that whatever meagre fare sustained the prisoners, the warden ensured he was well supplied with treats.

The guard put the tray on the desk and left, closing the door behind him. There were only two cups on the tray. It had not occurred to the warden or the cook that Manning might be offered a cup. Seeing this, Bear indicated he didn't need tea, so Wolf went to pour for himself and Manning. But his butlering habits were so well-ingrained, even in his present unfortunate circumstances, that Manning stood and refused to let Wolf serve him. Instead, the exhausted, bedraggled man poured and served the tea as if he was back in the dowager's drawing room.

Wolf indicated the food and said, "I ordered this for you, Mr Manning. You look as if you have not eaten much recently."

"I couldn't possibly, your lordship. By all rights, I should not even be sitting in your presence."

Wolf shook his head, "Mr Manning, I am sure you are an exemplary butler, but just now, can we put such formalities aside? You are a wrongly accused man." Wolf wasn't convinced that was the case but decided to at least work from that assumption. "And I am here to try to help you. You are hungry, and there is food. Please, do not stand on ceremony. Eat until you are full, and perhaps we can talk while you do so." In the hopes of encouraging the man to eat, Wolf helped himself to one of the iced cakes and took a bite. While it wasn't up to Mrs Smith's standards, it was far better fare than one might expect to be served in prison.

Manning looked at the food hesitantly but also hungrily. Finally, hunger won out, and he took a few finger sandwiches and a scone. Wolf allowed the man to satiate his initial hunger before continuing the conversation. Finally, after three sandwiches and a few bites of a scone, followed by some gulps of tea, Manning looked up and said, "I will be eternally grateful to her ladyship for her faith in me. But I fear my fate is sealed. Hopefully, by the time my case comes up for a trial, there will be something more sensational to splash across the front pages of the journals, and I will bring no more shame to the Pembroke name."

Wolf shook his head in frustration at the man's hardheadedness. Or maybe he was guilty and was merely accepting his just punishment. Ignoring this possibility, Wolf persisted, "Mr Manning, you know the punishment for murder is capital punishment. Do you wish to die for a crime you didn't commit?"

"Milord, with all due respect, how can you be sure I didn't commit it?"

"Did you commit the crime? Did you murder Collette DuBois?" Wolf noticed an expression flit across the butler's face at the woman's name. If he had to put any name to the emotion he saw for a brief instance, it would have been regret. But what did the man regret? Perhaps he regretted murdering a beautiful young woman in the prime of her life.

"No, I didn't murder her. I could never have done such a thing," Manning finally answered.

"Then let me help prove that. Why would you want to accept a conviction if you're innocent?"

"I wish to cause her ladyship no more trouble and bring no more shame on the family than I already have. I will plead guilty, and the trial will be swift with nothing to interest the scandal sheets."

Wolf sighed at the man's misguided loyalty. "Mr Manning, while your loyalty and devotion to Lady Pembroke, indeed to the whole family, are admirable and much appreciated, you must know that the dowager countess is lost without you. In fact, those were almost her very words. You have been in her household since she was a young married woman and care for her now that she is older, as no one else will ever do. You must see that she values you and your continued service in her household beyond all things. Let me prove your innocence and enable you to return to an employer beside herself at your fate and your absence from her home."

Manning looked down, deep in thought for a few moments, then said, "If you truly believe it is in her ladyship's best interests, I will accept your help with gratitude, your lordship." At that, he took more sandwiches and cakes and poured them both more tea.

After a few minutes of eating and drinking, Wolf steepled his fingers, considering for a moment how he wanted to begin his questioning. The warden had set no time limit on the visit, and Wolf was sure the sycophantic little man could be persuaded to give them more time if necessary. Nevertheless, he thought it prudent not to push his luck and set about the task at hand.

"Mr Manning, I realise these questions may seem intrusive into your private life, and any answers you provide may give rise to feelings of embarrassment, even shame. But, I beg of you, answer to the best of your ability and tell the truth. Anything less will hinder me from fulfilling Lady Pembroke's dearest wish; to have you back at her side." Wolf knew he was manipulating the man. Manning may not be concerned for his well-being, but he cared deeply about his mistress. Hopefully, his fear of causing her pain would override his discomfort about answering fully and honestly.

It was apparent from the look on Manning's face that Wolf's words hit home. He sat straight, looked Wolf directly in the eye, and said, "What do you want to know?"

Aware that time was of the essence, Wolf didn't beat around the bush, "I know Collette DuBois was a high-end prostitute." Curiously, Manning winced at this statement. Wolf continued, "Were you a client of hers?"

"No, I was not!" Manning replied with surprising fierceness.

"I'm sorry if the question offends you, Mr Manning, but you must see why it had to be asked. If you were not visiting her in a professional capacity, why were you there?"

Watching emotions play across the man's face, it was clear Manning was struggling with how much of the truth to tell. Wolf tried to pre-empt a possible lie, saying, "Mr Manning, I reiterate, I can only help you if you tell me the full truth. So, I'll ask you again, what was your relationship to Collette DuBois, and why were you in her house that night?"

After a few more moments of visible inner turmoil, the man's shoulders slumped, and he replied, "Her name wasn't Collette DuBois. It was Claire Murphy. But, in reality, it should have been Claire Manning. She was my daughter." Whatever Wolf had been expecting to hear, it wasn't that, and his surprise was obvious. Manning continued, "As you may know, before becoming the butler at Chesterton House, I had worked my way up through the household. By the time I was about twenty-five or so, I was the lower footman. There was a new Irish housemaid at the time named Jenny Murphy. She was a lovely lass with pitch-black hair and green eyes like a cat.

"I think every man on the staff fell slightly in love with her. Well, perhaps everyone but old Jennings, the butler at the time. But Jenny had a sharp tongue on her, and she brooked no nonsense. I never even considered I had a chance, a gangly, callow lad like me. Of course, I made eyes at her; we all did. But I left the flirting and such to the gardener's lad and even the upper footman, Charles. He was the kind of strapping young man you'd expect to turn the head of a beauty such as Jenny Murphy.

"So, you can imagine my surprise when, suddenly, out of nowhere, she took a liking to me. I honestly have no idea why; I was just grateful. We started walking out, and I thought I was the luckiest man alive. It was only a matter of a few weeks until I asked her to marry me, and she said yes. You have to understand that not all mistresses will allow relations amongst their staff, but Lady Pembroke has always had a heart of gold and promised us married quarters.

"We married quickly because neither of us saw a reason to postpone it. Before we knew it, Jenny was expecting a baby. She wasn't far along yet, but we were so happy planning for our family. We talked about what to do when the child was born. We needed Jenny's income, and she had ambitions to become a lady's maid. We were trying to work out what best to do when, one day, Jenny just disappeared. No one saw her leave, but her belongings were gone. She'd left a note for me saying she was sorry. And that was that."

Wolf had questions, but now that he'd got the man to start talking, he didn't want to interrupt his flow. Manning sipped tea and continued, "I didn't know anything about her family except that she had been raised by grandparents in Ireland and had come to England only recently to find work. I didn't even know where in Ireland she was from. I never heard from her again. I didn't even know if she and the baby had survived the birth. I searched as best I could and finally resigned myself to losing Jenny and the baby.

"Then one day, about two months ago, I was taking my day off and strolling in Hyde Park when I saw a landau with a young woman in it who could have been the twin to my Jenny. I was so shocked I called out her name, and the woman turned to me, and the look she gave me, well, I can't explain it, but it was a combination of shock and fear, but mostly recognition.

"I knew the woman couldn't be my Jenny after twenty-five years, but I was sure she was a relative. The landau left the park, and I ran after it. I was quite the sprinter in my time, and thanks to London traffic congestion these days, I managed to keep up with it well enough, even though, that was quite the distance, I can tell you.

"I saw the landau pull up to a smart house in Chelsea. My daughter, for I was convinced it was she, entered the building with the authority of the mistress of the house. By then, I was sweaty and in no fit state to be admitted to any decent home, so I left, determined to return the following Sunday. I was unsure what reception I might receive when I knocked on the door later that week. What I did not expect was to be immediately welcomed into the house and the presence of its mistress. She had seen me following her landau and, anticipating a visit, had told her butler to admit me whenever I turned up."

Wolf was caught up in the story and intrigued to discover what had happened next. His anticipation was such that he forgot his determination not to interrupt and said, "And was she, in fact, your daughter?"

"Well, she greeted me with a French accent and told me her name was Collette DuBois, but I could see the truth in her eyes. Whatever else she was, she wasn't a good enough actress to hide her true identity from me. Ignoring the sham of the French identity, I asked her if my Jenny was alive. That question seemed to break her. She sat down and started crying. Her tears answered two questions: clearly, she was my daughter, and equally clearly, Jenny was dead. When she finally answered me, now in a heavy Irish brogue, she told me her mother had died when she was young, and she missed her every day. She also told me her name was Claire."

"I'm sorry to ask this question, Mr Manning, but I must. At what point did you discover your daughter's profession?" Wolf asked.

Manning's face became taut with barely restrained emotions, "I began visiting Claire every Sunday on my afternoon off. Early on, nothing about the house or my daughter indicated how she supported herself. Of course, I wondered about the French accent and name, but I assumed she had somehow reinvented herself from a poor Irish farm girl. It turns out I was right. At first, I didn't want to pry. Deep down, I had my suspicions. There seemed to be no husband, but I told myself she might be a widow. But she never mentioned a husband. I'm not a man of the world, Lord Pembroke, but even I realise there are only so many ways a poor girl ends up a grand lady in a house in Chelsea. And when you add in the accent and the new name, well, it wasn't hard to guess.

Wolf felt he had to interject at this point, "Mr Manning, did she ever tell you how she went from Irish farmgirl to being able to set herself up in such a way in Chelsea? Because, I have to tell you, most girls who enter that profession are lucky if they find themselves in a brothel in Whitechapel. The unlucky are plying their trade on the streets."

Manning shook his head, "As you can imagine, this was not a topic I cared to pursue too deeply. I was more concerned about hearing what had happened to her mother and perhaps learning why she had left me. But this was a topic Claire was very unwilling to talk about. I'm unsure what she knew, but I felt sure she knew more than she said. It was clear enough that she had known she had a father in London. And she never rebuked me, so it was also clear she knew I hadn't abandoned her and Jenny. But more than that, I was never able to find out. All she would say was that Jenny had died in childbirth. After that, Claire was raised by her grandparents near Limerick.

"She told me she had come to London seven years before. She didn't tell me why she'd come or how she'd found herself in that profession. I was happy to have found my daughter and didn't want to jeopardise my fledgling relationship with her by demanding too many answers."

Wolf had one more question, "Mr Manning, if your routine was to visit Claire on Sunday afternoons, what were you doing in her home at seven o'clock that evening?"

Manning looked him in the eye and answered, "She had sent me a note instructing me to come later that day." Wolf believed the man.

CHAPTER 8

Wolf didn't speak much during the carriage ride home; he wanted to think about what Manning had told him. He knew Tabitha would want a full account of the meeting, and he wanted to ensure he had his thoughts and observations straight in his head.

On entering the house, Wolf asked Talbot where he would find Tabitha and was told she was in the parlour. He entered the cosy room where he and Tabitha usually sat after dinner and found her hunched over the low tea table, busy cutting up paper squares. Wolf immediately knew what she was doing. During their previous investigation, Tabitha had devised an ingenious method for organising their findings, theories and outstanding questions; she wrote each thought on a square of paper and pinned it to a makeshift board they had constructed by sewing fabric tightly over a rather ugly old painting on the wall.

Attaching the notecards to the board with pins enabled them to be moved around as relevant connections arose. They also used yarn to connect groupings of notes. Wolf had been impressed by how visualising their various clues in such a way helped spur creative problem-solving and also highlighted what they had yet to learn. It seemed Tabitha intended to use the same process for their current case.

Tabitha looked up when he entered and said, "Can you ask Talbot to bring some tea and cake?" That request made, Wolf took his usual armchair and asked, "How did your questioning of the staff go?"

With a shake of her head, Tabitha said, "Oh no, you're going first. I can't imagine anything I have to tell comparing with your afternoon."

Wolf smiled; he had expected nothing less. He relayed his conversation with Manning as faithfully as possible. Tabitha's shock was almost comical when Wolf revealed that not only was Collette DuBois, in reality, Claire Murphy, but she was Manning's long-lost daughter.

Tabitha interrupted, "Did he ever work up the courage to ask her for the truth about why her mother had left him?"

Wolf shook his head, "He tried to bring it up a few times, but she avoided answering the question. Eventually, he decided it was obvious she didn't want to talk about the subject and that he was putting his relationship with her at risk by pressing the point. As to why she pretended to be French, well, that's obvious enough. Colette DuBois, the exotic Parisian, is far more appealing as a courtesan than Claire Murphy from Limerick."

"I agree. I don't think there's any mystery over that point," Tabitha agreed. "So, he's been going to see his daughter every Sunday afternoon for two months?" Wolf nodded his assent, and Tabitha continued, "We know she gave her staff the evening off every Sunday. Did this usually include the times Manning was visiting?"

"I asked that question, and he said no. When he visited, there was often staff working in the house."

Tabitha sat back, digesting the information Wolf had learned from Manning. Taking one of the sublime ginger biscuits they'd started getting regular deliveries from Mickey D's wife, she savoured its light, buttery texture, then asked, "I'm assuming Manning hasn't revealed any of this to the police? If he has, it certainly hasn't hit the newspapers."

"No, the man was determined to be a martyr, to save the dowager from as much embarrassment as possible. I persuaded him she cared more for his life and continued service than any shame the case might bring to the Pembroke name. Before I did that, he was determined not to try to clear his name."

Tabitha let go for the moment of the absurdity of the man's willingness to die for the dowager's good name and continued, "So what could Manning's motive possibly be for killing his long-lost daughter? This is a daughter he went out of his way to build a relationship with and one who probably made far more money in a day than Manning did in a year. He built this relationship with her knowing, or at least suspecting, how she made that money. Where's the motive? She couldn't have been blackmailing him."

"Maybe she was. Perhaps she didn't have as much money as we're assuming she did. First thing tomorrow, I will instruct my man of business to see what he can find out about the house and her finances. Perhaps she was struggling for money. While she couldn't have believed Manning had much money of his own, perhaps she was trying to persuade him to steal from the dowager. One thing is true; he places what he sees as your erstwhile mother-in-law's best interests above all others. Perhaps, the one thing he could not do for Claire was to betray the dowager's trust, so he killed her instead."

Tabitha could see some logic in this but had questions, "But what could she have been blackmailing him with? That she would reveal her relationship with him? Would the scandal have been so great? He was legally married to her mother, who had been the one to abandon him and take their child. Yes, his daughter was a prostitute, but he's a butler, not a duke. Who was going to be scandalised, the maids?"

Wolf agreed with her but pointed out, "I don't believe he would care for any scandal for himself, but even the thought that his daughter's profession would cause any sordid gossip about the dowager might have been enough to drive the man to murder. After all, if he's prepared to go to the gallows for her, what would he not be prepared to do? And perhaps this was his plan all along, to kill his daughter and then hang for the crime, thereby keeping the scandal as far from the dowager's door as possible. Though," he added, "if that was the plan, it was poorly thought out. Having a butler with a prostitute as a daughter would hardly cause the dowager to be more than a mild object of titillation at a couple of evening parties. To have one whose arrest for murder is splashed across all the worst newspapers in

London is infinitely worse."

Tabitha agreed and said, "Nevertheless, it is a credible motive. I'll put it on the board. Of course, it relies on the presumption that Collete, sorry Claire's, finances were in trouble. Let's see what we can find out about that." Tabitha wrote up a notecard as she spoke with the question, "Did Claire/Collette need money?" on it. When she finished writing, she paused and said, "I don't understand why he was visiting in the evening on the day of the murder. What brought him there later than usual if his normal visiting time was in the afternoon?"

"Well," Wolf pointed out, "her staff was around during his visits but given the evening off on Sundays. Assuming the murder was premeditated, waiting until the staff were gone would make perfect sense. Though he claims he received a note asking him to come later. But who was it that usually came on Sunday evenings? We've already posited that perhaps Collete had a patron whose visits needed particular secrecy, which is why she regularly gave her staff the evening off. But who might that be, and how can we find out? If so, did this patron ever show up?"

Tabitha had a thought, "What has happened to her house? Is her staff still there?"

"Well," Wolf said thoughtfully, "if Manning is her nearest relative, there is a good chance the house now belongs to him. But those are good questions. We need to visit the house, talk to the staff if they're still in residence, and search for any information we can. Now tell me what you found out from our staff."

Tabitha settled back in her chair with yet another biscuit, "Well, most of them weren't here when Manning was young. In fact, only Mrs Jenkins was here as a young housemaid. She and I had a nice long chat. Her narrative both validates and gives some more colour to the story told to you by Manning.

"Even though Mrs Jenkins is younger than he is, they joined the household at about the same time. She said he was a somewhat awkward but kindly young man. Given his height, he was sometimes asked to help the maids with chores beyond their reach, and he was always happy to be of assistance, often volunteering even before being asked. Jenny Murphy joined the household about two years after Mrs Jenkins did. Even thirty years later, I could hear the girlish jealousy in her tone when she talked about the beautiful, vivacious new maid."

Wolf interjected, "Manning said that every man on the staff was making eyes at her. He couldn't understand why she chose him."

"Well, Mrs Jenkins told me the gossip below stairs about that. There was speculation that perhaps she was already in the family way. Mrs Jenkins said that, while she didn't indulge in such talk at the time, or so she claims, she had wondered why such a beautiful young woman had chosen a gangly dolt like Manning. She told me that Jenny hadn't noticed the young Manning for months, instead flirting with the far more handsome upper footman and even making eyes at the young gardener. But then suddenly, out of nowhere, she was encouraging Manning, and before anyone knew it, they were betrothed and then married."

Tabitha paused, and Wolf said, "Given those circumstances, I can see why there might be gossip that Jenny was already with child. Perhaps she saw Manning as the man who would happily marry her and not ask questions if the baby came early."

"That was exactly what Mrs Jenkins implied. She told me they had been married for only three months when Jenny started to show more than one might expect, even if she'd fallen pregnant on her wedding night, and this only fuelled the rumours. Then one day, Jenny was gone. She packed her stuff and snuck out of the house before anyone was up, leaving nothing but a brief note for Manning. The housekeeper at the time discovered a small amount of money missing, and a few trinkets belonging to the family had also been taken. But the dowager seemed disinclined to press charges."

At that moment, Talbot informed them that luncheon was served, so they moved their conversation to the dining room.

Over one of Mrs Smith's excellent raised game pies, they continued to discuss the findings they had gathered that morning and their next steps. "I believe we need to pursue separate threads this afternoon," Wolf concluded. "I want to go and talk to Dr Blackwell and learn more about the autopsy results."

"Do you think he will talk to you? Even if you two do have a history?" Tabitha asked.

Wolf chuckled, "Tabitha, you're the one who keeps telling me how being a peer of the realm opens doors. Whether or not Blackwell would have given this information to Wolf, the thief-taker, he may give it to the Earl of Pembroke." Tabitha smiled; Wolf was learning.

"And what will I be doing?" she asked.

"You will visit your favourite person, the dowager countess. After all, it's Thursday afternoon."

Tabitha groaned, "I'd almost forgotten that decree. But I was hoping I could send Mary with Melody rather than have to go myself. I certainly have no intention of visiting her three times a week, heaven forbid. And I'm sure the dowager has even less interest in seeing me than I do in seeing her."

"While I'm sure that is the case," Wolf concurred, "this is Melody's first visit. I'm sure even the dowager would accept your desire to accompany the child and ensure she is comfortable." Tabitha acknowledged the truth of the sentiment, and Wolf continued. "Take Ginny with you instead of Mary. It's not as if the dowager knows one servant from the other. And Melly won't need Mary there if you're with her. I want Ginny to go down and get the dowager's servants talking. Let's see what they thought of Manning and what gossip might be circulating."

Tabitha could think of many things she would rather do than visit with the Dowager Countess of Pembroke, but she realised the sense in Wolf's suggestion. She also realised, with a twinge of guilt, that it should have occurred to her anyway to be the one to accompany Melody on this first visit.

After lunch, Tabitha asked Talbot to have Ginny meet her

in the nursery. Peeking through the doorway at the four-year-old girl and her nursemaid, previously the housemaid, Mary, Tabitha was struck again by how the child had acclimated to her circumstances. It had not been that many weeks since Melody had been homeless and sleeping rough in the dank basement of a public house.

But watching Melody now, singing with Mary while she brushed her doll, Gemmy's, hair, it was hard to believe what poverty and hardship she'd experienced in her young life. She seemed like any other happy, well-fed, comfortable child. Tabitha's knowledge that she'd managed to save the innocence, and perhaps the life, of at least one young child brought her a sense of purpose and contentment she hadn't known since it had become apparent during her marriage that she was unlikely ever to conceive and carry a baby to term.

For many years, Tabitha had a recurring dream about mothering two small children, a little girl with red-gold ringlets and freckles called Maryann and her brother Peter. When she had first laid eyes on Melody, it had been as if that dream daughter had come to life. When she had convinced an unwilling Wolf to bring Melody and Rat into the household, he had asked what she would do if Rat decided to leave his employment at Chesterton House and wished to take his sister with him. Tabitha hadn't been able to answer that question then, and she was even less willing to confront it now. Back then, the best answer she could come up with was, "I will just have to make sure that Rat is happy here and doesn't want to leave." Now, she acknowledged that giving up Melody and sending her back to a life of uncertainty and deprivation would be unthinkable. No, it wouldn't be unthinkable; it would be unbearable. Tabitha sighed and thought, yet again, "Let us hope it never comes to that."

Tabitha walked into the room, and the little girl ran over to hug her, "Tabby Cat, come and play."

"Melly, you and I are going out this afternoon. Do you remember the nice lady who visited the other day and gave you the sweetie?" It almost stuck in her throat to describe the dowager countess in such benign terms. Still, Wolf's advice resonated with her, and she knew she could not communicate any of her true feelings about the older woman to Melody in word or deed.

"Granny?" Melody asked. "Are we going to see Granny?" The childish delight in the thought of the visit charmed Tabitha, even though she wasn't looking forward to it.

"Yes, Melly. We're going to have tea with Granny. And Ginny will come with us." Luckily, Melody was comfortable with Ginny, Tabitha's lady's maid, who occasionally helped Mary out with Melody and watched her on Mary's afternoon off.

"Mary isn't coming?" Melody asked.

"Not today. Mary will have some time off, just as she does on Sundays when Ginny comes to play with you." Tabitha then turned to the nursery maid and said, "Mary, please help Miss Melody change into one of her pretty new dresses.

As Mary changed Melody's clothes and shoes, Ginny entered the nursery. Tabitha took her aside to explain the plan. Ginny had been extremely helpful during their last investigation. She was a friendly, plain-spoken Irish girl from Whitechapel. Tabitha had found that Ginny could mingle with the staff in other people's households, encouraging them to open up to her. Previously, Tabitha and Wolf had gleaned vital information from Ginny's seemingly innocent gossip in servant halls. Ginny had admitted she had enjoyed playing her role in solving the duke's murder, and Tabitha had no doubt she would jump at the chance to be involved in another case. Ginny didn't disappoint.

On their arrival at the dowager countess' home, it was disconcerting to have the door opened by the upper footman, Michael, rather than by Manning. He took their outerwear and led them into the drawing room. Meanwhile, Ginny made her way down to the servant's hall.

If the dowager had been born a male, she could have been one of the great military minds of all time. As it was, she navigated society as if it were a giant chessboard, keeping her eyes at all times on how she might gain a tactical upper hand over an opponent. Ensuring they were sitting uncomfortably lower than her was just one of the dowager's many ways of tilting the board in her favour. Tabitha wondered in the past if the furniture had originally been made for a nursery, but now she acknowledged the setup was very accommodating to a small child.

On entering the room, the first thing that caught Tabitha's eye was a vast, elaborate dolls' house set on a low table in the middle of the room. The house was exquisite in every detail. Tabitha could sense Melody's excitement at seeing it and kept a firm hold of her hand to prevent the child from running straight over to it. Tabitha was determined that bad parenting would not be something else the dowager could add to her long list of her daughter-in-law's sins.

"Ah, Melody. Come and give Granny a kiss," the dowager said. It wasn't lost on Tabitha that she received no greeting or acknowledgement. However, she led the little girl over and to her amazement, the dowager indicated to her own lap that Tabitha should lift the child onto it. This accomplished, the dowager patted one of her age-lined cheeks where Melody should kiss. The child threw her little arms around the dowager's neck and kissed and hugged her. If Tabitha hadn't known better, she would have sworn the other woman's eyes were wet with unshed tears. But, she rationalised that she must be wrong, and it must be nothing more than the rheumy eyes of an old woman.

The dowager seemed so preoccupied with Melody that Tabitha questioned if she would ever invite Tabitha to take a seat and decided to buck protocol and sit. This went unnoticed and unremarked upon. Tabitha was unsure if it was worse to be the focus of the dowager's unrelenting criticism or ignored altogether.

"Melody, did you see what Granny has for you?" the dowager asked, pointing at the dolls' house. The little girl needed no more encouragement than that and hopped off the dowager's lap and ran over to the extravagant doll's house to play. Tabitha realised this now left the adults to make polite conversation. Or it left Tabitha to make polite conversation and the dowager to say whatever came to mind, however harsh or unfair.

Luckily, Michael entered with a tray of tea and cakes. It was a testament to how enthralled Melody was by the dolls' house that she ignored the cakes altogether. Michael served Tabitha and the dowager tea and a slice of Madeira cake each, and they managed to fill a few minutes with genteel sipping of tea and nibbling of cake.

Finally, knowing conversation could no longer be avoided, Tabitha said, "It feels very strange seeing Michael perform Manning's duties. I can only imagine how much harder it is for you. I know he's served you well for a very long time." Even as she said these words, Tabitha knew the likely response. And she wasn't disappointed.

"If you can imagine how hard this must be for me, I can't imagine why you haven't been able to resolve this misunderstanding yet and return my butler to me."

Tabitha ignored that the dowager had never actually asked Tabitha to prove Manning's innocence; she'd asked "Dear Jeremy." Well, she had demanded more than asked. But either way, Tabitha was only part of the investigation because of her insistence and Wolf's consent. That the dowager saw Manning's arrest for the capital crime of murder primarily through the lens of her own inconvenience was hardly surprising. But her characterisation of it as a misunderstanding that could be resolved in a matter of days needed to be addressed. Actually, it gave Tabitha an excellent opening to ask some questions of the dowager.

"Mama," Tabitha said as gently as she could stomach. While referring to her mother-in-law in such an informal manner felt uncomfortable to Tabitha, she had realised a while ago that she needed to pretend they maintained friendly familial relations. "The charges against Manning are more than a misunderstanding. He was discovered at the crime scene, kneeling over the victim and covered in her blood. When arrested, he gave the police no explanation for why he was there and has still said nothing officially to counter their assumptions. This is not something that Lord Pembroke and myself can magically fix overnight."

The dowager harrumphed as she often did when she found herself on the losing side of an argument she was unwilling to concede. "So, what have you managed to find out so far?" she asked aggressively.

"Did you know Manning had a daughter?" Tabitha asked. She assumed the dowager remembered the circumstances of his marriage to Jenny, her pregnancy, and her abandonment of her new husband. But she wanted to hear the dowager's take on the subject.

"It is hardly for me to pry into and concern myself with the personal lives of my servants," she admonished. Tabitha had a hard time believing that there were any personal lives, from a duchess to a scullery maid, that the dowager wouldn't consider prying into and interfering with, but she kept this thought to herself. The dowager continued, "However, I think I recall a brief marriage to one of our housemaids, a pretty little thing; I can't remember her name."

"Jenny Murphy," Tabitha provided. "Her name was Jenny Murphy."

"If you say so," the dowager conceded. "I believe I have some memory of the girl being with child when she upped and left poor Manning. Of course," the dowager continued in a rather gossipy tone, "it was always unlikely that a gangly, awkward lad like Manning was back in those days could keep the attention of a beautiful girl like Jenny Murphy. It was beyond belief that he caught her eye to begin with. Certainly, she had all the men running after her." The dowager, Tabitha reflected, could suddenly recall quite a lot about the beautiful housemaid she had just claimed to barely remember.

There was something about the way the dowager had said "all the men" that Tabitha noticed. Had Jenny Murphy caught the eye of a man beyond the household staff? She decided to roll the dice and feed the dowager a piece of information she was sure she would seize on with her talons like a bird of prey with carrion, "The murder victim, Collette DuBois, was Jenny Murphy's daughter. Her real name was Claire Murphy." Tabitha phrased that shocking piece of news very carefully. She hadn't said Claire was Manning's daughter because that was still unclear, and she wondered if the dowager had the same doubts.

The gleam in the dowager's eyes told her how titillating she had found that information. As genuinely distressed as she was by the situation her butler found himself in, her insatiable need for gossip, and to be the first person to know such gossip, trumped all.

"So the French tart was nothing more than a common Colleen after all! Like mother, like daughter," the dowager said triumphantly. Tabitha was appalled at the dowager's crude terminology and use of the derogatory slang, Colleen, denoting a female Irish peasant girl. However, she said nothing and schooled her face not to reflect her feelings on the subject. The dowager continued, "So, Manning thought he'd found his long-lost daughter, did he?" The very phrasing of the question indicated the dowager shared the same doubts about Claire Murphy's parentage as Mrs Jenkins had.

"Silly man! How was it not obvious to Manning, even back then, that Jenny had found herself in trouble and, when the father refused to make an honest woman of her, saw him as precisely the kind of stooge who would marry her and not ask too many questions." Tabitha thought it was telling that the dowager had phrased these suspicions in almost the exact words Mrs Jenkins had. "When the girl upped and ran off, that should have confirmed for him that the child was not his. Who knows why she left? Maybe her young man thought better of it, and they ran away together. It's hard to believe that all these years later, Manning was fool enough to be taken in by another Murphy girl."

Tabitha decided it would do no harm at this point, or no more harm, to tell the rest of the story as Manning had relayed it to Wolf, "He tracked her down, rather than the other way around. He happened to see her in her landau one day in the park. Apparently, her resemblance to her mother was uncanny. He followed her to her home and presented himself at her door a few days later. He had been visiting her on his afternoon off for months since then. At least on the surface, it seems she did not need anything from Manning except the love of a father." The dowager harrumphed again.

With no gossip left to reveal, Tabitha was somewhat at a loss for what small talk to make and was relieved when the dowager abruptly stood up and moved to another equally small chair already placed near the dolls' house. She then spent the next thirty minutes ignoring Tabitha and playing with dolls with Melody. Unperturbed by the dowager's rude disregard for her adult guest, Tabitha used the time to sip tea, eat cake, and consider what they had learned. She was eager to hear what Ginny had heard from the servants and to go home and add all these details to her notecards.

Forty-five minutes was a long time for any game, even one as novel as playing with a palatial dolls' house, to keep the attention of an energetic four-year-old. Eventually, it was clear Tabitha could make their excuses based on more than her readiness to depart.

"Yes, it is probably for the best. I expect Lady Willis this afternoon, and I would not subject even you to the company of that harpy, Tabitha." Overlooking this indirect insult and just happy to be able to take her leave, Tabitha sent Michael to inform Ginny of their departure.

In the carriage, Ginny told her what little she had gleaned from the dowager's staff. No one had ever questioned where Manning went on his days off. He might have seemed a little happier of late, but as a butler, that was hardly an emotion he'd be quick to display. As to how he had appeared on the day of the murder, the housekeeper remembered that a note had come for him in the morning and that he hadn't gone out as usual in the early afternoon but had waited until later. The housekeeper had said the only reason he'd managed to slip away when he did was that the dowager hadn't been dining at home that evening.

"That is interesting," Tabitha mused. "It explains how he could visit his daughter later than usual. But what did the note say that made him change his usual visiting time? Good work, Ginny."

Back home, Mary accompanied Melody back to the nursery, and Tabitha, with Ginny in tow, went to look for Wolf, only to find he hadn't returned yet from his expedition.

CHAPTER 9

For so many of his trips around London for investigations, Wolf had tried to hide, or at least downplay, his new position as Earl of Pembroke. But for the trip to see Dr Blackwell at St Thomas' Hospital, Wolf intended to wrap himself in as much of the cloak of hereditary entitlement that titles seemed to confer on men and to burnish the effect with the lustre of great wealth. If Wolf hadn't realised before he visited Pentonville Prison the extraordinary effect power and prestige had on people, Warden Featherstone's obsequiousness had made clear how useful it could be to flaunt that he was now a peer of the realm.

Usually unconcerned about whether his clothes befitted a man of his rank and stature, Wolf took special care to radiate sartorial splendour for his trip to see the doctor. He even shaved and tried to tame his usually unruly and unkempt hair. Normally uncomfortable travelling around London in his magnificent carriage replete with gilded flourishes and Pembroke crests, today he was happy to be delivered to St Thomas in a manner befitting an earl.

His reception at the hospital was all such an effort deserved. Located on the south bank of the River Thames, St Thomas' Hospital was impressive for its size and architecture. It was one of the most prominent hospitals in London, with a long medical innovation and research history. The hospital had a range of departments, including surgical, medicine, and pathology, and a fine reputation for serving the sick of London.

Upon arrival at the hospital, the carriage attracted attention from passersby and hospital staff alike. The sight of a wealthy and influential individual arriving in such a grand manner was unusual; people of wealth usually had doctors visit them rather than the other way around.

If Wolf had anticipated any possible resistance when he requested to speak to the pathologist, he was gratified to see that the trappings of his earldom had achieved the desired effect. He was quickly whisked down a rabbit's warren of hallways to the pathology department by the guard on duty.

Dr Blackwell was the chief pathologist, and his office was near the department's autopsy room. Wolf hadn't seen Dr Blackwell since he had concluded the man's blackmail case. His first impression was that the man's girth had expanded and his hairline had decreased. When Wolf strode into his office accompanied by the fawning guard who had directed him there, Blackwell's eyebrows raised in surprise, and he eyed Wolf carefully.

"Dr Blackwell, sir," the guard simpered, "this is the Earl of Pembroke to see you, sir." The guard puffed up as he said this as if he were responsible for bringing someone as illustrious as an earl to visit.

Dr Blackwell was a portly man in his late fifties. He sported a well-trimmed grey beard and a pair of impressive, shaggy, equally grey eyebrows. On hearing Wolf's title, those eyebrows shot up again, and a look somewhere between confusion and suspicion came over his face. Wolf could tell what the man was wondering, and he didn't blame him. The last time he'd seen Wolf had been during a particularly lean time for thief-taking work, and Wolf had looked especially slovenly and roguish. The doctor had only employed him because he'd come with such excellent recommendations from a former client, a fellow doctor, and he probably had no other options. Wolf would have respected the man less if he hadn't been sceptical that Wolf's title was anything other than an elaborate ruse.

Wolf had spent his childhood and young adult life knowing his grandfather, the old earl, had only tolerated his grandson's occasional presence as a backup plan. Wolf's father and grandfather had fallen out over his father's refusal to kowtow to the earl's wishes. When it became clear that Jonathan's father, then Viscount Chesterton, was not going to have any more sons, the grandfather paid just enough attention to Wolf to ensure he had the appropriate education, Eton and Oxford and enough exposure to his more illustrious family to step into the earldom if the worst came to the worst.

Remembering those occasional visits to his grandfather's home, Wolf impersonated the imperiousness the late earl always had projected. He tried to mimic the languid manner in which the man moved, even in old age, as if he had better places to be and people to see than whomever he happened to be with at the time. The man had looked down his aquiline nose and stared with disdain, seemingly for any conversation with anyone. He always exuded an air of, "My time is precious, and I don't have any of it to spare for you and your petty concerns."

Wolf summoned every one of those memories at that moment and strode into the doctor's office, uninvited and took a chair in front of the man's desk. Wolf crossed his legs, affecting the same languid manner. He attempted to copy his grandfather's haughty look and brushed an imaginary speck of dust off his impeccably tailored jacket sleeve for good measure.

"Blackwell, good to see you again. I imagine you have questions," Wolf began in a tone that ten generations of the Earl of Pembroke had used to indicate they would brook no dissent. "I inherited the earldom after my cousin Jonathan, the previous earl, died unexpectedly last year."

Wolf could see the man assess the situation, taking in Wolf's clothes, posture, and attitude, and decide, "Your lordship, I'm honoured to see you again." Wolf inclined his head to acknowledge what an honour it must indeed be. "You can leave us, Johnson," the doctor said to the guard. The man reluctantly left the office, almost falling over his feet on his way out.

"Let me get to the point, Blackwell," Wolf said. "I believe you recently conducted the autopsy of a young woman brought in under the name Collette DuBois." The doctor nodded warily, unsure where this conversation was going. Wolf continued, "I wish to know the details of your report."

"My lord," Dr Blackwell began cautiously, "as I'm sure you're aware, my report is confidential until it is handed to the coroner, who then presents it at the inquest. Your request is quite unorthodox, to say the least."

Wolf intensified his glare, summoned every ounce of his grandfather's arrogance, and said, "I am a peer of the realm. I sit in the House of Lords, and these orthodoxies do not apply to me." Wolf had no idea if this was or wasn't true, and he suspected the doctor didn't either.

After a few moments, it was evident by the man's body language that he had decided to err on the side of deference and said, "Of course, your lordship. What can I tell you?"

"I assume the facts, as reported in the newspapers, were correct, if incomplete, and that she died from being stabbed in her heart?"

"That is all correct," the doctor confirmed.

"What can you tell me about the young woman from the autopsy report?"

"There were two items of note; the first is that she was pregnant. The pregnancy was quite pronounced, even on her slim frame, so I'd guess perhaps six months along." This was a very interesting titbit of information, but Wolf didn't want to interrupt the man's flow and kept his face passive. The doctor continued, "The only other noteworthy abnormality on the body was that the young woman had six toes on one foot.

"In the medical profession, we call such a deformity Polydactyly. Interesting irregularity," the doctor continued thoughtfully, almost as if he were now talking with a student. "Of course, there was a time when such deformities were seen as signs of the devil, but we've known for quite a while now that it is merely a medical condition. Indeed, I have read many papers discussing how the condition seems to be passed down through the family and suggesting that it may have a hereditary basis. I find the new study of genetic inheritance fascinating. So, I was delighted to observe that the fetus also had six toes. Quite thrilling."

Wolf found the doctor's cold, scientific fascination with a child killed in its mother's womb quite gruesome, but he kept his thoughts to himself. "Is there anything else you can tell me, Dr Blackwell? Anything about the stabbing itself, perhaps?"

"Only that the knife entered the heart with surgical precision. Whoever killed her did not do so in a random fit of anger; this was a calculated attack. It is doubtful that someone managed to stab her accidentally in such a way as to guarantee immediate and certain death. I've seen stabbings such as this one before on occasion. It had all the marks of a trained killer."

Now, this was interesting information. "Will you be reporting this to the coroner?" Wolf asked. The doctor nodded, and Wolf continued, "I assume you know the police have arrested the Dowager Countess of Pembroke's butler for the crime. Would it be a fair conclusion to say that, unless Mr Manning, the butler, was sneaking out at night to perform a second job as a trained assassin, it's unlikely he was the murderer?"

"It is not for me to draw conclusions about who may or may not have committed the crime, nor to weave a narrative about motive or circumstance. However, if the question posed is, was this murder the work of a trained killer? Then, my answer is yes. As to the likelihood that a butler might moonlight as such a killer, I have no professional opinion."

Wolf considered what Dr Blackwell had told him in the carriage on the way home. He also took a moment to marvel at the power he held just in virtue of his title. Doors opened, and people spoke to him as the Earl of Pembroke, who would not have given him the time of day as Jeremy Wolfson Chesterton. He was appalled by this knowledge but also aware of what such power meant.

He found it ridiculous, laughable even, that he had Lord in front of his name only because of the random confluence of two events: his cousin having died childless and an ancestor hundreds of years before having done something to please a monarch enough to have been granted a title. These events and primogeniture suddenly gave him people's time, attention, and respect. But none of it changed who he was before or after inheriting the earldom. Fundamentally, Wolf had no respect for the system he had benefitted from so greatly. He was determined to find ways at least to have other unluckier souls reap some benefit from his elevation. As he considered this, he realised he was happy to be helping Manning because this was a perfect example of using his good fortune to help someone who was unable to help themselves.

Wolf was still mulling this over as he entered the house. He didn't care about the formalities of having his butler open the front door and take his coat. It still made him quite uncomfortable to have so many servants waiting on him hand and foot. But, he did wonder what had happened since he'd been gone to make Talbot abandon his post.

After depositing his coat, he followed a cacophony of voices from the parlour. As he opened the door, the primary sound he heard over all the voices was wailing. As he stepped into the room, he saw Mary sitting on the sofa, tears streaming down her cheeks, with Tabitha sitting beside her, arms around the young servant girl. Tabitha wasn't crying, but it looked like she might start any moment. She was pale and drawn, and he noticed her shoulders were shaking with barely controlled emotion. Ginny was in the room, also crying. Talbot was pouring tea for everyone, but even he looked shaken.

At Wolf's entrance, they all looked up. Tabitha jumped to her feet, exclaiming, "Thank heavens you're home, Wolf. Melody has been abducted."

Whatever Wolf had expected had caused such consternation, it wasn't that. He strode across the room and, without even considering what he was doing and that the servants were witnesses, pulled Tabitha into his arms. She had been trying to stay strong to comfort Mary, who was almost beyond reason by this point. But as Wolf's strong arms wrapped around her and he gently stroked her hair, murmuring soothing sounds in her ear, she lost all self-control and began to sob.

Wolf pulled her down to sit beside him on the sofa and let her cry while turning to Talbot and asking, "What happened?"

"It seems that on their return from visiting the dowager countess, Miss Melody had a lot of energy, and Mary thought it might do her some good to run around in the park for a little while. They were playing with a ball on the grass, and, at one point, it rolled away. Mary went to get it and, while her back was turned, which she swears was no more than a moment or two, a man grabbed Melody. When she turned back, she could only see him running away carrying the child. She tried to call out and chase him but was grabbed from behind and a hand put over her mouth. A voice said, 'If you want to see the little girl alive again, give your master a message from me. Tell him to leave well enough alone.'

"The man shoved Mary to the ground and ran away before she could get a good look at his face. By the time Mary had arrived back here, she was in such hysterics that we could barely get the story out of her. Mrs Jenkins has gone to get her a tincture of valerian root so we can put her to bed. The shock and the guilt are too much for the girl."

Tabitha's sobbing had stopped, and she pulled away from Wolf and asked, "Who could have done such a thing? Who is sending you a message?"

"Truly, I have no idea. But Mary, listen to me." At the sound of her master's voice, the girl's crying calmed down a little, and he continued, "Mary, this was not your fault. This was not a random abduction. This wasn't because of any negligence on your part. This was planned. Someone was waiting for just the right moment to grab Melody. And if you hadn't turned, he likely would have taken her in front of your eyes. There was nothing you could do against two men."

At that moment, Mrs Jenkins entered the room with the tincture and led Mary away to put her to bed. Wolf asked Talbot, "Was Mary able to describe the two men?"

"No, milord. However, as you can see, she was not in a state to be able to say much. Though she did say something that may be interesting. She said that the man who whispered in her ear sounded like a," the man paused, "sorry, milord, but to use her terminology, he sounded like a toff."

Tabitha had taken a fortifying gulp of tea and was now more composed, "A toff? That is what she said, isn't it."

"Yes, milady, and if I may be as bold to say, while someone of Mary's class might, under normal circumstances, use that term quite broadly, Mary has been in service for quite a few years. I believe when Mary says toff, she means he sounded like a far smaller circle of people."

"He sounded like an aristocrat," Wolf said, finishing Talbot's thought. "Thank you, Talbot. I'm sure all the staff has heard about this by now. Please go and reassure them we will do everything in our power to find Miss Melody."

As Wolf said these words, there was a noise at the door, and Rat rushed into the room, "Wolf, they took Melly!"

It had taken Rat some time to get used to addressing him as anything other than Wolf, and the best he usually managed was m'lord Wolf. But, his distress was so evident that even Talbot let the informality slide.

Wolf gestured that the boy should take a seat and, once he had, replied, "I'm just hearing all the details now. I will get her back, Rat."

"We'll get 'er back. She's my little sister, and I'm supposed to look after 'er."

Despite sensing Tabitha tense next to him, he conceded the point to the boy, "Yes, we will get her back. Rat, have you or the staff noticed anyone lurking around the house over the past few days? Anyone who looked out of place?"

The boy considered the question and then answered, "There was something. Mrs Jenkins sent me to run an errand this morning. On my way out, I did see this boy 'anging about. 'E was supposed to be shining shoes, but what was odd was 'e didn't seem like 'e was all that bothered about the business. I saw one man come up to get 'is boots shined, and the boy sent 'im away. I didn't think much more about it at the time. Do you think 'e was a lookout?"

"I think there's a very good chance that's exactly what he was. Someone was waiting for Melody to go out with Mary. Once the boy saw them leave, he must have alerted his master, who waited for an opportune moment to grab the child." As he said these words, Tabitha lost her composure again and flung herself back onto Wolf's shoulder, crying.

"She must be so scared. She's just a little girl. What if they hurt her, Wolf?"

Rat stood up, his young face contorted by anger, "If anyone lays one 'and on Melly, I'll kill 'im. And I don't care if I 'ang for it."

"Don't worry, lad, we'll make sure no one hurts her. What can you remember about this boy watching the house?"

Rat sat back down and thought, "You know, now you're asking; I did think somefink at the time. I thought that looks like Billy James' kid brother. 'Aven't seen him since before Ma and Pa died, but it looked like 'im. And when I saw 'im, 'e tried to pull 'is 'at down over his face like 'e didn't want me seeing 'im."

"Excellent, Rat. Then we have somewhere to start. Do you know where to find Billy James or his family?"

"Last I 'eard, Billy worked for a baker down Whitechapel Road. Want me to go down there and see what 'e 'as to say?"

"That's exactly what I want you to do." Under normal circumstances, Wolf would have expected Tabitha to resist sending Rat back into his old neighbourhood, even as a messenger boy. But, such was her emotional state that she barely even registered Wolf's conversation with the boy. Rat left to head out to Whitechapel. Talbot left the room with the tea tray, and Wolf and Tabitha were left alone. He decided they both needed something stronger than tea and poured himself a brandy and Tabitha an extra-large glass of sherry.

Reluctant at first, Tabitha finally had a few sips. She then took a few deep breaths and seemed to grow less agitated. Finally, she felt composed enough to speak, took one more sip of sherry and asked, "Someone took Melody to get to you. Who and why?"

"I've certainly made some enemies over the years, but this

doesn't sound as if it's about a past case. It sounds as if we're being warned off this case. This is about Manning. Someone has been watching us and knows we're investigating. Suddenly, I'm sure Manning is innocent. This feels much larger than a butler killing his long-lost daughter."

Wolf realised he'd had no opportunity to tell Tabitha what he'd learned from Dr Blackwell. He quickly brought her up to speed. "He said this was no random stabbing done in anger. This murder was committed by someone who knew how to strike in the heart and ensure the victim didn't survive. This was the work of a trained assassin."

Then, almost as an aside, Wolf told Tabitha about Claire Murphy's deformity. "She had six toes?" Tabitha asked with what sounded like more than idle curiosity. "How odd. So did Jonathan."

"Wait, your husband had six toes on one foot?"

Tabitha nodded. "Is that important?" she asked. "I mean, I can see it's a bizarre coincidence, but why is it anything more than that?"

"Blackwell said that having an extra finger or toe is called some name I can't remember now. But he said it's often hereditary."

"What are you saying?" Tabitha asked, even though she had a pretty good idea what Wolf was implying.

"I'm saying that I think we just found out who got Jenny Murphy pregnant. It wasn't the footman; it was your father-in-law."

The notion that peers of the realm often bedded young girls in their households was hardly new. And even in her naivety, Tabitha had long known that men in Jonathan's austere circle, and even above, often had children born on the wrong side of the blanket. She wouldn't be surprised to find out one day that Jonathan also had. She could only imagine his ire if a servant or showgirl had given him a son when his wife could not. She almost relished such a thought.

Tabitha wasn't sure how such situations were usually

handled. She suspected that Jonathan and his ilk rarely did the right thing and cared for their illegitimate progeny as they should. However, she wondered if Jenny Murphy's situation, where she had found a servant in the same household to marry her and claim her child was unusual.

Wolf spoke aloud where her thoughts were headed, "Do you think the dowager knew?"

Tabitha sighed, considered the question, and said, "I think she may have suspected. The way she talked about Jenny and her daughter was laced with vitriol. Of course, she talks about me like that all the time. And about her so-called friends. But that kind of nastiness about a servant and a young woman supposedly wholly unconnected to her seemed uncalled for. Now I think about it, it sounded personal. I think she knew."

"I wonder if she played a role in Jenny's sudden departure," Wolf suggested.

"I wouldn't be at all surprised," Tabitha said. "Most women of our class harbour few illusions about their husband's fidelity. In fact, from what the dowager has revealed, she had closed the door to her boudoir to my father-in-law quite early in the marriage. So, she may have been more than happy for him to turn his attention elsewhere. However, no woman would be happy seeing a beautiful young woman like Jenny Murphy grow large with her husband's child in her household."

Wolf wasn't entirely comfortable having such a conversation with Tabitha, but he had accused her of not facing the harsh realities of life. Now that she was discussing some of them bluntly, he could hardly complain. "And let's not forget," he added. "Once Jenny was safely married to Manning, there was no reason the affair couldn't continue beneath the dowager's very nose with any subsequent pregnancies being easily explained away."

"That may have been the final straw for my mother-in-law. Her husband carrying on with a housemaid was hardly something worth her notice. But the prospect of her husband's by-blows raised in the same house as her child, I'm sure, was intolerable. She's not someone I can see allowing a cuckoo in her nest. Even if I'm correct, is this merely an interesting side note to the case? Is it relevant to Claire's murder?" Tabitha asked.

"Well, if you'd told me this earlier, I would have said yes. Perhaps Manning discovered Claire wasn't his daughter. Perhaps, the dowager found out about his visits to Claire and told him the truth. Before, I might have suggested he killed Claire in a moment of misplaced anger. However, after what has happened with Melly, I doubt this has anything to do with the case. As I said, this isn't about Manning. I think it's about something more sinister."

As they discussed the case for a few minutes, Tabitha had almost forgotten what had happened to Melody, but Wolf's last statement was like a slap across her face, bringing her back to the moment. "How are we going to find her, Wolf?" she asked.

He had been sitting in his armchair while he drank his brandy, but at this question, he moved to sit back next to her on the sofa and took her in his arms. "We will find her, Tabitha. I swear to you. Remember, this is what I'm good at; finding people. I have people who can help. People from my old life."

"You do?" she asked with a whisper of hope.

"If necessary, I will even ask Mickey D for help." As he said these words, Wolf knew he would indeed ask the Whitechapel gangster for help if it came to it. Mickey and his boys were part of the dark underbelly of London. They knew who was working for whom. They knew when someone suddenly was flush with money. If the "toff" had people working for him, there was a good chance Mickey could find out who they were.

But Wolf also knew that having finally managed to get himself out from under Mickey's thumb after the last case, asking for this favour would put him, yet again, in the man's power. But if that was what he had to do to return Melody to Tabitha unharmed, he would do so willingly.

CHAPTER 10

Neither Tabitha nor Wolf had much appetite for dinner that night. They sat at the dining room table, pushing Mrs Smith's delicious food around the plate. Tabitha jumped at every noise, alert for the possibility of Melody's return. After dinner, they retired to the parlour, and Tabitha tried to read a book but found she couldn't concentrate and was rereading the same page repeatedly.

When she was ready to give up any pretence she could think of anything but Melody, the door opened, and Rat entered. Tabitha jumped up, unable to contain herself, "What did you find out?"

"Let the boy sit and catch his breath, Tabitha."

"Yes, of course. I'm sorry, Rat. Sit down. Have a biscuit."

Never one to turn down any sweet treat, Rat helped himself. But he could see Tabitha's impatience to hear what he had found out needed to be satiated before he could enjoy the biscuit. "So, I couldn't find Billy James. The butcher's shop was closed for the day." Tabitha's heart sank, but Rat continued, "But I did run into a kid me and Billy used to run with when we were nippers."

It broke Tabitha's heart to hear a boy of nine speak as if his childhood was long behind him. Rat continued, "I asked him if 'e knew what Billy's brother, Ollie, 'is name is, was up to. He said, "I thought I might 'ave seen 'im polishing boots on the street in Toff Town. This kid laughs and says that Ollie claims 'e's polishing boots, but 'e suddenly seems very flush. Mrs James even 'ad a new 'at on in church last Sunday. So there's brass coming from somewhere, 'ain't there?"

"Did this friend of yours know who Ollie is working for?"

"Nah. But, said Ollie's been tight-lipped. Except, 'e said the other day, Ollie was showing off, like, and 'e did say something about working for a toff. But then, 'e must have realised wot 'e said, and 'e clammed up."

Tabitha was disappointed Rat didn't have more to tell, but Wolf pointed out, "We now know for sure the boy Rat saw outside the house works for the man who grabbed Melody."

"We do?" Tabitha asked. "How can you be so sure?"

"I spent a long time as a thief-catcher. Hunting someone down is rarely about knowing things for absolute certain. It's about having hunches, hearing suspicions, and then trying to verify them as best you can. We know a boy was behaving oddly outside our house yesterday. Rat has every reason to believe it is this Ollie James. We know Melody was taken by someone whose voice sounded aristocratic. We now know Ollie is suddenly flush with money and is working for someone who sounds aristocratic. The likelihood is that Ollie is working for the man who abducted Melody. Remember Occam's Razor, Tabitha?"

"Yes, the simplest answer is normally the correct one."

"Exactly. This is progress, Tabitha. It really is. Well done, Rat, really excellent job."

The boy flushed with pride. Tabitha knew how much he idolised Wolf. His given name was Matt. Still, he refused to answer to any name besides Rat because the nickname bonded him with Wolf and Bear.

"Rat, head back to the kitchen and have Mrs Smith make you some hot milk. It's been a long day, and you should try to get some rest." Tabitha could see him about to protest and continued, "Rat, I know waiting to hear a word of Melly is torture; it is for me as well. But we will do better tomorrow if we're not exhausted and have clear heads. There is no higher priority for his lordship and me than to bring your sister home unharmed."

Reluctantly, the boy left. Wolf asked Tabitha, "Are you going to be able to take your own stellar advice and get some sleep tonight?"

Tabitha shook her head, "I doubt I'll sleep a wink. How can I?"

Wolf went and sat beside Tabitha, took her hand in his much

larger one, and said very gently, "I'm as concerned as you are. As determined as I've been to remain detached, Miss Melly has wormed her way into my heart, into all our hearts, and no one in this house will sleep well until she's safely back in the nursery, where she belongs."

These words warmed Tabitha more than she could express. She had understood Wolf's concerns when Melody and Rat came to live at Chesterton House. Rationally, she had agreed with all of them. But from the first moment she had set eyes on the little girl, she knew she had no choice but to protect and nurture her. It meant a lot to know that, despite his own attempts at rational indifference, Wolf now felt the same.

Wolf encouraged her to take some hot milk to bed and try to sleep. Tabitha shook her head, "Not yet. I want to write up everything we know, including what Ginny learned from the dowager's staff. I forgot to tell you in the chaos of the afternoon. Though, it's hard to care about Manning when Melly is missing."

"I understand. You feel as if every second spent investigating the murder is a moment we could be using trying to find Melody. But these are not separate cases; they're inextricably linked. Melody's abduction was a warning for us to stop investigating. As I said, this tells me the case is about something much bigger and darker than Manning and Claire Murphy. Finding the answers will lead us to whoever has Melody."

Wolf still had hold of Tabitha's hand. She turned towards him and asked in a scared voice that broke his heart, "If we don't do what they demanded and let this case go, how do we know they won't hurt her?"

Wolf considered her question and realised he couldn't lie to her, even though every fibre of his being pushed him to say anything that might ease her concerns. "We don't know that." He paused and then said the words he'd been dreading having to say to Tabitha, "But we don't know they haven't already hurt her." At this, she burst into tears, sobbing on his shoulder. He put his arm around her shoulders and pulled her close. And then he let her cry.

Finally, when she seemed to have cried her eyes dry, Wolf asked, "Maybe do the notecards tomorrow?" But Tabitha insisted. Pulling herself from his embrace, she wiped her eyes. She insisted that if she didn't organise her thoughts tonight, she definitely wouldn't get any sleep that night.

Writing out the notecards calmed Tabitha's nerves somewhat, giving her a practical task to focus on. As she wrote, Tabitha told Wolf what Ginny had discovered. "Well, that confirms what Manning told me, that he'd gone later that day because he'd received a note from Claire asking him to," Wolf said. "But why did she want to see him later?"

Tabitha stopped writing and tapped the pen against her lips absent-mindedly, "Is it possible Claire Murphy didn't send the note?" she mused. "After all, if Dr Blackwell is correct and a professional assassin killed her, he may have known her movements and that Manning visited on Sundays. It would be a perfect crime to frame Manning for the murder. I wonder if Manning kept the letter".

"That's an interesting theory, but even if he did keep the letter, we'd have to find a sample of Claire Murphy's handwriting to compare it to, which comes back to the fact that we need to gain admittance to that house. I wrote to my man of business and my solicitor this morning, and I hope they have some news for me by tomorrow."

Tabitha finished writing up all their notecards. As she pinned them to the board, it became clear they had discovered a lot. Pieces of red yarn crisscrossed the board connecting cards. They had multiple narrative strings to pull on, but an obvious pattern had yet to emerge. Wolf came and stood beside her, and they stared at the board in silence for some time.

Finally, Tabitha summarised what they were looking at, "Jenny Murphy fell pregnant. We believe the late Earl of Pembroke was the father. Manning marries Jenny, presumably unaware that she is already pregnant. Before the baby is born, Jenny runs away. Did the dowager know the baby was her husband's, and did she facilitate Jenny's departure?

"Thirty years later, Manning believes he's found his long-lost daughter, now posing as the elegant Parisian courtesan Collette DuBois. Somehow, she has set herself up with a house in Chelsea. We know that Claire/Collette gave her staff the evening off every Sunday. Who did she meet with during that time whose presence needed to be kept secret, even from her loyal staff?

"Finally, Manning receives a note telling him to come in the evening rather than Sunday afternoon. Did Claire send the note? Manning arrives at the house to find Claire stabbed through the heart. He bends over her body just as the butler arrives home earlier than usual and catches him with blood on his hands. He seems to have been caught in the act, yet Dr Blackwell's autopsy report will say that the murder was committed with a surgical precision that indicates the murderer knew exactly where to strike. Have I missed anything?" Tabitha asked.

"Well, we now know Claire Murphy was pregnant," Wolf answered.

"Is that relevant? She was a prostitute. Presumably, even when care is taken, such things are occasionally occupational hazards."

Wolf was so uncomfortable discussing such things with Tabitha that his first instinct was to say it wasn't relevant and quickly move on. But he knew that was neither doing Tabitha's intelligence nor the case justice. "Tabitha, you know by now not to discard any evidence at this stage of an investigation. Perhaps Claire was making demands on the baby's father, and he had her killed."

"Of course, you're right," Tabitha conceded. She took a deep breath and said, "And now Melody has been abducted by an aristocratic-sounding man as a warning to us to stop investigating. Who is this man, and what is his involvement? Is he the killer?"

"There's one more thing I want us to put on this board before I insist you go to bed," Wolf said. "We've been assuming the killer was a professional assassin because of the accuracy of the stabbing. But, of course, there's another kind of person who knows exactly where to stab to cause instant death; an actual surgeon. It's just something to consider." Tabitha agreed and wrote up one last notecard before calling for hot milk and heading up to her bed for what she was sure would be a restless night.

CHAPTER 11

Tabitha slept as badly as she had expected to, tossing and turning all night. When she finally fell asleep, she was plagued with nightmares. When Ginny entered her room the following morning with tea and toast, Tabitha felt as if she hadn't slept a wink of sleep all night. She had no patience for anything but minimal effort with her dress and hair, but a glance in the mirror showed the dark circles under her eyes. She was grateful for the tea but had no appetite for the toast.

She found Wolf at breakfast, though he seemed not to have much more appetite than she did. He was reading letters which he put down as she sat. Refusing food, she was happy to drink some coffee and try to clear the heaviness from her head.

The letters were from Wolf's man of business and solicitor. As Tabitha sipped her coffee, Wolf continued perusing the information the men had managed to glean. "So, it seems Claire Murphy did not own the house," Wolf summarised. "However, it's unclear who does own it. My solicitor Anderson writes that the house is owned by something called a limited liability company. He advises that this is often done to shield the actual owners. The company can be set up with a director acting as a front for the real owners."

"Is it possible to discover those real owners?" Tabitha asked.

He says, and I quote, "As a legal matter, one potential avenue for piercing the shield is to argue the company is being used to commit fraud or other illegal activities. If it can be shown that the company is a sham, with no legitimate business purpose, a court could potentially set aside the corporate structure and hold the individual shareholders liable for any damages or debts incurred by the company." He continued, "Another potential approach is to obtain a court order requiring the company to disclose the identity of its shareholders. However, there must be a compelling reason for a court to grant such an order, such as suspected criminal activity or a threat to public safety.'"

Wolf continued, "He ends by saying that neither of the above is a quick solution for finding out who owns the house. He does provide the name of the company director and a registered address for the company. Which I suppose is something. A Mr Fitzpatrick, in Bloomsbury."

"Does your man of business have much to add to this?" Tabitha asked.

"Not a lot. However, what he says mostly confirms Anderson's findings: Claire Murphy didn't seem to have much of a financial situation as far as he can see. She seems to have had no obvious assets besides the house, which we now know wasn't hers."

Tabitha hesitated before asking her next question. She knew it made Wolf very uncomfortable when she questioned him about the more lascivious aspects of society. Still, there were many things a young woman of her class knew nothing about, but Tabitha suspected Wolf did. "Thanks to our last investigation, I now know a bit more about brothels and prostitution," she laughed nervously as she said this. "But, I know nothing of the more high-end situation Claire Murphy seems to have been in. I realise men like my husband have long supported mistresses, providing them with houses and jewels. Is it normal to do so via this kind of legal structure?"

Wolf was as uncomfortable with this discussion as she knew he would be. However, he steeled himself and said, "Truthfully, this is not a matter of which I have any personal experience. However, in my professional life, I have encountered such situations. I suspect that such a legal structure is unusual and unnecessarily complicated. After all, as you've said, it is hardly a secret or in any way socially unacceptable for men in the highest echelons of society to keep mistresses."

"Indeed, Bertie has made it quite fashionable even," Tabitha said, referring to the Prince of Wales and his notorious string of mistresses. Is that what you think Claire Murphy was, a mistress?"

"I'm not going to try to parse the subtle differences between mistress, courtesan and prostitute," Wolf answered. "I will say, the French name does indicate she was playing the part of a cultured sophisticate, and that certainly fits with the persona of a more refined companion. Though to pull off such a ruse and turn from Claire Murphy to Collette DuBois, there would have to have been some kind of initial expenditure. The gowns, the jewels, a woman doesn't catch an earl or a duke, certainly not a prince, if she's selling vegetables in Covent Garden. Somehow, Claire Murphy would have had to get herself on enough of a footing to catch the eye of a man who could set her up in style."

"We need to know more about her life. And for that, we need to know what happened to her mother when she left Chesterton House. Where did she go?" Tabitha continued, "I hate to say this, but we must talk with the dowager again. If our suspicions are correct, she knows more about this than she is saying. Perhaps finding out about Melly's abduction will be incentive enough for her to be honest. Wolf, I cannot face her alone today."

"Of course, I'll come with you. There are a few things I need to do before we go. I'd like to understand why the police assumed she was a courtesan, or as Bruiser put it, a high-end prostitute. The headlines' sensationalism was partly the idea of Manning as a client. But how did that idea even get started? I need to talk to Andrews." At Tabitha's look of confusion, Wolf explained, "He's the news hound I had Anthony go to with the photographs. As these ink-slingers go, Andrews is okay. I want to understand how they ended up with this information."

"Wolf," Tabitha asked hesitantly, "do we need to be more circumspect in our investigations? Are we being watched? Someone knows we are looking into Claire's death and took Melly to force us to stop. What will happen if this person suspects we're still investigating?"

Wolf had no comforting answer for her, but he had considered that question during his own sleepless night. "We have not been operating with much stealth to date; I had Somerset request access to Manning through the Secretary of State's office. I turned up at the prison and St Thomas' with all the pomp and circumstances possible. It would not have taken much for word of this to get back to someone important enough to have eyes and ears everywhere. From now on, this investigation cannot be conducted by the Earl of Pembroke." He saw alarm flash in Tabitha's eyes and quickly added, "It must be conducted by Wolf, the thief-taker."

"But what role will I have?" she demanded.

"Tabitha, as I have said before, I have nothing but respect and admiration for your intelligence, insight and bravery. But we both know the most important thing at this point is to get Melody home safely. You are a countess, not a person who skulks in the shadows, which is what is called for now. But there is still help you can provide. Cataloguing and analysing the clues was a key part of solving our last investigation, and I believe it will be so again."

Of course, Tabitha knew he was right and that he'd known what to say to counter any resistance she might put up. All that mattered was getting Melody back home safely. Anything else was merely ego, and she felt somewhat ashamed for questioning why she was being left out.

"The other thing we must do is gain access to that house. Claire must have kept some kind of correspondence or papers," Wolf continued. "I'm sending Rat to watch the house. Are the servants still there? Now that we know Claire Murphy didn't own the house, I'm assuming she didn't engage the staff. If they're being kept around, why?"

He saw Tabitha about to debate Rat's participation and said, "It's his sister, Tabitha. He needs to feel he's doing something to help find her. This is probably the safest thing he can do at this point. All he has to do is to watch the house. Maybe he can speak to the neighbours' staff. He can be an engaging lad when he wants to. He's certainly an intelligent one. He'll be fine doing this." Tabitha's shoulders slumped, and he knew he'd won that round.

Talbot entered the room with fresh coffee, and Wolf asked him to send Bear in. Tabitha quirked an eyebrow, and he answered, "I said I would ask Mickey D for help if it came to it, and I think it has. The Irish community is tight, and their families and histories are interwoven. He may know something about Jenny Murphy or Claire and that household."

Tabitha could see the stress lines around his mouth as he spoke. She'd never asked exactly what hold the Irish gangster from Whitechapel had over Wolf. But whatever it was, she knew Mickey had agreed that the successful conclusion of their last case, which had allowed his nephew Seamus to emigrate to America with a nice nest egg to get him started, had been considered full payment of the debt. If Wolf asked the man for help now, he would be putting himself willingly under a new obligation, and she knew Mickey would cash that chit in at some point. She also knew Wolf was right; they had no choice.

They sipped their fresh coffee in silence for a few minutes. Wolf contemplated how best to manage Mickey D; Tabitha could think of little but Melody and how the little girl was being treated. She could only hope Melody didn't realise what was happening. The thought of her being scared, perhaps hungry, or worse. No! She couldn't even consider anything worse. She needed to stay focused and not let herself be pulled under by her emotions. That wouldn't help Melody.

There was a knock at the door, and Bear entered. Tabitha had become used to Bear's size and misleadingly intimidating visage and had grown very fond of the gentle giant. "Ah, Bear, good. Come and take a seat," Wolf said, gesturing to one of the dining room chairs. He and Bear had been friends and partners for many years, and neither was inclined to stand on ceremony merely because a twist of fate had given Wolf a title.

Bear took a chair, helping himself to coffee. "Any word on Miss Melody?" he asked. It seemed that Bear had also formed a strong attachment to the adorable, charming little girl.

"Unfortunately, no," Wolf admitted. "There is something off about this whole case, not the least of which is that someone wants to scare us off it. That speaks to something more than a crime of passion committed by Manning or anyone else. Lady Pembroke and I believe Manning may have been set up, lured to the house just in time to find the body."

Wolf paused momentarily and then said to Tabitha, "That's something we missed last night while working through the supposed narrative of events. The butler came home earlier than expected, just in time to discover Manning leaning over the body and covered in blood. That's quite the coincidence, isn't it?"

Tabitha leaned forward and clasped her hands together, suddenly excited by Wolf's observation, "When a mistress gives her staff the evening off and very explicitly orders them to leave the house, to come home early is not only unusual, it would smack of insubordination. Unless..."

Wolf picked up her thought, "Unless someone ordered the butler to return home in time to be a witness. We know Claire Murphy didn't own that house. Therefore, it's likely she also didn't employ the staff. Perhaps their loyalty didn't sit with the putative mistress of the house at all. If this is true, then I do not have a choice." Wolf turned to look at Bear, "I need you to go to Whitechapel and find Mickey D. Ask him," he paused, thought for a moment, then said with resignation in his voice, "if he and Angie would be kind enough to be our guests for dinner tonight, please."

Wolf wasn't sure who looked more surprised by that request, Tabitha or Bear, "Dinner?" Tabitha asked.

"Yes, dinner. The man owes me nothing. In fact, I was the one who said I wanted nothing more to do with him once Seamus was safely packed off to America. We need his goodwill. If there's one thing Mickey D craves, it's respect. And as for Angie, well, the chance to dine like a fine lady at an earl's table in Mayfair won't be something she'll let Mickey turn down. In fact," Wolf considered for a minute, "don't deliver the invitation to Mickey. Go to the house and ask Angie. That'll ensure they come. And honestly, Angie is as likely to know something about the Murphy women as Mickey."

Tabitha smiled at Wolf's deviousness. This would be the first formal dinner Wolf had thrown as the Earl of Pembroke. How ironic, and yet fitting, that the guests were to be an Irish gangster and his common-law wife.

"Oh, and Bear," Wolf added as the large man stood up from the table, "on your way back, go and see how Rat is doing watching the house. Take the lad a pie or something. Tell him to gather all the information he has and report back before dinner." Wolf glanced at Tabitha as he said this last part and noted her approval. He knew she would never tolerate Rat keeping watch past dark. "Tabitha, I will send a note around to the dowager asking if we can call on her at her convenience this morning. Actually," he said, "given the unsociable hour we'd like to call, I may just say that I wish to call on her." Tabitha smiled and agreed.

Within the hour, Wolf received a note from the dowager expressing how delighted she would be to receive dear Jeremy at his convenience. The dowager never received company in the morning and was rarely seen out of her boudoir before noon, preferring to take breakfast in bed, so Tabitha recognised the honour she was bestowing on her new favourite.

CHAPTER 12

Tabitha gave Mrs Smith, the cook, instructions for their dinner party that evening, and then she and Wolf went to change their clothes. Wolf refused to dress formally when in his own home. Instead, he normally wore neither jacket nor cravat, his shirt open at the neck and rolled up at the sleeves. Tabitha's husband, Jonathan, the previous earl, had always been perfectly turned out. He never left his rooms looking anything less than ready to greet the queen at a moment's notice. Wolf couldn't be less like his cousin in that and so many other ways. Initially shocked by this informality, Tabitha had not only become used to seeing Wolf dressed in such a way, but she'd also come to appreciate how pleasant it must be to be that comfortable.

Wolf, in turn, had come to see the wisdom in Tabitha's lessons on how an earl should dress and behave when out in society. Certainly, the dowager countess seemed to find him charming. She enjoyed innocently flirting with him - or he at least hoped it was innocent, which had been very useful on multiple occasions. So, Wolf could see that dressing the part and presenting himself at his best occasionally had its uses.

The footman, Michael, again opened the door and took their outer clothes before showing them into the drawing room. Tabitha saw that the room was arranged with a full-sized, comfortable chair placed beside the dowager's own, almost nursery-sized one. Clearly, she was preparing for a very intimate tête-à-tête with Wolf. That presumption of intimacy was confirmed by the unhappy look on the dowager's face at Tabitha's entrance into the room.

"Tabitha, I had not realised you would be accompanying

dear Jeremy," the older woman sniffed, not trying to hide her disappointment.

"Mama, how lovely to see you," Tabitha answered with barely concealed sarcasm. Tabitha sat on the sofa opposite her mother-in-law while Wolf kissed the dowager's hand gallantly and then sat beside her.

Tabitha decided to dispense with any pleasantries. It couldn't be clearer that the dowager wasn't happy to see her, and Tabitha was too tired from her sleepless night to pretend she felt differently. And so she came straight to the point, "Claire Murphy had six toes on one foot, as did the child she was carrying." Tabitha observed the dowager's face carefully as she said this and noted no surprise, shock, or confusion. The woman understood the import of what Tabitha was implying, that Claire Murphy was the old earl's by-blow. More pertinently, it was obvious the dowager had already known this fact.

"What is your point, Tabitha?" the dowager asked coldly.

"Did you pay Jenny Murphy to leave Manning and your house?"

The dowager didn't answer immediately, weighing her response very carefully. A great general knew when to retreat and regroup the troops. "Yes, I paid the harlot off. My husband Philip was an earl. But he was also a man, with a man's desires and vices. Desires I had no wish to help satiate for a moment longer than I had to. It was mutually satisfactory that he inflict himself elsewhere. He had a mistress, of course; what man of his stature didn't? But it was not unusual for men like my husband to occasionally meddle with servant girls. As soon as I laid eyes on Jenny Murphy, I knew he wouldn't be able to keep his hands off her. And that was all very well. It was always inconvenient to send a maid away just as she was trained up, but once they fell pregnant, we had no choice. "

Tabitha was horrified to hear the dowager speak flippantly about abandoning vulnerable young women whose only crime was to become impregnated by their master. But she knew better than to express such sentiments at that moment. Instead, she bit her tongue as the dowager continued, "But that little chit, Jenny Murphy, was sharper than most of the other girls and sweet-talked Manning, who was such a dolt back in those days, into marrying her."

At this point in her narrative, the dowager's face became harder and angrier, "Once they were married, the girl became unbearable. She could boldly entice Philip, knowing there could be no repercussions; she was already pregnant. I could tell he continued to lust for the girl. She brazenly made eye contact with him while I was in the room, giving him this wanton look and then turning a triumphant smile on me. I could not continue to be humiliated thus in my own home. And the idea of her raising Philip's by-blow under my roof was intolerable. And so, yes, I went to her and offered her a sum of money she could not turn down.

"Jenny was a smart girl; she knew she would never replace me as countess. Perhaps, she had nurtured some hopes of eventually being set up in a household of her own as Philip's mistress, but she also realised the short attention span a man like Philip had. If she had to make a bet between an immediate payoff and a possible but not guaranteed future one, she would choose what was on offer there and then.

"I told her I would only pay if she returned to Ireland. I didn't trust her; she was too pretty, sharp, and ambitious. I needed her as far away as possible. I made sure my coachman drove her to Bristol and watched her get on the boat back to Ireland."

"And what of Manning?" Tabitha couldn't help asking.

"Manning? I did the man an enormous favour. Jenny Murphy never loved him. She cuckolded him from the start of their marriage and would have continued to, if not with my husband, then undoubtedly with someone else's. He was going to raise another man's child, and undoubtedly, at some point, the hussy would have received a better offer and left Manning and taken the child with her. He would have his heart broken one day. I merely saved him the pain of it coming after years of being a devoted husband and father. I feel no remorse about my actions, particularly concerning Manning."

Tabitha felt this was neither a point worth debating nor a topic she felt moral clarity about. But she had one last question, "Did you ever hear anything more of or from Jenny Murphy after your coachman saw her onto the boat to Ireland?"

"No, I'm happy to say I never saw, heard from or thought of the girl again until this unfortunate incident."

"And her child?" Tabitha asked. Despite being the instigator of their investigation, the dowager had been less than forthcoming so far. Tabitha couldn't help wondering if they were finally being told the truth.

"I confess that when you told me Manning had found his long-lost daughter, I realised this young woman was likely Philip's by-blow. The news you delivered today merely confirms it. However, given that I didn't tell a living soul, not even my lady's maid, that I had sent Jenny away, or why, it was entirely believable that Manning still considered this Claire Murphy his daughter. If the question you are skulking around is, could Manning have discovered the truth and perhaps killed her in a fit of anger, the answer is, he never heard it from me or anyone in my orbit. What Jenny might have told her daughter is another matter."

Wolf and Tabitha doubted Claire Murphy had entertained Manning for two months, knowing he wasn't her real father, only to disabuse him of the idea. It was clear the dowager had nothing else to share. As Tabitha prepared to make their excuses, the dowager said, "Do not forget that tomorrow is Saturday, and I expect to see Melody here promptly at two o'clock. I intend to take her to the Natural History Museum. It is never too early to spark curiosity in a child, even a girl. "

Tabitha had completely forgotten they would need to share the news of Melody's abduction with the dowager at some point, and the dowager's words caught her off-guard, so much so that she burst into tears.

"Tabitha!" the dowager commanded. "Get a hold of yourself, woman. I cannot imagine what could possibly warrant such a display of uncontrolled emotion in my drawing room."

It was clear to Wolf that Tabitha was in no state to describe the events of the past twenty-four hours to the dowager, so he took it upon himself to explain what had happened to Melody.

The dowager had never been at a loss for words in her many years on earth, but at that moment, she was. Finally, with tears in her eyes, she uttered, "They took the child? Because I asked you to prove Manning's innocence, someone abducted an innocent little girl? How do we get her back, and what can I do to help? I will do anything you ask."

Tabitha's shock at the dowager's display of emotion stemmed her own tears. She and Wolf exchanged looks and came to an unspoken agreement. During their last case, they had been economical with the version of the truth they had finally told the dowager. She may have guessed something about Wolf's prior career as a thief-taker but knew nothing of his association with Mickey D and some of London's more notorious criminal elements. But, perhaps, it was time to share more with the dowager. It felt like they were no closer to finding Melody and needed all the help they could get. They knew that whoever had taken her was from aristocratic circles, and no one knew the people in those circles and their sordid secrets better than the dowager. And so they told her, if not everything, at least more about Wolf's prior life.

When Wolf reached the part where he was preparing to knowingly put himself under a new debt to the Irish gangster, she put up her hand for him to pause. "I must confess to being quite astounded by this story, Jeremy," she announced. Tabitha considered it a good sign that she was still using Wolf's given name, the only person who did. The dowager continued, "Let me understand this correctly; you believe your movements are being watched and that if this devil who abducted Melody realises you are still investigating the murder, he will hurt the child?"

"That is the threat, at least," Wolf said. "We believe Melody's abduction was meant to force us to stop investigating and that my inquiries so far, conducted as the Earl of Pembroke, have been too high profile."

"If you are being watched, won't having a notorious Irish gangster over for dinner seem suspicious?" the dowager asked.

"I suppose it will be," Tabitha answered. "We were going to have Mickey D and his wife Angie come in through the back of the house, but of course, we don't know that's not under observation. I'm not sure what else to do."

"Well, that I can at least answer," the dowager said, clapping her hands together and calling for Michael. When the footman, now butler, entered the room, the dowager said, "Michael, tell Cook we will be entertaining tonight. We will be six for dinner."

Neither Tabitha nor Wolf knew what to say; was the dowager suggesting she host Mickey D and Angie in her house? And who was the sixth person? "Oh, and Michael, she continued, I'm sending a note round to the Duke of Somerset, so please have someone ready to take it in a few minutes." The dowager then rose from her chair, walked to a little writing desk against the wall, quickly penned a note, and gave it to the returning footman. All the while, Tabitha and Wolf looked on in confusion and amazement.

Finally, with the note sent and the cook alerted, the dowager returned to her chair and said, "Tabitha, your mouth is hanging open like a fish. It is most unbecoming. What has so surprised you? For anyone watching your movements, it will not cause any comment if you come to a dinner party at my home. And my guests will come under far less scrutiny than any you might play host to. I am the Dowager Countess of Pembroke, beyond reproach and certainly beyond suspicion of inviting gangsters to my home."

Wolf couldn't hold back and said, "Lady Pembroke, while the idea has merit, you cannot possibly be serious about hosting such people. I would certainly never ask it of you."

"Pish posh, Jeremy. You are not asking anything of me. If I am going to be an integral part of the efforts to return Melody," Tabitha tried not to react to this statement, "then let me start from this moment on. I'm sure this so-called gangster is not as bad as you claim. He certainly can't be worse than some of the appalling creatures I've dealt with in society over the years."

Wolf highly doubted that any society harpy and her machinations were in the same league as a notorious Whitechapel criminal. Still, he doubted anything he could say would disabuse the dowager of this belief, so he let it be. However, he did have one question he needed to ask, "Why is the Duke of Somerset invited?"

"Jeremy, dear, you are an impressive man in so many ways." As she said this, the dowager's glance ran up and down Wolf's form in a rather disconcerting way, "But you are not yet well connected. Somerset is. Even before his father's death, he had made a name for himself in important circles. He was never one of those young rakes whoring and gambling their days away. If, as you suspect, this murder is an assassination with deep and nefarious roots and, more importantly, an aristocratic villain at its heart, then we will need someone with Somerset's connections and standing in society to help. I realise I was never given the full story about his father's murder, but I know the two of you were instrumental in helping his family, and I'm sure he feels that debt keenly."

There seemed to be nothing else to be said to answer this logic, so Wolf and Tabitha soon left. If the dinner party was being relocated, they needed to get word to Mickey D. Wolf also wanted to hear Rat's report before they regrouped for the evening.

CHAPTER 13

Tabitha's first task on returning home was to rush to the kitchen and beg forgiveness from her cook, who was already well on her way to creating a sumptuous feast for that night. The only thing that appeased the woman was the news that the venue change was to facilitate finding Melody. Like everyone else in the house, Mrs Smith had a soft spot for the little girl.

By the time Tabitha and Wolf had returned, Bear had completed his errands, delivering the dinner invitation to Whitechapel and checking in on Rat. He found Wolf in his study and reported back.

"So?" Wolf asked.

"As expected, Angie was thrilled to get the invitation and assured me they would both be there. And as for Rat, from what the boy has observed so far, not much seems to have changed. It doesn't seem to be a household in mourning for its mistress. There's no black wreath on the door or other signs of a recent death. The servants are going about their daily routines as if nothing has changed. He saw deliveries received, maids sweeping the steps, nothing to suggest any pause in the household routine."

"Well, that's certainly interesting, isn't it?" Wolf observed. "Did he see anyone coming or going?"

"Yes, he did. Late this morning, a fancy carriage pulled up, and a well-dressed man got out with a very pretty young woman. He said she had a trunk and some bags with her. They went inside the house, and an hour later, the man came out alone."

"It seems as if, whoever owns this house, has lost no time replacing Claire Murphy as its titular mistress." Wolf told Bear he needed to return to Whitechapel and amend the invitation to dinner at the dowager countess' home. He also instructed him to bring Rat back with him. He felt they had learned a lot from the boy's observations of the house, and he'd rather have him give a good description of the well-dressed man than spend any more time there.

"Oh, and Bear, go and talk to Andrews. See what he knows about how the papers had so much information on Claire Murphy's profession and Manning's supposed involvement. Something doesn't sit right. Someone leaked something, and perhaps Andrews has a sense who that was."

Bear shook his head, "Even if he does, why do you think he'll tell us?"

Wolf laughed darkly, "Besides the fact that he owes me a favour or two, not the least of which is the scoop he received from the Duke of Somerset thanks to me, remind him that I'm an earl now. Andrews is too good a journalist not to understand the value of having such a source in his debt.

After talking to Mrs Smith, Tabitha retired to the parlour to put the new information on notecards on the board. Wolf found her there, deep in thought, as she stared at the information they had gathered. Wolf quickly brought her up-to-date on the intelligence Rat had collected, and she wrote up notecards and added them to the board. They then both considered it in silence.

Finally, Tabitha asked, "Who is running that house? And is it merely a high-end brothel where one courtesan has replaced another?"

"Something is going on here. It is certainly possible that the house is owned by one well-placed client who is now moving in a new woman. But it feels like it's more than that. I want to hear more from Rat and see what Bear can find out from Andrews. But more than anything, I want to understand more about Claire Murphy and how she went from Limerick farm girl to Collette DuBois, the courtesan.

"We need to get in that house. I hoped it would be possible to gain entry through the front door, but the servants clearly have a loyalty beyond whatever they may or may not have had towards their putative mistress."

Tabitha held up her hand to stop him before he could take that thought any further, "Don't even think about having Rat break in." Wolf had used the boy to break into a house during their last investigation, and Tabitha still hadn't forgiven him for putting the child at risk.

"Don't worry, even if I were inclined to use Rat for such a job," Wolf saw the look on his face and hurriedly added, "which I'm not; this job is one I must do." Wolf saw her look of warning turn to concern mixed with a healthy dose of scepticism. "Tabitha, lest you doubt my abilities in this arena, suffice it to say, this will not be the first time I have accomplished such a task. I know what I'm doing." Anticipating her next words, he added, "And no, you will not be coming with me."

Talbot's entrance into the room with a letter interrupted any further debate on the topic. "Milady, this was slipped under the front door. Unfortunately, I did not see who left it."

The envelope was of good quality, and the handwriting was elegant. Tabitha wasted no time ripping it open. As she unfolded the letter, a red-gold lock of hair fell into her lap. There was no doubt whose hair it was. Tabitha's hand flew to her mouth as she gasped, "Wolf, what have they done to Melody?"

Wolf took the letter from her and read, "You seem to be following instructions. But please don't play me for a fool. I will know if you continue to investigate. The child is safe for now."

Tears rolled down Tabitha's face as she said, "Perhaps we should stop, Wolf. I feel for Manning, I really do. But I can't jeopardise Melody's life to save his."

Wolf considered how to address Tabitha's fears. His first inclination was to try to placate her somehow, but he respected her intelligence too much and knew she was unlikely to be so easily swayed. "Tabitha, whoever is behind this believes we have stopped investigating, yet Melody still has not been returned. I want Melody returned safely as much as you do, but I believe the only way to ensure that is to find this person and stop them. Nothing else guarantees her return." He paused, unsure how to articulate his next thought, and then realised there was no good way to say it. "We can't even be sure she is still alive."

At this, Tabitha broke down into great gulping sobs. Wolf sat beside her, pulling her in to weep on his chest in what was becoming a regular occurrence. "We also don't know she's not. Finding this monster is our best course of action if Melody is alive. If she isn't, we must find him and ensure he is held accountable. Either way, I need you to be strong. I know it's hard, but we can't and won't give up hope until we know for sure. And until that moment, every second counts."

As Wolf suspected, this last statement was the call to action Tabitha needed. She sat up, wiped her tears and said, "You are right, of course. I'm being self-indulgently emotional, and Melody cannot afford for me to be thus."

Wolf took her hand in his and pressed it gently, "That's not what I meant to say, Tabitha. Of course, you're upset. I'm upset. This note is terrifying. But that is what it was supposed to be. Why send the lock of hair except to cause this reaction? It neither proves nor disproves that she's alive. The intention was to shock. You notice it was addressed to you, not to me."

"Whoever sent this believes I'm the weak link," Tabitha said. This was stated rather than a question. "They think I will demand you stop investigating."

"Yes. That was exactly the intention."

Tabitha stood up, dry-eyed now, "You are right. We cannot stop. We must redouble our discretion while using all the means at our disposal to discover the killer. I am going to lie down. I have a terrible headache and need my head clear tonight."

"I believe that is a good idea. If I am going to break into that house, I need to do it as soon as possible. I am going to slip out during dinner tonight. It will be far safer for me to leave from the dowager's house than from here. And if there is anyone who won't bat an eyelid at a fellow guest leaving dinner early to do a spot of housebreaking, it's Mickey D."

Tabitha retired to her bedroom, and Wolf went to his study. He tried to read through some of the estate's ledgers but couldn't concentrate. Finally, he gave up, poured himself a brandy, settled into an armchair with a book and waited for Bear and Rat to return.

Finally, there was a knock on the study door, and the incongruous-looking pair entered. The enormous man and the small boy each quivered excitedly, and Wolf indicated that they both sit. "So, Rat, Bear told me what you've observed about a new woman installed in the house. Tell me what happened today and what you saw. "

The young boy idolised Wolf, something Tabitha had warned him about previously. She was concerned about what actions this hero worship might cause Rat to emulate. He secretly considered her concerns overblown. Nevertheless, over the short time Rat had been part of his household, Wolf had come to feel more of a sense of responsibility towards the lad. But the boy was sharp, street smart, and observant. Wolf was trying harder to utilise these skills in ways that didn't put him in harm's way. He hoped that merely observing the house had been one of those fairly benign jobs.

The boy launched into his tale, "Bear told you about the geezer bringing the new dollymop. She's quite the looker, this one. I was standing there across the street, when this big, black carriage turns up, and they get out. They go up to the door, some butler, looking like old Talbot, answers the door. The geezer almost thrusts 'er at 'im and then leaves."

"What did the 'geezer' look like?" Wolf asked.

"'E had dark 'air with this white stripe in it like. He was dressed very fancy looking."

"Was the carriage marked in any way?"

"Nah, nuffink. All black. Even the 'orses were black."

"Did anyone else come or go all day?"

At this question, Rat began positively vibrating with energy and excitement, "Not out front, but some of the servants were coming and going. And the boot boy was sent out to run some errands and turns out, I know 'im from Whitechapel. 'E's Brody Farley's brother, Liam. I see 'im and call out. 'E stops and then says 'e's gotta run to the wine merchants 'cause the order is wrong. So, I say I'll come along. 'E wasn't sure but then I tell 'im I've a penny to buy some buns, and I'll share with 'im."

"Very enterprising lad. I hope it was money well spent."

"It was, 'E's been in the 'ouse a while now, and seems it's a rum sort of place. When the other dollymop was there, nuffink went on all week. It was just a normal 'ouse. But three times a week, this toff would come, and the 'ousehold would get all upside down. A fancy dinner, fancy wines. The dollymop would gussy herself up. The man always got full up to the knocker he'd drink so much booze. The servants were all told to stay away. After the dinner, she did all the waiting on him."

"What did this gentleman look like?" Bear asked.

"Liam didn't say much. Just that he was older. He didn't get to see him much, just heard what the maids gossiped about."

"Very good work, Rat. Anything else?"

"Just that, after the first dollymop was killed, he wondered if 'e'd be out of a job. But things just carried on the same. Then one day, the butler, O'Reilly, tells him a new mistress is coming, and 'e is to call her Madame Franchesca. The maids got the old dollymop's bedroom ready. They didn't even bother to redo the room."

Wolf picked up on an interesting part of the story, "The butler is Irish?"

"Yeah, every one of them is a Mick or a Bridget."

Wolf considered this. While the servant population of London was heavily Irish, it was unusual for every servant to be. On the other hand, he reflected, if the mistress was Irish, even if she was pretending to be French, perhaps it made sense. Except that she wasn't the real mistress of the house. So, was there another reason?

Turning to Bear, he asked, "And what of Andrews? Did he have anything useful to say?"

While Rat had been talking, Bear had poured himself a Brandy.

Now, he swirled it around in his glass while considering his answer, "Well, yes and no. There was definitely a tip-off. But he has no idea where it came from. It didn't come through any of the journalists. It didn't even come in through his editor, who seemed clueless. The first he heard of it, he was handed a statement that he was told to write for the front page. When he asked about the source, his editor said to stop asking questions and that this had come from the top. "

"The top? What does that mean?"

"No idea."

Wolf sent Rat back to the kitchen to get some food and told Bear about their plans for the evening. "When we've left for the dowager's house, I want you to go out for the evening. Find a public house, and have a few drinks. Then meet me at the Chelsea house. I'm going to set out after dinner sometime. I can't use the carriage, so I'll try to get a hackney cab, but it may take a while. Meet me around the back. I want you there in case there's a problem."

CHAPTER 14

Since coming out of mourning, Tabitha had been experimenting, even if somewhat gingerly, with a new, less severe style of dress. Her deceased husband, Jonathan, had harshly enforced his conservative views of how his wife should carry herself throughout their marriage. Finally free of his draconian rule, she was starting to experiment with what her sense of style might be. However, she knew the dowager was appalled that she was even out of mourning after less than a year, so this wasn't the evening to explore how daring a neckline she might feel comfortable with.

Instead, she had her maid Ginny lay out a dark, wine-coloured silk that was elegant but modest enough, even for the dowager's critical eye. However, Tabitha wasn't entirely prepared to pander to her mother-in-law's whims and did allow Ginny to style her hair in a softer, more playful style than she had worn during her marriage.

Wolf had also dressed with care that evening. He wanted to leave the house looking like an earl about to dine with a dowager countess. But he also had to dress for housebreaking. It occurred to him to take his thief-taking clothes with him, but he didn't want to do anything that might draw attention from whoever was watching their house. Luckily, the appropriate trousers to match his de rigour tailcoat were black. He happened to have a silk dress shirt that was black. He wore it with a silk, jade-coloured waistcoat that he could jettison before setting out for his adventure. The only concern he had was shoes. While his patent leather Oxfords were black, they were new. He needed well-worn shoes that wouldn't make a sound as he broke into the house.

Bear's official title in the household was valet, but he didn't know much more about the services such a person was supposed to render than Wolf. However, as much to keep up appearances as anything else, he was in Wolf's room as he dressed for the evening. Wolf voiced his concerns about his shoes. Bear thought for a minute and then snapped his fingers, "Madison! Madison can wear your old shoes to drive the carriage. He's about your height, so the shoes should fit. While you eat dinner, he can go into the servants' hall for a bite to eat. When you're ready, get your shoes from him."

Wolf clapped him on the back, "Inspired thinking."

Dressed elegantly, if rather severely, for what was supposed to be a frivolous evening out, Wolf went downstairs to wait for Tabitha in the drawing room. When he first arrived at Chesterton House, he considered her a handsome woman with her lustrous, wavy chestnut hair and hazel eyes flecked with gold. Handsome but somewhat austere. But in the relatively short time he'd known her, she had begun to emerge from her cocoon and spread her wings as a glorious multi-hued butterfly. The days of his distant, reserved appreciation of her as handsome were long behind him, and Wolf now considered her one of the most beautiful, radiant women he had ever known. Seeing her enter the drawing room in a still conservative but gorgeous gown that brought out all the fiery highlights in her hair made him audibly gasp.

"I'll take that as a sign of approval," Tabitha quipped lightly. Despite the flippancy of her tone, she was gratified by Wolf's evident admiration. Although not a dandy, Jonathan had nevertheless been meticulous in his attire. Despite Wolf's refusal to emulate his deceased cousin in his own home, when he chose to, Wolf wore fine tailoring as well as any man Tabitha had ever seen. His broad shoulders filled out his top coat, and his long legs showed to great advantage in the high-waisted, fitted dress trousers. Tabitha knew they made a fine-looking couple.

Wolf approached her and kissed her hand with all the gallantry worthy of an Arthurian knight, saying, "You look beautiful, Tabitha."

She blushed as if she were a debutante again, attending her first ball. Trying to cover her blushes, she crossed the room and poured herself a small sherry. "I need a little of the spirit of Bachus before we leave," she explained.

"Tabitha, there's nothing to be nervous about," Wolf assured her.

"Well, we're spending the evening with the dowager, which is always a fraught experience for me. And we're being joined by a notorious Whitechapel gangster and a duke. Oh, and then you're sneaking out to break into a house. I'm sorry, but I believe there is much to be nervous about," Tabitha said.

Wolf laughed rather hollowly, "You're right, of course. I stand corrected. All I can say is that we need to look for all the world as if we have nothing to be nervous about. We need to leave this house in high spirits. I have no doubt we will be followed and must similarly enter the dowager's house.

"As for the evening itself, this is happening at the dowager's instigation. She may have no love for you, but she appears to care deeply about Melody and Manning. And as for Mickey, well, as you've observed, he is a man of many parts. He may surprise us."

Entering the dowager's drawing room, Tabitha was confronted with multiple surprises. The first was that Mickey D and Angie were already there. On reflection, Tabitha realised they were not familiar with the timekeeping norms of the upper classes and probably considered a seven o'clock dinner invitation to mean arriving at six-thirty. The second surprise was the furniture. The dowager had augmented her usual nursery-sized chairs with normal-sized ones that an adult could sit in comfortably.

But, far and away, the most shocking thing confronting her was smiles, even laughter. Mickey D was sitting in a chair next to the dowager, sipping brandy, and in the middle of telling what seemed to be a riotously funny story. At least the dowager seemed to find it so. Her head was tipped back, and she was laughing out loud. Tabitha wasn't sure she'd ever seen the woman laugh or even sure she'd ever seen her smile genuinely. She had seen her smile wolfishly when she had caught her prey. She'd seen the smirk of triumph when she bested an enemy on the battlefield. But this crinkling of the eyes, gleaming eyes kind of smile, accompanied by a rather unladylike chuckle, was something she had never encountered.

Angie was sitting on another chair, sipping sherry and smiling ear-to-ear. While hardly dressed in what the aristocracy would consider the height of fashion, she looked for the whole world like the wife of a solidly middle-class solicitor or clergyman. In fact, Mickey D himself could have passed for a prosperous merchant.

"Ah, Tabitha and dear Jeremy, do join us. Mr Doherty has been entertaining me with some delightful stories of his misspent youth."

Wolf almost asked who Mr Doherty was before realising that must be what the D in Mickey D stood for. "Your lordship," Mickey said, standing and bowing slightly. "How good to see you again. And your ladyship, you look as radiant as ever."

Wolf inclined his head and crossed the room to greet Angie. At least he could do that with a straight face. He would have bent and kissed her hand, but she stood up and clasped him to her ample chest. "Wolf! How fine you look in your grand clothes."

"Wolf?" the dowager asked. Before introducing Wolf to the dowager for the first time, Tabitha made it clear that his nickname was never to be mentioned. It seemed that ship had now sailed.

"A nickname," he said hesitantly.

"I'm not sure I approve," she continued imperiously. What is wrong with Pembroke?"

"Well," he explained, "until recently, I was not Pembroke. For all the years Mickey and Angie have known me, I've been Wolf."

Neither Wolf nor Tabitha knew how the dowager might take this, but they had not expected her to say, "Well, of course, for such old, dear friends as Mr and Mrs Doherty, allowances must be made. But please don't make a habit of it, Jeremy." Wolf wasn't sure what he wasn't to make a habit of. He could hardly control how others addressed him. But, as he dearly hoped this would be the only time the dowager would cross paths with people from his old life as a thief-taker, it sufficed to acquiesce.

The entrance of Anthony Rowley, the Duke of Somerset, curtailed any further discussion of Wolf's name. During their last investigation, Wolf had come to see that any physical appearance of delicacy belied the man's iron inner strength and integrity. He might not have the physical strength, but Anthony Rowley was a man Wolf would gladly take as a comrade in arms any day. And more to the point, the Duke of Somerset was one of the few people who knew the entire story of the theft of the Somerset Diamonds and the murder of the old Duke of Somerset. Because of this, he was aware he was, in a twisted way, in the debt of the gangster before him.

Wolf made the introductions. Angie curtsied as if she were meeting the queen, and even Mickey seemed uncharacteristically unsure of himself. He was a man who prided himself on his achievements, the life he had built for himself and his family, and the esteem in which his community held him. But even Mickey D had never met a duke before.

Anthony was a man who wore his title lightly. He grasped Mickey's hand and said with real warmth, "It is a pleasure to meet you. Thank you for your services to my family." At these words, the dowager's eyebrows shot up. She had not been told the entire story and was unaware of Mickey D's involvement. The Dowager Countess of Pembroke was far too well-mannered to say anything at that moment, but Wolf exchanged looks with Tabitha, and it was clear they both knew they had not heard the last of this.

The small talk and banter, mainly between the dowager and Mickey D, continued until dinner. Over a delicious vichyssoise, the dowager began, "As delightful as the conversation has been so far, I believe we have more serious things to discuss."

Wolf quickly brought Anthony, Mickey, and Angie up to speed on what they knew. When they finished, Mickey sipped the fine burgundy wine he had just been served and said, "Jenny Murphy. I'm sorry, but I'm not sure that name rings a bell."

Angie interrupted, "It may not ring a bell to you, Mick, but it does to me. We grew up not far from each other. Sure, she was a year or two younger than me. But I remember the lass well. She was a beauty but always trouble in the making. Even when she was still in pigtails, she was making eyes at the boys, and they were running after her. It's amazing she didn't get herself into trouble earlier. As my mother, God bless her soul, used to say, 'That Jenny Murphy is no better than she should be.'

"Anyway, I came to London when I was 14 and eventually met Mickey here. A year or two later, I heard her mother had sent her over to try to keep her out of trouble back home. A lot of good that did. She'd barely been in London a year or so, and I heard from Ma she was back in Limerick again, and this time heavy with a baba. She said she was married, but Ma didn't credit that story. Looks like it was true."

Wolf considered what Angie had said, "We already knew she had been put on the boat back to Ireland" he looked at the dowager as he said this, "but it's useful to know she went home to Limerick. What more did you hear of her over the years?"

"Not a lot," Angie admitted. "Ma died soon after that, and Da couldn't read or write. But I did stay in touch occasionally with a friend, Marigold, and she would keep me up on the local gossip. After the baba was born, it was no surprise that Jenny found herself a new man. One day, Marigold told me in passing that Jenny had died in childbirth, and the baba too. It must have been about ten years after she went back. Her wee lass, Claire, was raised by Jenny's parents, poor thing."

"Why do you say that?" Tabitha asked.

"That Mr Murphy was a crazy old man. All the wee ones were scared of him when I was a lass. No one loved the English in Limerick, but that man was rabid about Home Rule. My Ma used to say he took part in the Land War and spent some time in prison. She reckoned it made him a little doolally."

"So Claire Murphy was raised by a fervent Irish Nationalist, a

Fenian?" Wolf mused. "That's interesting."

"Irish nationalism!" the dowager exclaimed. "This is hardly conversation appropriate for the dining table."

Tabitha and Wolf held their breaths, worried about what would come out of the dowager's mouth next and how much she might insult her guests. She did not disappoint. "Mr and Mrs Doherty, I have no desire to offend, but you must agree what a misguided notion it is that the Irish, of all people, should have a say in their own affairs. How absurd!" the dowager looked across the table with an air of superiority as if the thought of Irish self-determination offended her refined sensibilities. "I mean, what do they think they're capable of? Governing themselves? It's positively laughable. They simply lack the sophistication and refinement that we, the noble British aristocracy, possess. Surely, you must agree.

"Of course," she continued before anyone could contradict her, "such absurd notions are hardly unique to the Irish. Why, even in England, notions of equality amongst people are being voiced. The British Empire is God-given, as is the divine right of the ruling class."

As appalled as Tabitha was to hear these thoughts spoken aloud, it did at least right the topsy-turvy world she had fallen into so far that evening, where the dowager was charmed by Whitechapel gangsters.

Mickey D put down his knife and fork and cleared his throat, and Tabitha and Wolf waited for the inevitable furor. "I couldn't agree more with your ladyship," he said to the dowager. "It is one of the reasons why I left Ireland and came to seek my fortune in London."

While Tabitha did not claim to understand the details of the Irish cause, she nevertheless recognised the harshness and bigotry in the dowager's words. She wasn't sure if she was more appalled or relieved that Mickey D seemed to share her sentiments.

Luckily, before the dowager could espouse any more of her political philosophy, Anthony stepped in and said, "The Irish question is a thorny one and perhaps best not debated over such a delightful dinner. However, there is no doubt that the cause of Irish nationalism, whether right or wrong, inspires great passions and, in many cases, great violence."

Wolf agreed, "I think we cannot ignore the fact that a young woman was killed in, what for all the world looks like a professional assassination, and that she had been raised by a man militantly dedicated to the cause of Irish nationalism." He turned to Anthony and asked, "Somerset, what do you know of Fenian activities in London and what, if anything, the British government is doing about them?"

Anthony was a young man, only recently elevated to his ducal title. But unlike so many men his age who filled their misspent youths with gambling, drinking and whoring, the new Duke of Somerset had long been interested in and engaged with politics. "Well, as I'm sure you all know," he said, "Fenian activities are illegal. Of course, that does not mean they aren't happening. The government keeps a close eye on certain persons of interest.

"From what I understand, these people are actively engaged in recruitment, fundraising, and even arms procurement. They operate within a clandestine and secretive environment, relying on their network, commitment, and resourcefulness to advance their cause while attempting to avoid detection and apprehension by the authorities." As he said this, Anthony glanced over at Mickey D, a wariness in his eyes.

Mickey saw the glance and replied, "Your Grace, I can assure you that I am not a supporter of the Fenian cause, and even if I was, it's no secret that the British government has eyes and ears everywhere."

Tabitha asked, "So, they are operating here, in London? I always assumed that the cause of Irish nationalism occurred in, well, in Ireland."

"Ha! If only that were the case. But yes, there are Fenians in London planning and conspiring towards their goal. And we have reason to believe that such plans often involve sabotage and, sometimes, targeted assassinations. If this young woman,

Claire Murphy, was caught up with such a group, she was involved with dangerous people."

CHAPTER 15

Wolf knew there was no point in leaving dinner too early. As it was, he had to hope that the inhabitants of the Chelsea house would take to their beds at a reasonably early hour. He had no desire to break into a home where the servants were still up. But by the end of dinner, he knew it was time he took his leave. The dowager had made it clear she had no time for the practice of the women demurely leaving the men to port and cigars, and so the entire party rose to retire to the drawing room. He had explained over dinner what his plans were for the night. The duke seemed shocked, and Mickey gave him a look that clearly said, "Old habits die hard."

"How long do you think you'll be?" Tabitha asked.

"Hopefully, not long. But I will have to wait if people are still up and about. If that household is full of Fenians, I'm not just breaking into a house full of harmless servants. I would rather I don't encounter anyone."

"I assume you're armed, lad," Mickey said almost paternalistically. Wolf nodded but didn't elaborate.

"Lady Pembroke," he said, turning to the dowager, "I apologise for imposing on your hospitality, but Tabitha must stay here until I return. We must be seen leaving together. Anything else will immediately cause suspicion."

"Jeremy, dear. Do not concern yourself with such things. I am not yet so decrepit that I must be abed before ten o'clock. We will play cards, and perhaps Mr Doherty will entertain us with more tall stories. Take all the time you need. Whatever is needed to return that darling child."

Wolf excused himself and went to find Madison to swap shoes.

That done, he removed his waistcoat and tailcoat; he'd rather go in just a shirt than try breaking into a house wearing formal attire. He let himself out the back door and, keeping to the shadows, crept through the garden to the alleyway abutting the carriage house. He was thankful for an almost moonless night. As far as he could see, no one was watching the back of the house, and he could slip away and make his way down the street. He didn't want to draw attention to himself, so he walked briefly before finally feeling safe enough to hail a hackney cab.

Rat hadn't reported anyone watching the Chelsea house except for him, but Wolf didn't want to take any chances. He had the cab drop him off a few streets away and then quietly and carefully made his way to the back of the houses. Bear's enormous size had never made him an ideal choice for covert surveillance. But, he was surprisingly good at staying out of sight for a man of his height and girth. Walking into the alley, Wolf gave their signal, an owl's coot. He heard the answering call come from the shadows ahead.

Like most London townhouses, the Chelsea house backed onto a small garden with a gate leading out to the alley. He found Bear crouching by the gate. Joining him, Wolf asked in a whisper, "What can you tell me?"

"The gate wasn't even locked. I've been in the garden for a while, observing movements in the house. The study is on the ground floor at the back of the house, As luck would have it. I saw the maid come in to tamp down the fire in the hearth for the night. Whoever the new mistress is, she retired early. Her bedroom is also at the back of the house. I talked to Rat before I left, and he had managed to get some intelligence on the servant makeup of the house from the boot boy. It's a pretty sparse household; the butler, a housekeeper, a housemaid who acts as a lady's maid, and a cook. Do you know what you're looking for and where you might find it?"

Wolf shook his head, "Not really. But we learned some things tonight that have given me some thoughts about where to start." He quickly told Bear what they'd learned about Claire Murphy over dinner.

"Fenians? You really think so?" Bear asked. "This case just took a very unexpected turn."

Wolf agreed, "We don't know anything for sure. It may be nothing more than a coincidence that a rabid Irish Nationalist raised Claire Murphy. But something tells me it isn't. We still don't understand why she was set up in this house as a courtesan, but perhaps we now know who set her up. So, what of the servants?"

"You're in luck. With the so-called mistress of the house asleep a while ago, it looks as if the staff finished up early for the night. I saw the lights go off in the kitchen an hour ago and haven't seen any movement since. I believe the servants' quarters are at the top of the house. I saw some candlelight up there, but even that was extinguished about thirty minutes ago."

"Then, I guess it's time. Come through the garden and wait outside the study window for me. Just in case." Wolf opened the garden door, grateful for well-oiled hinges. He then followed Bear to a window to the left of the house. Wolf had climbed trees to second and even third-floor windows aplenty in his time. But, given the dress trousers he was wearing, he was grateful not to have to do so tonight.

"I picked the lock for you already," Bear said. He handed his lockpicking kit to Wolf. "Here you go, in case there are any locked drawers." He gently pushed up the window frame, and with a litheness barely hampered by his less-than-ideal clothing, Wolf sprang up on the window sill and entered the room.

The lack of moonlight had been to his advantage earlier, but now it made it difficult to see anything in the darkened room. The only illumination was the still glowing embers in the fireplace. He let his eyes get accustomed to the darkness for a few moments while he tried to judge the room's layout. He hadn't been an earl long enough to lose the skills he had long honed as a thief-taker; he had broken into many houses over the years and had a good sense of what to look for.

This was the study in a house that was, at least nominally, run by a woman. But if, as they now believed, someone else owned and ran this house, then perhaps that person used this study as their own. In fact, he was counting on this. If that were the case, then Claire Murphy's death would not have changed anything significant about who used this house and its study.

Just as with his own house, the desk, a large mahogany affair, was close to the window. He sat down in the chair behind it and started opening drawers. There were papers stacked neatly in the first unlocked drawer he opened. He realised he would have to light a candle to read anything. It was a chance he would have to take. He was sure the house had gaslights, but that was a risk he wasn't prepared to take. He went to the window, sure Bear would carry a candle and matches with him.

Back at the desk, he carefully lit the candle and hoped its light didn't attract attention. The papers he had pulled out of the unlocked drawer weren't interesting. They were merely household accounts by the looks of things. The only notable thing was how much Laphroaig single-malt scotch whisky this household seemed to go through. Wolf couldn't abide the stuff himself. He found the peaty taste quite overwhelming. But clearly, someone visiting this house had quite a taste for it.

Putting the papers back, he found the next drawer was locked. Grateful for Bear's lockpicks, he quickly opened the drawer. He wasn't sure what he expected to find inside, but it wasn't a lone book at the bottom of the drawer. Picking the book up, he saw it was in German. Wolf couldn't read German. The book was titled *Effi Briest*. It was well-thumbed, but there was nothing obvious about the book to make it worthy of a locked drawer. Of course, other things could have been put in this drawer but taken out at some point recently.

A quick perusal of the other unlocked drawers didn't turn up anything interesting. Wolf quickly relocked the book back in the drawer, blew out his candle and exited the window. Bear shut and locked it behind him. He and Bear silently left the garden and didn't talk until they were far from the house.

"Did you find anything?" Bear asked.

"I don't think so. Actually, I'm not sure. I need to get back to the dowager's dinner. I'm sure there is only so much Tabitha can bear this evening. I'll see you back at Chesterton House. And Bear, thank you."

Bear put a meaty paw on his old friend, now master's shoulder, "Always, Wolf."

Wolf was afraid he wouldn't find a hackney cab to hail, but eventually, he did, having it drop him a few streets from the dowager's home. Retracing his steps back through the kitchen, he swapped his shoes again with Madison and returned to the drawing room. Mickey was in fine form from the sounds of things, and the dowager's laughter rang through the hallway.

The laughter stopped quite abruptly at his entrance. Without thinking, Tabitha jumped to her feet and ran to embrace him. "Wolf, you're safe. I've been so worried." If the dowager thought anything about this demonstration of emotion, and he was sure she did, she kept it to herself for now. She did, however, point to the brandy decanters, and he gladly went and poured himself a glass.

He sat down and took a large sip of brandy. "Come, Jeremy, don't keep us in suspense. This is almost as bad as waiting for Lady Willis to get to the point of a story. Did you manage to get into the house?" the dowager demanded.

"I did," Wolf answered.

"And?" the dowager asked impatiently.

"Honestly, I'm not sure what I found. Someone in that house or visiting it seems to be very fond of Laphroaig whisky. But for the life of me, I can't imagine what that tells us. And in a locked drawer, I found a German book. I don't speak German, so I don't know what it's about. But there were no annotations. It looked like a perfectly ordinary book to me."

"You don't speak German?" the dowager asked in undisguised horror. "What kind of education did you receive, Jeremy? Were you raised by wolves? What was the title of the book?"

Wolf thought for a moment, "I think it was *Effi Briest*. Or something like that."

"Ah, by Fontane. A little melodramatic for my tastes, but certainly popular."

"So, it's a novel?" Wolf asked.

"It is. Though the ideas it contains are rather radical. If memory serves me correctly, it is about a young woman from a bourgeois background who is married off to an aristocratic man. The book makes a lot of her stifling marriage, loneliness and subsequent affair. As if there is anything new and surprising about such things. My word, if there were, I could write a bestselling autobiography. Anyway, the author, Fontane, seems to use this story to criticise what he claims are the oppressive conventions and hypocritical values of the aristocratic class. As I said, melodramatic claptrap."

"There certainly doesn't seem to be anything in such a book to warrant locking it away," Tabitha observed.

"Unless," Anthony said, the book is used as a cypher."

"A cypher, dear boy? What on earth do you mean? Please speak clearly," the dowager exclaimed.

"This is not something I know much about," Anthony admitted. "But as far as I understand it, a cypher is used to help decode secret messages. The message's sender and the recipient agree on a specific book as their shared key. They then use predetermined rules to identify specific words or letters within the book corresponding to what they want to encode or decode."

"So, the book itself is useless, except to the people who know how to use it to pass secret messages?" Tabitha asked.

"I don't believe it's common to use novels for such things, though it would add complexity and obscurity to the encryption process. It would work as long as both people knew and had access to the book and there was careful coordination and precise rules to ensure accurate encryption and decryption. Having the book in German would add a further level of complexity.

"And as for the Laphroaig whisky," the duke added, "that is not a drink to everyone's tastes. Even my late father, a man known for his hard-drinking, was not a fan. He used to say it was like drinking iodine. This might help narrow down the universe of people we're investigating."

"How so?" Wolf asked.

"It is the rare aristocrat who isn't a member of White's. And the club steward there prides himself on knowing the members' favourite drinks. If someone is a regular Laphroaig drinker, he will know."

"But will he tell us?" Tabitha wondered. "That seems like a lady's maid spilling the secrets of the boudoir."

"I am a duke," Anthony said with no trace of arrogance, merely stating a fact. "He'll tell me."

CHAPTER 16

The hour was late, and Wolf could tell that Tabitha's energy was flagging, but there was one more thing they needed to discuss before leaving, discovering who owned the house.

"So, you have an address for this holding company, do you, Wolf?" Mickey D asked. He'd very much enjoyed the food and drink that evening and was currently savouring an excellent vintage port. He could see Angie's eyes shining with happiness. He'd do anything to make his best lass smile. He'd never had any aspirations higher than being the head of his own gang and providing for his family. But, tonight had given him a peek into what it might be like to partake of the finer things in life, and he liked it.

"Yes. A Mr Fitzpatrick in Bloomsbury," Wolf answered.

"Leave it to me," Mickey said decisively.

"Are you sure?" Wolf asked.

"Jeremy, dear," the dowager interjected, "as we've seen tonight, it is not a trivial endeavour for you to skulk around London. And I suspect, and dear Mr Doherty, do excuse me if I slander you by saying this, that my esteemed guest and his men are not unused to breaking into safes and taking what isn't theirs."

Neither Wolf nor Tabitha had gone into great detail with the dowager about Mickey's activities in Whitechapel. He did wonder about the stories the man had been telling while he was gone. He glanced at Tabitha, who cocked her head slightly and raised her eyebrows. It seemed he'd missed quite a bit that evening. However, the dowager seemed not at all put out to be hosting a known thief for dinner. The woman never ceased to amaze.

The dowager continued, "Would you be able to help with this small task, Mr Doherty?"

"My dear Lady P, it would be an honour to be of service." Lady P? Wolf had missed a lot that evening if this was how it ended. Rather than being put out by the diminution of her title, the dowager seemed even more charmed, if possible. "Wolf, we'll do the job tomorrow night," Mickey continued. "Send the lad the next day, and I'll report what we find." He added, "It may be necessary to have a conversation, but don't worry, Lady P." He winked as he said this. Wolf wondered if the dowager understood what Mickey and his boys "having a conversation" with someone meant. But he kept that thought to himself.

"Meanwhile," Anthony said, "Pembroke, you and I should spend tomorrow evening at White's and see what we can discover." Wolf nodded in agreement. With all their business concluded for the evening, he and Tabitha gave their thanks for what had been a fascinating evening.

"It was my pleasure, dear Jeremy. I am happy to do anything that will help my poor Manning and bring Melody home to us." The dowager turned to Mickey D and Angie. "Please allow me to give you the use of my carriage to get home, Mrs Doherty. No guests of mine should be hailing hackney cabs at this hour." She paused and then added, "This was quite a delightful evening. Perhaps the most delightful I've had in a long time. You might find this hard to believe, Mr and Mrs Doherty, but the aristocracy is filled with crashing bores. You have been a breath of fresh air. I hope I can count on you to dine with me again soon."

Tabitha and Wolf looked at each other. It was one thing for the dowager to offer to host such a motley crew for the sake of an investigation; it was quite another for evenings such as this one to be a part of the regular social calendar. Wolf had long had an awkward and often strained relationship with the Whitechapel gangster. He wasn't sure he was ready for that relationship to morph into one filled with regular Mayfair drawing room soirees. But, it seemed the monster they had created was now beyond either of their abilities to control.

"Lady P, nothing would give Angie or me greater pleasure. You're a rare one, if I can say that. A true lady." Tabitha could have sworn the dowager actually blushed at that compliment. Blushed! "And we'll be grateful for the offer of your carriage." He then bowed low over the dowager's hand and kissed it.

As Mickey turned to leave, the dowager put a bejewelled hand on his arm. She said in as mild a tone as if she were asking about the weather, "Oh, and Mr Doherty, I'll take it as a given that any knowledge you might have gleaned of my home tonight will not be used against me and my possessions?"

Mickey chuckled, clearly not offended by the insinuation, "Lady P, I can assure you that you could now walk through Whitechapel itself wearing your best diamonds, and no one will lay a hand on you."

Of course, as Tabitha reflected, the dowager had never walked anywhere and had certainly never been in Whitechapel. And yet she turned and said to Tabitha, "Really, Tabitha, I can't imagine why you haven't introduced me to Mr Doherty before. Amusing, charming, and apparently a guarantor of personal safety. I consider you quite remiss in keeping him to yourself all this time. Wait until I tell Lady Willis that I may safely walk through Whitechapel. I'm tempted to do so just for the thrill of invulnerability."

Tabitha shook her head in bemusement and didn't even address such absurdity.

Finally extricated from the dowager's carnival hall of mirrors, Tabitha and Wolf were seated in their carriage for the short ride home. "I can honestly say that was the most surreal evening of my life," Wolf admitted. "I'm not sure what was most unbelievable, Mickey D's behaviour or the dowager's."

"She liked him. The woman who has found fault with my every word and action for over three years is a brutal gangster's biggest fan." Tabitha said, shaking her head in amazement. "Do you think she realises what the word gangster implies?" she asked.

"Probably not," Wolf acknowledged. "Though, to be fair, Mickey D is no killer. Don't get me wrong, he can be a brutal thug when he has to be. You don't get to be the head of a notorious London gang by being a gentle soul, but he's always been more bark than bite. But when he bites, he ensures everyone knows about it, which has always been an excellent deterrent. And she clearly is under no illusions about his tendency to relieve wealthy aristocrats of their riches."

When they arrived home, Tabitha was too tired to record the evening's findings on the notecards. But, she rose early the following day, and Wolf found her in the parlour transcribing all their new information and arranging the cards on the board.

Wolf had asked Talbot to bring some coffee, and the butler entered soon enough with a tray laden with cups, a flask of coffee, and some of Angie's delicious biscuits that Wolf had become quite addicted to having daily.

Tabitha was standing in a pose he had become familiar with: hands on her hips in front of the board, deep in thought. She turned when he entered and said, "Perhaps this is making more sense. I'm not sure."

Wolf nibbled on a biscuit and said, "Well, I believe we've confirmed that Manning did not kill Claire Murphy. He has no motive, and everything points to him being set up. And now, we have possible evidence of spy activity in the house. Of course, I still don't understand Claire Murphy's involvement. I am highly doubtful that she spoke German. And how would a poor Irish girl from Limerick become a German spy?"

"Well, I hope we learn something from your outing to White's tonight. It's good for you to spend time with Anthony. He's the perfect person to help you acclimate to your new title. I know he's quite a bit younger than you are, but he's a good man."

"I have nothing but the greatest respect and admiration for Somerset and appreciate his help on this case. What are your plans for the day? I am going to use the time to catch up on estate matters. I feel I've rather neglected them of late."

Tabitha sat down and took a cup of coffee and one of the

biscuits. Under normal circumstances, she might have spent time in the nursery with Melody. It hadn't been three months since Wolf and then Melody joined the household, yet Tabitha couldn't remember how she used to fill her days. However, she did have one thing she could productively do with the spare time she found herself with that day, "I believe I will go out to Dulwich to see how Mrs Caruthers and the girls are getting along. I feel I have neglected them. I promised to help interview possible teachers."

Wolf spoke gently, "Tabitha, the girls are fine in Mrs Caruthers' more than capable hands. While I agree it's important to restore some sense of normalcy in their lives, unfortunately, they've missed so many years of schooling, if they ever had any, that a few more weeks here or there will make no difference. It's more important that they recover emotionally, and I believe Mrs Caruthers is more than capable of ensuring that. Fresh air, good wholesome food, love and care, that's what they need now. And it's what they're receiving in abundance thanks to your efforts."

Tabitha blushed at his words, "Thank you for that, Wolf. It means a lot. But I do want to go and see for myself. I particularly want to see how Becky is coming along." Becky was a slightly older girl who had aged out of the Holborn brothel run by the deceased Duke of Somerset. Wolf and Tabitha had found her in another brothel run by a Mrs Hutchins. Tabitha insisted they take Becky home with them, where she had helped Mary with Melody in the nursery. But Becky wanted to stay behind with her friends when they liberated the other girls. Tabitha had grown very fond of the young girl in the short time she had lived at Chesterton House, and she wanted to ensure Becky had not thought twice about her decision to stay in Dulwich.

On arrival at the Dulwich house, Tabitha was delighted to hear the sounds of childish laughter and chatter from the orchard. The house had wonderful grounds, and the orchard was full of trees bursting with apple blossoms. Girls ran in and out of the trees, engaging in a game. Mrs Caruthers, who both in size and facial features, looked for all the world like her son

Bear, in a grey wig and dress, sat in a chair knitting. Known by everyone as Mother Lizzy, the woman exuded a no-nonsense, big-hearted sense of capable practicality, which was exactly what the broken, traumatised young girls needed.

When Mother Lizzy and the girls saw Tabitha approaching, everyone stopped what they were doing, and the girls ran up to her. Tabitha had quickly become a favourite, and she delighted in their hugs and greetings.

"I don't mean to interrupt your activities, Mrs Caruthers," Tabitha said. "But I did want to visit the girls and see how you are all settling in."

"Lady Pembroke, you are always welcome here. But come, let me take you inside, and we can have some tea." She clapped, "Girls, I would like Lady Pembroke to see us all at our best. Please go inside, wash your hands, and take up some activity, perhaps reading or needlework. Big girls, you can help the younger girls. Once Lady Pembroke and I have had a nice natter, we'll come to the schoolroom, and you can show her your progress."

With a burst of girlish excitement, the girls entered the house. Mrs Caruthers led the way into the house's cosy parlour and rang the bell for the maid to bring tea.

"I'm so happy to hear the girls are practising their reading, even before we've hired a teacher," Tabitha said, sinking into an inelegant but very comfortable green velvet armchair.

"Yes, well, I don't believe in idle hands. Some girls have their letters, and a few can even read. It seemed to make sense to have those girls work with the others. And while the duke has been generosity itself with an allowance for clothes for the girls, I don't believe in waste. The girls should be able to mend their clothes."

"I think that is all very sensible, Mrs Caruthers. And I'm sure I speak for the duke when I say how much we appreciate everything you've done here. I'm not sure how we would have managed without your help."

Now it was time for the older woman to blush, "Pshh, lass, it's my pleasure to be able to do something to help these poor girls."

"And as to a teacher, have you received many applications?"

"Aye, a goodly number, in fact. I'm particularly hopeful about one young woman who can also teach the girls the pianoforte. She has taught young girls before and wrote a very sensible letter. She is coming this afternoon, in fact, if your ladyship would like to stay to help me interview her."

"I would love that, Mrs Caruthers. As you know, the duke and I strongly believe these girls should be given all the educational advantages possible. I don't wish to train them up for service merely. I want these girls to have a real chance to make something of themselves. We are almost in a new century, and I hope these girls will have options open to them that I could never even have dreamed of. That they might be doctors, lawyers, engineers."

The other woman smiled kindly, if sceptically, at Tabitha's enthusiasm for the future of women in the workplace, "Well, wouldn't that be something. But even if we can help them be governesses and teachers, that would be such a step up from their prospects if they had stayed in Whitechapel." The woman paused, "Well, it doesn't make up for what they went through, but it's something. Isn't it?"

"I hope so," Tabitha sighed. "I really hope we can help make up for what they've all suffered, at least in some small way."

Changing topics, Mrs Caruthers said, "My Albert came to visit the other day." Much to his chagrin, Bear's mother insisted on using his given name, Albert. "He told me about this new case you're working on. That poor girl, stabbed in the heart."

Tabitha took a sip of her tea. In the short time she had known Bear's mother, she had found her to be an intelligent, sensible sort of woman. Tabitha hoped that she might even consider her a friend. Perhaps the case would benefit from a fresh take from such a person. She told Mrs Caruthers all they knew so far.

"So, this lass, Claire Murphy, had been set up as a courtesan in a house you believe is being used for spying?"

"That's the long and short of it," Tabitha admitted. "But we still can't understand Claire Murphy's role in all this."

Mrs Caruthers let out a deep belly laugh that sounded an awful lot like Bear's laugh, "Why, dear, isn't it obvious?"

"No, I'm sorry, it isn't. At least to me," Tabitha said.

"Aye, well, that's because you're a fine lady who shouldn't know about such things. But to a woman like me who has been around and seen it all in her time, I'd say it's quite obvious what was going on."

Tabitha leaned forward in suspense, intrigued by what the woman would reveal.

"That girl was a lure," Mrs Caruthers said, delighted with herself.

"A lure? I don't understand," Tabitha said, utterly confused.

"She had lured in someone high up and was plying them with alcohol and her favours, and in return, they were speaking out of turn. Men are absurd creatures. No, not Wolf and my Albert," she quickly said. "And I'm sure the duke is as upstanding a man as there is, but as for the rest of them." She waved her hand dismissively as if passing judgement on the entire male population. "It's amazing how a pretty lass can get them to loosen their tongues."

Tabitha thought about what Mrs Caruthers had said and realised the great insight the woman had provided. "So, you're saying someone had set her up as a courtesan to pry information out of a well-placed man?"

"That I am. You told me it didn't seem like her activities were occurring frequently. And why would they? I'm sure she had a very particular man she was targeting, and all her energies went into making sure he was as loose-lipped as possible."

"Laphroaig!" Tabitha exclaimed.

"Now, what are you saying?" Mrs Caruthers asked with a bemused look.

"It's an excellent scotch whisky that the household bought in large amounts. Apparently, it's quite an acquired taste and was probably just the thing to ensure Claire's guest was lubricated enough to lose any inhibitions he might have." Tabitha was suddenly quite sure they had hit on the truth.

"Mrs Caruthers, you are brilliant," Tabitha said excitedly. "I believe you have provided one of the key missing pieces of this puzzle. I think that's exactly the role Claire Murphy played. And it explains why the house owner quickly moved a new girl in. I wonder if that girl was to target the same man or another. Either way, I'm sure that's exactly what is happening in that house. I don't know who is behind it or who they're targeting. And I still don't understand why Claire was killed. But I think we now know what has been happening. Mrs Caruthers, I don't know what we'd do without you."

By now, the older woman was blushing at her hair roots. She was used to being praised for her cooking and neat stitching, but there had not been many times in Elizabeth Caruthers' fifty years on this earth when she had been praised for her insightful thinking. To cover her embarrassment, she suggested they go up to the schoolroom to see how the girls were getting on.

The Dulwich house had been a fine old manor from the 18th century when the duke bought it to house the girls. It had a large, sun-filled schoolroom from when the family's sons spent their formative years learning before being sent to Eton. The duke had been sure to equip it with everything he could think young girls might need for their education and more. Plenty of wooden desks and chairs filled the room. A large slate blackboard was mounted on the wall at the front of the room, and plenty of chalk was on the teacher's table. A large collection of books and educational materials lined the bookshelves around the walls. A glance at them showed they covered many subjects, including mathematics, history, geography, grammar, and literature.

There was a magnificent-looking globe and various maps, both of the local area and the world, for geography lessons and to enhance students' understanding of different regions. In addition, there were multiple abaci and other aids for teaching arithmetic lessons. The entire room was as well-equipped as anything Tabitha might expect in the duke's schoolroom.

Girls sat at the desks and in small groups on sofas at the

back of the room. Some were reading silently, and some of the older ones were helping the younger girls with their letters and numbers. The whole room buzzed with happy, engaged energy. Becky was particularly delighted to see Tabitha and happily showed off her reading. Tabitha was comforted to see how at home and happy Becky was.

Tabitha spent a pleasant hour going from group to group, watching and listening. She sometimes stepped in to help, but for the most part, she was just content to see the girls so settled. Before she knew it, it was time for lunch. The large dining room had been transformed into canteen-style seating. The older girls helped the maid serve food. Tabitha sat with Mrs Caruthers and enjoyed the hearty, wholesome food.

After lunch, the girls went outside with the older girls supervising while Tabitha and Mrs Caruthers interviewed the prospective teacher. Miss Jones was a soft-spoken young woman, very pretty, with striking auburn hair and green eyes that shone with intelligence and honesty. She seemed like just the person to take charge of a group of rambunctious young people.

Mrs Caruthers didn't believe in beating around the bush. Without melodrama but with great compassion, she told Miss Jones the circumstances that had led to the girls being in her care. The young woman was visibly shocked by the story, and who wouldn't be? But she didn't shirk from taking on the students, "That is an awful story Mrs Caruthers, and I can only be thankful that these poor children were lucky enough to be rescued by yourself and Lady Pembroke. If you should choose me for this role, I will treat the girls with all the sensitivity and kindness they deserve after such an ordeal."

This all sounded wonderful, but Tabitha had one last question: "Miss Jones, why do you believe it is worth educating girls? Are they not merely destined for wives and mothers?"

Miss Jones sat up straighter in her chair and answered in a very clear and sure voice, "Your ladyship, while that is what many of us have been raised to believe, I feel otherwise. The new century will bring opportunities for women that we cannot even begin to imagine. To take full advantage of these opportunities, young girls should be educated on par with boys." She paused and said apologetically, "I realise these are quite radical thoughts and perhaps more than you had hoped for in an educator. However, that is what I believe."

Tabitha shook her head, "Far from it, Miss Jones. I find myself captivated by your enthusiasm for the subject. Mrs Caruthers, I hope you will forgive me for saying so without consulting you, but I believe Miss Jones is exactly the teacher we need for our girls."

Mrs Caruthers had been prepared to defer to the countess and wasn't offended. It was quickly agreed that Miss Jones would live in the Dulwich house and help Mrs Caruthers oversee the girls' day-to-day lives. Tabitha was thrilled with the hire and felt sure they were placing the girls in hands that would nurture and care for them.

Tabitha stayed for the rest of the afternoon, losing herself and the troubles surrounding the case for a few hours in the laughter and silliness of the children. The carriage ride home took over an hour, and she had plenty of time to reflect on the joy that had so unexpectedly come into her life with the girls at the Dulwich house. When they first discovered the girls at the brothel, Tabitha was horrified that anyone could abuse innocent children in such a way. And while that horror hadn't disappeared, it had become more muted, more of a background hum as the girls had begun to heal from their trauma and start to laugh, sing, play, and just act like the children they were. Her part in that liberation and healing was one of the most rewarding things Tabitha had ever done with her life.

Not long ago, there had been a time when her shunning by society had stung. The rational part of her had said she had no interest in being welcomed by such fork-tongued, hypocritical harpies. Still, another, albeit small, voice had said she had lost something of value in losing her place in society. But now, she could barely remember what she had believed that value to be. It wasn't often Tabitha felt in complete agreement with the dowager. But when she told Mickey D that aristocratic society was filled with crashing bores, the dowager spoke a truth Tabitha had long felt.

Life these days was anything but boring. Tabitha could even understand the dowager's fascination with Mickey D, at least to a point. Whatever the man was, he wasn't boring. Wolf and Bear had brought a wonderful kaleidoscope of people into her life. People from walks of life she had never considered in her prior existence. People who were kind, wise, patient, and generous. People who accepted her as she was and passed no judgement. Mrs Caruthers was one of those people. Reflecting on her challenging relationship with her mother, Tabitha felt Bear was a fortunate man to have grown up at the knee of such a woman.

CHAPTER 17

Wolf had visited White's once during their last investigation. He had been surprised to learn that he had inherited his membership in the storied club when he inherited the earldom. He knew Tabitha was right and that he had to make more of an effort to mix socially with other peers and men of influence. And White's was definitely the place to do that. He just had a hard time summoning much enthusiasm for such activities.

Wolf had mixed with men, such as the members of White's when he was at Eton and then Oxford. Back then, he had been a nobody. The son of a younger son of an earl with no fortune. For the most part, his fellow students had looked down their noses at him. Wolf's only friend, Jack, was the youngest son of a marquis whose coffers were running dry. At the time, Jack had three older brothers and few prospects of inheriting the title. Jack had gone to Cambridge when Wolf went to Oxford, and they had lost touch. The last Wolf had heard of him, Jack had entered the military.

Now that he found himself unexpectedly the Earl of Pembroke, he had little interest in what might pass for friendship from men who had no time for him when he was merely Jeremy Wolfson Chesterton. However, he genuinely liked Antony, the Duke of Somerset, and felt spending an evening in the younger man's company was no great hardship. He sometimes wondered whether he should try to track down his old friend Jack.

He and Anthony had arranged to dine at the club. Wolf dressed carefully and was downstairs just in time to see Tabitha return home. She quickly told him Mrs Caruthers' insight about

Claire Murphy's role before entering the parlour to make a new notecard. He waited a few minutes for Madison to switch the horses, then took the carriage and headed over the short distance to White's.

Moved from its original location in 1778, White's stood as a stately testament to the exclusive company within. Approaching the club, Wolf encountered the grand entrance, a masterpiece of craftsmanship, offering a subtle reminder of the exclusivity awaiting its members.

As Wolf made his way up the steps, he was greeted by an exquisite façade crafted from locally sourced Bath stone. The pale, creamy hue of the stone added a touch of grandeur to the exterior, radiating a sense of timeless elegance. Large windows framed by ornate mouldings punctuated the façade, offering glimpses of the vibrant world within. Thick, velvet drapes in regal hues of crimson and gold hung behind the glass, hinting at the extravagance and intrigue that unfolded behind closed doors.

In the evenings, the exterior of White's took on a special allure. Gas lamps cast a soft, warm glow on the surrounding area, illuminating the intricate details of the façade. The play of light and shadows created an atmosphere of mystery, enticing those passing by to imagine the secrets and revelries unfolding within.

Even Wolf had to admit that White's was a sight to behold with its majestic entrance and awe-inspiring architectural details. Its exterior radiated an aura of exclusivity and refinement, enticing the discerning few to step inside and immerse themselves in the world of privilege, power and intrigue that awaited within its hallowed walls. The club's interior was a symphony of elegance and sophistication, designed to envelop guests in a world of opulence and ease.

The main hall, with its high ceilings and marble columns, exuded an air of grandeur. Soft golden light cascaded from ornate crystal chandeliers, glowing warmly upon the polished marble floors below. Plush velvet drapes adorned the walls, enhancing the sense of intimacy and exclusivity. The room was filled with clusters of comfortable armchairs and plush sofas, inviting guests to gather and engage in conversation.

As guests ventured further into the club, they encountered private salons nestled behind intricately carved wooden doors. These sanctuaries of seclusion were adorned with lavish tapestries, creating an ambience of refined taste and privacy. Deep mahogany bookshelves lined the walls, filled with leather-bound tomes, artfully arranged to captivate the eye. Soft lighting emanated from ornate wall sconces, casting a warm glow on the richly-hued Persian rugs that adorned the hardwood floors.

A well-stocked bar stood as a beacon of liquid indulgence in a private alcove. Crystal decanters lined the shelves, filled with the finest spirits and aged wines, their amber hues catching the light and enticing the discerning palate.

Every detail within White's was meticulously curated, from the delicate lace doilies that adorned the tables to the scent of fragrant flowers that permeated the air. The atmosphere was one of refined allure, where every guest felt transported to a world where indulgence and pleasure reigned supreme.

Entering this rarefied space, Wolf asked after Anthony and was told that the Duke of Somerset was waiting for him in the dining room. Wolf made his way in the direction he had been pointed in. Members were sitting or standing in groups throughout the club. He had been introduced to some of the men at the dowager's soiree and at the ball he and Tabitha had attended some weeks before. Those men nodded their heads in greeting, and Wolf responded in kind.

He noticed he was the recipient of many curious looks. Wolf knew that his living situation with Tabitha was seen as unusual at best and scandalous at worst. Even though he was technically a family member, he was unmarried, and she was a beautiful young widow. It was not surprising that tongues were wagging. Added to this was Tabitha's own low standing in the eyes of society. It wasn't surprising they were keeping society's gossips busy. He cared not a whit for his reputation, but he did care about Tabitha's, even if she claimed not to.

After taking a wrong turn and finding himself in the billiards room, he finally found the dining room and was pleased to spot Anthony easily. The young duke seemed to hold Wolf in as warm a regard as he was held in, and they greeted each other with genuine pleasure. After ordering food, Anthony asked the waiter to send over the chief steward. While they waited, Wolf filled Anthony in on Mrs Caruthers insights about what Claire Murphy may have been attempting to do under cover of being a courtesan. They speculated that their Laphroaig drinker could indeed be the person she was supposed to be soliciting information from.

The chief steward was an insipid-looking man with thinning hair and a pronounced beaky nose. He approached the table with all the obsequiousness he believed was owed to a duke and an earl.

"Your Grace and your lordship, how may I be of assistance to you this evening?" the man asked in a voice dripping with servility.

"Smithers, I wonder if you could help me settle a little bet with Lord Pembroke here. We were discussing Scotch whiskies. As you know, I am quite partial to a Balvenie, but I refuse to believe that any gentleman in his right mind can tolerate Laphroaig. Perhaps a Scotsman can tolerate it, but surely not an Englishman. However, Pembroke believes that even some of the members of White's might have a tolerance for it. I know you have every member's favourite tipple committed to memory and so could easily settle this dispute."

An interesting range of emotions played over Smither's face. The first was gratification at such praise and acknowledgement. But then, that pleasure was replaced with what almost looked like pain that he would have to prove an earl correct over a duke. "Your Grace, while I hate to cause you to lose a bet, I must concur with his lordship; there are indeed members of White's who regularly drink Laphroaig."

Anthony displayed amazement at this news and said, "Surely, there isn't more than one such member?"

The steward saw this as an opportunity to prove his total loyalty to any position the duke might take, "I could not agree with you more, Your Grace, as to the unsuitability of such a beverage for an Englishman. I was commenting on such an outrage to Mr Johns the other day. However, as appalling as it is, there are actually three members who seem to have an actual preference for the disgusting drink."

Anthony's face showed all the horror that such a revelation seemed to deserve. Then beckoning the man a little closer, he said in a lowered tone, "I know you are normally the soul of discretion, but I find I must know the identities of such men. I am sure there is something suspect about any man with such tastes. What other unnatural predilections might they harbour?"

Smithers glanced around him to ensure none of the offending gentlemen was within earshot and replied, "Mr Coleman, Sir Desmond Chambers, and Lord Antioch."

"Antioch? Really?" Anthony exclaimed. "He is the last man of whom I would have expected that."

"Indeed, Your Grace, "Smithers continued, clearly getting into his theme now, "I've heard rumours that Lord Antioch also likes to eat haggis with his Laphroaig."

"Was the man raised in the wilds of Scotland?" Anthony asked in faux horror. "I thought he was from the home counties."

"I couldn't possibly say, Your Grace. But I share your revulsion."

"Indeed, Smithers. Well, thank you for settling our bet."

With a last bow, the man slithered away.

Anthony sipped on the fine claret they were drinking with dinner and said, "That is very interesting."

The entire exchange had been the height of absurdity to Wolf's ear. He knew Anthony had been playing a part to encourage the steward to gossip, but nevertheless, he was appalled at the thought that kind of behaviour might even be expected of him in his new role. "Did we learn something useful?" he asked.

"I don't know Coleman well, but I believe he's a young pup with more money than good sense. His father is an industrialist, but I don't believe the son has ever done a day's work. I can't imagine there's anything in that drink-addled bird brain of his that is worth learning. Honestly, I'm surprised to hear he enjoys a drink as unsuited to the average palate as Laphroaig. It might actually make me think more highly of him.

"As for the apparently haggis-eating Antioch, he's 85 if he's a day. I doubt he does more with his time than nap here. But Sir Desmond Chambers, now there's an interesting twist to our plot."

Wolf could appreciate why Tabitha had suggested Anthony be the man to help identify their Laphroaig drinker; he did seem to know something about every member of White's.

Anthony continued, "Chambers works in government. Something high up in the war office, I believe. If memory serves me correctly, he has some kind of civilian role related to the Royal Navy. Maybe a budgetary position."

Wolf thought about this, "So, quite likely to be privy to some interesting highly sensitive information of national importance?"

"Definitely. In fact, when I think back to a rather drunken, loud conversation I overheard not long ago, he may even have access to plans for new naval ships. I'm not sure why such a loose-lipped, bad drunk would be given that kind of access, but there you have it."

"And presumably, such a man might be easy to weasel information out of," Wolf mused.

"Indeed," Anthony concurred.

After dinner, they retired to the main lounge. Comfortable, over-stuffed armchairs were scattered around the room. Some men sat in small groupings, sipping their preferred tipple, others read, while a few snored away as they enjoyed their evening nap. As they entered the room, Anthony pointed out a wizened old man snoring loudly in a leather armchair by the fireplace, "That's Antioch." Looking at the frail, octogenarian, Wolf agreed it was highly unlikely he was their man.

Anthony and Wolf selected chairs set a little away from the other groupings to afford them privacy but a good view of men entering the lounge. They ordered a brandy each and settled in, preparing to wait a few hours to see if they could spot their prey. They had sat there for a little more than an hour when Anthony subtly indicated a man who had just walked in alone. He was about fifty years old, of middling height, with a large stomach that spoke of a man who enjoyed the finer things in life. A protruding, bulbous, heavily veined nose completed the picture of a man who overindulged regularly.

The man, presumably Sir Desmond Chambers, glanced around the room, seemingly looking for company. He seemed very surprised to find the Duke of Somerset gesturing to him. Under normal circumstances, Sir Desmond wouldn't have expected to be recognised by as illustrious member of the peerage as a duke. He came from solidly middle-class stock but had worked hard as a young man to ingratiate himself in circles likely to benefit a moderately intelligent but highly ambitious striver. He'd managed to land himself a knighthood at some point for some service to the Crown, now remembered by no one, perhaps not even Sir Desmond.

Whatever energy and drive the man had exhibited in his youth that enabled him to pull himself up by his bootstraps into the ranks of the lower nobility had now fully dissipated. Lacking discipline and having a hearty appreciation for the finer things in life, Sir Desmond needed to work and was grateful to have the role he'd landed some years ago at the War Office. The work demanded of him was not onerous. He had a pair of young clerks who worked hard to keep the wheels turning. His role had become mostly ceremonial, reporting monthly to the Royal Navy budgetary committee and attending the occasional launch of a new battleship.

Sir Desmond liked to boast about his pivotal role in ensuring the preeminence of Her Majesty's naval fleet. But whatever world dominance the British Empire enjoyed, thanks to ships that were the envy of other nations, had little to do with Sir Desmond. His higher-ups viewed Sir Desmond as lazy and inept but benign. This led to a certain institutional laxness when considering the highly sensitive, classified information the bumbling bureaucrat had access to.

CHAPTER 18

Wolf and Anthony had been sure to choose a grouping of a few chairs so Sir Desmond could join them. While he'd been surprised to be hailed by the Duke of Somerset, Sir Desmond was a vain, self-important man, and he quickly convinced himself of the normalcy of such a welcome.

Anthony gestured for the man to sit and join them. It only took a few moments for the steward to join them with a glass of what Wolf assumed was the infamous Laphroaig. "Chambers! How good to see you," Anthony began. Again, Sir Desmond's vanity prevented him from considering too deeply why he was suddenly being hailed after quite a few years of sharing the same club.

"Ah, Your Grace. How well you look, sir. And your companion..." he looked at Wolf.

"Let me introduce the Earl of Pembroke," Anthony said.

"Pembroke, this is Sir Desmond Chambers. Sir Desmond has a key role in government. Navy ships, I believe, is that not the case?"

"Yes, that is it, Your Grace. I'm honoured to find that you recognise my humble role in keeping Her Majesty's navy at the peak of performance."

"Your humility does credit to you, Chambers, but I have heard the truth; you are vital in keeping the cogs turning." Anthony didn't know what Sir Desmond did but doubted he was vital to anything. However, the man's vanity was flattered, and he happily preened his feathers.

As Anthony continued indulging Sir Desmond's puffed-up ego, Wolf caught sight of a familiar face out of the corner of his eye, Maxwell Sandworth, Earl of Langley. A handsome man, in a rather cold, reptilian way. It was a little-known fact that he was Anthony's natural father. Cassandra, the Duchess of Somerset, had fallen in love with Lord Langley when she first came out. At that point, he was only a penniless third son, and her father had refused to permit the marriage. Instead, she had been hastily married off to Viscount Rowley, later the Duke of Somerset. Unbeknownst to Cassandra, she was carrying Langley's child as she went to her marriage bed. The now-deceased Duke of Somerset had been a man with unnatural tastes and unable to bed his new wife. Even so, Somerset had acknowledged Anthony as his son and heir.

During their previous investigation into the old duke's death, Wolf and Tabitha had discovered that Anthony had known the old duke hadn't been his natural father for many years. While neither he nor Langley had acknowledged their relationship, there was some tentative hope on both sides that the old duke's death might enable them to become better acquainted.

However, if the sharp glares that Langley was sending their way at that moment were any indication, tonight was not the night he intended to pursue a more paternal relationship. He seemed to edge closer surreptitiously as if trying to overhear their conversation. Lord Langley had been one of their suspects in the old duke's murder. He continued to pine after Cassandra, and his desire one day to claim his first love seemed to provide a strong motive. While they finally accepted his innocence, he was a man of whom it was easy to believe the worst. Wolf found it hard to accept that his eavesdropping had no darker motive.

Knowing Langley was listening, Wolf was unsure how deeply he wanted to probe Sir Desmond. However, he was curious about something but wasn't sure how to elegantly introduce his question into the conversation. Luckily, Sir Desmond inadvertently gave him an opening, "Lord Pembroke, I believe you are newly elevated to the earldom. How do you find the Dowager Countess of Pembroke? I hear the woman does not brook fools lightly."

"Indeed," Wolf said. "And her ladyship is particularly distressed at the moment because of the arrest of her butler for murder. Did you read about the case? It's been claimed that he murdered the courtesan, Collette DuBois." At the name, Sir Desmond visibly blanched. In fact, all the blood seemed to drain from his face. "Well," thought Wolf, "that confirms we have Claire Murphy's illustrious visitor and Laphroaig drinker."

"No, I don't believe I read anything about it," Sir Desmond lied. He suddenly found he had to leave because he had people to meet. He got up, blustered through his thanks and farewells and was gone.

"Interesting," Anthony observed. Before either man could say anything else, Lord Langley stood before them.

"May I?" he asked, indicating the recently vacated chair. Without waiting for permission, he sat down. He and Anthony eyed each other warily. While each man was aware of the nature of their relationship, they had never acknowledged it on the occasions they had found themselves together in company. Before the old duke's death, when they had seen each other at White's, they'd assiduously avoided intimate conversation as if by mutual agreement. But now that the main obstacle to forming a closer relationship was dead, they both seemed unsure how to begin.

"I was surprised to see you talking to Chambers," Langley observed. "He is not a man I would expect you to admit as an intimate."

"Really?" Anthony replied. "Why not?" Of course, he knew precisely what the other man was implying but decided to play dumb and see where this conversation led.

Lord Langley was not usually a man caught at a disadvantage. Still, it was clear he hadn't been expecting to have to justify his statement and was searching for the right way to phrase what he wanted to say. He paused, sipped his fine, aged cognac, and then pivoted the conversation rather than answering the challenge, "And what did you talk about with the loquacious Sir Desmond?"

Wolf eyed the other man. There was little warmth between

him and Langley, but he knew the man was no fool. This conversation didn't feel like idle banter. Langley wanted to know the answer but was trying, unsuccessfully, to appear nonchalant. Wolf decided to bait him, "Langley, as much as you claim to be surprised at our acknowledgement of Sir Desmond, I am equally surprised that you want to know about the contents of our conversation. Do you have a particular reason for asking?"

Langley stared at him, pursing his lips and trying to decide how far to push this interrogation. Wolf might not normally have cared about disclosing the subject matter of the conversation, except that Langley clearly seemed very interested. That same interest seemed a good enough reason to keep what was otherwise quite a banal conversation to himself.

Finally, determining he wasn't going to get the answers he sought, Lord Langley changed tack again, "I hear the Dowager Countess of Pembroke is quite distressed about the arrest of her butler. Indeed, she proclaims his innocence to anyone who will listen. Given your previous career, I'm surprised she hasn't tasked you with proving that innocence, Pembroke."

Now that was an interesting tangent for the conversation to take, Wolf reflected. He took his time answering, considering carefully what the subtext might be behind Langley's words. Even though the man had turned out to be innocent of the murder of the deceased duke, Wolf didn't trust him. Langley struck him as a man with deep, dark secrets, even if they hadn't happened to include murder this time.

Wolf decided to continue to play his cards very close to his chest. Instead, he took a leaf out of Langley's book, choosing not to answer the question posed, and instead, he stood and said, "Somerset, thank you for your company this evening. However, I am suddenly quite overcome with fatigue and longing for my own hearth."

"Indeed, if I were lucky enough to have a housemate as delightful as the younger Lady Pembroke waiting for me, I might also choose to rush home," Langley said with enough lascivious suggestion in his tone to make Wolf hate him even more.

Shaking Anthony's hand but making a point to do no more than nod at the other man, Wolf started to turn away.

As he did, Langley put a firm hand on his sleeve and said in a quiet, chilling tone, "I hear you've mislaid a young child in your care. I do hope she is returned unharmed soon."

Wolf pulled his arm away and said nothing. Only as he was retrieving his outerwear and going out to his carriage did he question how Langley knew Melody was missing. As evidenced by the dowager's surprise at Melody's residence at Chesterton House, it had hardly been common knowledge that he and Tabitha had taken in the orphaned girl. And why would it be? She was a street urchin from Whitechapel. Hardly someone the aristocrats of London would give a second thought to. At most, it might have been considered eccentric, perhaps somewhat maudlin charity, to take the child into the nursery of an earl as if she were a well-born child made parentless.

And yet, Langley didn't only know of Melody's existence. He knew she was missing. What did that mean? Wolf made a mental note to discuss it and his other findings with Tabitha over breakfast the following day. However, on entering Chesterton House, Talbot told him that not only was Tabitha still up, but that she wasn't alone.

For a moment, Wolf couldn't imagine who would pay a visit at that time of the evening. But as soon as he had the thought, he realised only one person would do so uninvited. As if reading his mind, Talbot said with a sniff of disapproval, "It's a 'gentleman'." The tone in which he said gentleman made it quite clear he considered Mickey D anything but.

"Thank you, Talbot. I'll go and join them." On Mickey D's previous visits to the house, he'd entered very discreetly and never had cause to be observed by Talbot. Wolf found it interesting that he chose to be more public during his visit this time. He suspected the dowager's dinner party had emboldened the gangster.

Indeed, entering the comfy parlour, Wolf found Mickey enjoying some of Wolf's finest brandy and making himself very at home in front of the fire. Tabitha was laughing at something he'd just said, and the entire scene looked for all the world as if they were entertaining an old family friend.

Mickey and Tabitha looked up at Wolf's entry, and Mickey said, "Ah, Wolf, about time. I wondered how long I'd have to inflict my company on the ever-charming Lady Pembroke."

"I didn't expect to see you again so soon, Mickey," Wolf said. "I thought the plan was for Rat to come and get your report tomorrow morning."

"Aye, that was the plan, but I thought you might want to hear this sooner rather than later."

"So, what did you discover was so important it needed to be personally delivered? I assume you sent your boys to talk to Mr Fitzpatrick?"

"Sent my boys? No, this was a job that needed my attention. Lady P deserves nothing less," Mickey exclaimed.

"And what did you get out of the man? Were you able to find out who owns that house?"

"Well, as you can imagine, Wolf, I can be very persuasive when necessary." Mickey D rubbed his hands together, making Wolf wonder how violent the persuasion had been. "He was very reluctant and claimed his life would be in danger if he squealed. But, I managed to persuade him that his life was already in danger, so the man made the smart decision, eventually."

Wolf asked impatiently, "So, who owns the house?"

Mickey D was enjoying the drama of his big reveal and seemed unwilling to give up the information without a little more of a theatrical flourish, but he could see Wolf's face and decided not to take his chances. Mickey D may have been able to terrify others with his threats, but Wolf knew him too well and wasn't scared enough of the man to hide his impatience.

"A Hun!" Mickey finally said. "And not just any Hun, but a count. Count Dieter von Kletzer. Apparently, he's quite a diplomatic bigwig. Or at least that's what Fitzpatrick said. Claimed he had no idea what the house was being used for or why this count wanted to hide his ownership."

"Do you believe him?" Tabitha asked.

"Yes and no. I believe he doesn't know exactly what the house is being used for. He's got a couple of broken fingers that say he was telling the truth." Tabitha winced at this image but said nothing. Mickey continued, "But I asked around about this Fitzpatrick before we went there. I didn't get much definitive information, but there was plenty of gossip to be had. If he's not a Fenian, he's definitely sympathetic to the cause. He's known as a man to go to when the Nationalists have business-related needs." Mickey finished his story with a triumphant grin, then sat back in his chair awaiting the plaudits.

Wolf and Tabitha digested this information for a few moments before replying. Tabitha was the first to speak, "So, we have a confirmation of the German connection implied by the book Wolf found. And we also seem to have confirmation of a Fenian connection suggested by Claire Murphy's involvement. And we have reason to believe her presence was to get some information from an unwitting patron, which presumably was then encrypted using the cypher. But what I don't understand is the Irish/German connection."

"That's an easy one, lassie," Mickey D observed. "The enemy of my enemy is my friend. The Irish Nationalists hate the English. The Huns are if not enemies these days, far from easy friends. Staffing a household full of Irish servants would cause far less notice than Germans."

It all seemed so diabolically simple when Mickey laid it out like that. Though, they still had no idea who killed Claire Murphy or why.

Tabitha expressed this frustration, and Wolf replied, "But we do suspect that the butler was involved somehow. If nothing else, he was almost certainly involved in framing Manning. If this von Kletzer owns the house, then he's also the person employing the servants. It seems likely that whatever efforts the butler made to frame Manning were performed at his employer's behest."

They sat in contemplation for a few more minutes, and then

Wolf said, "We need to speak to Rat. I want a fuller description of the man he saw escorting the new girl into the Chelsea house. If this von Kletzer is some kind of German diplomat, he won't be hard to track down. I want to know if he is pulling the strings in this scheme." He rang the bell for Talbot and then asked the butler to find Rat. It was barely five minutes later that the young boy came into the room. He seemed surprised to see Mickey D ensconced by the fire sipping Wolf's brandy.

"Come in, Rat," Wolf said encouragingly. "Mickey D has brought us some information, and I want to ask you again about the man you saw while watching the Chelsea house. The one who brought the new girl." Rat quickly gave a very detailed description of the man. He was an observant, sharp child who could remember pertinent details; as he'd said before, the man was tall with dark hair and a distinctive white stripe. But now, they asked about his age and clothes, and Rat more fully described a handsome, well-dressed man in perhaps his late thirties.

"That's very helpful, Rat. It shouldn't be hard to determine if this Count von Kletzer matches Rat's description." Rat blushed at Wolf's praise.

"But how does any of this help prove Manning's innocence or get Melly back?" Tabitha asked with a certain frustration clear in her voice. "Do you think Count von Kletzer is the person who took Melody?" she asked Wolf. "Mary mentioned nothing about a German accent,"

"I'm assuming von Kletzer must have something to do with it. Or someone associated with him who wanted to warn us off. Who else could possibly care if we're investigating?" Wolf mused.

They realised they weren't going to find the answers they were seeking that evening, and so, after a not-so-subtle hint from Wolf, Mickey finished up his brandy and left. Tabitha retired for the night, followed quickly by Wolf.

CHAPTER 19

The following morning, Tabitha was surprised to hear from Talbot that Wolf had already breakfasted and was in his study. Wolf normally liked to linger over his coffee while reading the newspapers. Tabitha instructed Talbot to bring fresh coffee to the study and, after a moment's consideration, some of Angie's biscuits.

Entering the study that had previously been her deceased husband Jonathan's domain, she was reminded yet again how different entering it felt. Even if she'd been inclined to seek Jonathan out, and she rarely had been, he had made it very clear the study was his sanctuary. Much to Mrs Jenkins, the housekeeper's chagrin, he hadn't even wanted the maids to do more than a very light dusting and to make up the fire. Actually, Tabitha had always thought of it as less a sanctuary than a lair. A lair to which Jonathan retreated to lick his wounds and growl to himself.

But since Wolf had taken up residence at Chesterton House, the study had become just another room. To Mrs Jenkins's relief, she and her staff were given free rein to clean and tidy. Tabitha wandered in and out as she saw fit, and Wolf was always happy to see her enter, eagerly offering her a chair and refreshments. It took Tabitha a few weeks to get beyond the dread she had always felt about the room. A sense of dread so pronounced that she hadn't even opened the study door in the six months after Jonathan's death. But now, everything about the room felt lighter, brighter, and more welcoming.

Wolf was studying estate accounts but looked up with a smile upon seeing Tabitha enter. She felt no need to stand on ceremony and moved to take the armchair in front of the heavy mahogany desk. "You're at work early this morning," she observed.

"I wanted to send a note to Somerset first thing this morning. If this so-called count is a diplomat, Somerset must know something about him."

"You think he's holding Melody?" Tabitha asked anxiously.

"Well, I think it's a fair assumption that he has her." Wolf could see the excitement in her eyes and knew he must not encourage false hopes. "But, Tabitha, this is just a theory at this point. Don't forget that, please."

Tabitha nodded, but Wolf could tell his words had done little to tamp down her hopes. This was their first real lead as to who might have taken Melody. Nevertheless, what Wolf didn't want to say out loud, at least to Tabitha, was that they couldn't even be sure the child was still alive.

"So, what is the plan? Do we break in and rescue her?" Tabitha demanded eagerly.

"Well, to begin with, if that were the plan, there would be no 'we' to it. However, that's not the plan."

"Why not? I thought breaking and entering was your forte!"

"Well, I take issue with that characterisation of my skillset. However, that aside, it is one thing to break into a lightly staffed house and poke around. It's quite another to break into what I'm sure will be a well-guarded diplomat's house and retrieve a talkative little girl. It would put Melody at far too much risk to attempt that." Seeing Tabitha's face fall with disappointment, Wolf continued hurriedly, "However, I do have a plan. As you know, I usually ignore most of the invitations you put on my desk daily."

Tabitha knew this all too well. As the new Earl of Pembroke, Wolf was in great demand socially. But his natural inclination was to avoid such affairs, and the absence of companion invitations for Tabitha compounded this. Even though she had told him often not to make her fight his fight, he refused to swan about while she languished at home, a social pariah. They had thrown propriety to the wind during their last investigation and attended a ball together. The whispers and looks shot their way had discomforted Wolf, even if Tabitha claimed not to care. In fact, the person most scandalised had been the dowager. Luckily, poking at her mother-in-law's sensibilities was something Tabitha quite enjoyed.

However, this morning, Wolf sorted through the large stack of invitations built up over the last few weeks. Tabitha lived in the hope that, eventually, Wolf could be persuaded to take his rightful place in society. And to this end, she instructed the maids not to throw the invitations away. Wolf shuffled the invitations until he found what he was looking for. "Here it is!" he announced triumphantly, pulling a particularly ornate-looking invitation out of the pile. "I knew I'd seen something from the new German ambassador. An invitation to a ball to introduce him to London society."

"And we're going to attend, I assume?" Tabitha asked. "But we don't know that's where von Kletzer is holding her," she pointed out.

"No, we don't. But it's as good a place as any. We know the Germans are involved in this up to their ears. Let's go and see what we can discover. A ball is the perfect cover for some snooping. And who knows, perhaps we'll get lucky, and they'll have Melody there. If they do, it'll be far easier to sneak her out of a crowded house unseen."

Tabitha took the invitation from Wolf, "Oh my, it's tonight. Luckily, you thought of this; we could have missed it altogether. I'm assuming I will be allowed to accompany you." Her voice was heavy with sarcasm. There was no doubt in Wolf's mind she would be going to this ball whether he liked it or not.

"Yes, I wouldn't dare attempt to get in your way. But," and he paused, "we're going to take the dowager with us."

"We are?" Tabitha demanded in surprise. "Why on earth would we do that?"

"Because we may need to create a diversion, and no one is better at forcing all eyes on her than the Dowager Countess of Pembroke. I'm assuming she will consent to join us?"

"Consent? Once she knows there's subterfuge afoot, nothing will prevent her from participating. Why don't we see if Anthony can join us? He knows everyone and can help us identify the various players in the German diplomatic circles."

"Great idea," Wolf said. I'll write notes to both of them now. As soon as Rat returns with Somerset's reply to my first note, I'll send him back out."

They spent twenty minutes talking about their strategy for the coming evening while drinking coffee and eating Angie's delectable biscuits. Finally, there was a knock at the door, and Rat appeared.

"I've got a reply, m'lord Wolf," Rat said eagerly. Tabitha's heart broke for the boy who wanted to do whatever he could to help bring his little sister home.

Wolf took the note and quickly perused it, "Anthony confirms von Kletzer is somehow involved with the German diplomatic entourage and suggests we all go to the ball tonight. So that makes things easier. Rat, take a note to the dowager and wait for a reply. Then go back to Rowley House with her reply." He turned to Tabitha, "I'm going to suggest that, assuming she can join us, she send a note to Somerset confirming when he should arrive to take her in his carriage."

"Well, if we are going to a ball tonight, I better get together with Ginny and determine my outfit. Fortunately, I had some new ballgowns made up recently." Tabitha noticed Wolf raising his eyebrows at this, "Yes, well, let's say it was a momentary lapse of judgement, given that my social standing doesn't seem to be improving. However, it seems lucky that I did so. I am making somewhat of a habit of flouting society's expectations and thumbing my nose at their judgements. I must say, it's more fun than I might have expected."

Yet again, Tabitha wanted to make use of her maid Ginny's friendly, outgoing nature. It was not unusual to have a lady's maid accompany aristocratic women to balls to help with last-minute repairs or other personal attentions. However, Tabitha did not need such fussing but instead wanted Ginny to mingle with the household staff and see what she could find out. If a child was staying in the house, particularly against her will, the servants had to know something about it. Of course, the staff would be run off their feet during a ball. But even more reason why Ginny, who was always willing to help wherever necessary, might make herself useful and glean some information in return.

Tabitha asked Talbot to send Ginny up to her room. When she told her maid about their plans for the evening, she wasn't sure what excited the other woman more, dressing her mistress up in one of her new ballgowns or the prospect of being involved in more subterfuge. Ginny had been Tabitha's maid for many years and had come with her to Chesterton House upon her marriage. Tabitha had selected her as her maid, much against her mother's wishes, and the two had formed a much closer relationship than the average mistress and maid.

Ginny was a sensible, plain-spoken woman, not much older than Tabitha who was grateful for the maid's loyalty over the years. During the darkest times of Tabitha's marriage and after Jonathan's death, when she was shunned, even by her own mother, Ginny was the only person Tabitha could confide in. Despite some initial reluctance to drag her maid into the investigations, Tabitha had come to appreciate Ginny's genuine enthusiasm for participating. And Tabitha acknowledged that if Wolf and Bear and the adventures they had brought with them to Chesterton House had made her life more exciting, why should Ginny not feel similarly? Apart from all this, Ginny, like everyone else in the household, was devoted to Melody and would do anything to see her safely returned.

Looking over the ballgowns she had recently ordered from the modiste, Tabitha couldn't decide how much she cared about provoking the dowager. The dowager would judge and criticise Tabitha no matter what she did or wore. Even if she was still in severe black, Tabitha had no doubt the woman would find something else to find fault with. She wasn't sure why she even tried not to provoke her mother-in-law's sharp tongue.

However, the woman was as invested in finding Melody and proving Manning innocent as Tabitha and Wolf were, so there was no need to attempt to appease her. Considering this, Tabitha reached for a beautiful pearly silver dress cut daringly low. She knew the dress would show off her figure to perfection. She decided to wear a stunning amethyst necklace and earrings she inherited from her grandmother.

Tabitha's dress, hairstyle, and makeup were quite risqué when she last attended a ball with Wolf. Or at least risqué by the standards Jonathan had enforced during their marriage. Tabitha had been gratified to see the undisguised admiration in Wolf's eyes when he first saw the outfit. Tabitha hoped he would be equally admiring of her that night. She stopped momentarily to question why his admiration was so important to her but shook off the thought as nothing more than vanity on her part. Wolf was very attractive, and she wouldn't be human if she didn't enjoy his attention. Dancing with him at the previous ball had been a delicious thrill, which she hoped they could repeat that evening at least once.

Ginny was thrilled by Tabitha's choice of dress and began excitedly discussing how she might style her hair. Tabitha was mindful that she was not an eighteen-year-old ingenue anymore and was nervous about being viewed as trying to dress as if she were. However, she trusted Ginny and her sense of what looked good on Tabitha.

CHAPTER 20

Julia Chesterton, the Dowager Countess of Pembroke, had no illusions about how society viewed her. Far from it, she relished her reputation as an old battle-axe. She would rather be respected, even feared, than beloved. Not many people were left who might even be inclined to love her. Certainly, her husband never had. She had considered herself lucky when he ignored her rather than using his fists to take his frustrations out on her. It was a great relief when he died in a hunting accident early in their marriage.

The dowager had not found motherhood at all fulfilling. Now that both of her daughters were long married and living somewhere in the wilds of Britain, the dowager felt any obligation to them to be at an end. The dowager had always assumed she had an open invitation to visit her daughters whenever she wanted. She just never wanted to. And so, she only saw her grandchildren on the rare occasions when the families came to town. Up until recently, that had been just as she wanted it. No one had been more surprised by her reaction to Melody than the dowager herself. From the little she had seen of her grandchildren over the years, she considered the girls mousey, insipid copies of their mothers and the boys weak-chinned replicas of their fathers. But Melody was different. She had reminded the dowager of, well, of herself.

Lady Pembroke had harboured no illusions that her son was a better man or husband than his father. Given this, one might have expected her to have more sympathy and compassion for Tabitha. But in the dowager's view, Tabitha's crime was a lack of stoicism. She had recently expressed this quite plainly to Wolf, "When one finds oneself in a marriage such as Tabitha's or mine, it is important to keep one's dignity, find a lady's maid who is good at concealing bruises and accept that such is a wife's lot. Instead, my daughter-in-law goaded her husband, fought back, and now he is dead." But perhaps Tabitha's greatest crime, in her mother-in-law's eyes, was her inability to provide an heir. Or indeed grandchildren of any gender.

Despite her constant criticism of Tabitha, she did feel for the girl, deep down, somewhere. She'd seen the bruises, carefully camouflaged by a lady's maid who had cause to be far too adept at such artifice. While she had publicly condemned Tabitha for in some way causing Jonathan's death - whether it was actually pushing him down the stairs or, at the very least, infuriating him to the point where he stumbled and fell - in truth, if she could have found a way to kill her own husband earlier, she would have.

Yes, when it came to Tabitha, Julia Chesterton found herself permanently conflicted, caught between the societal norms demanded of women of her class and a dim awareness that a new century was almost upon them. Women were starting to demand rights that, if not on par with a man's, at least would elevate them from chattel. Why, some women were even demanding the right to vote. Again, the dowager was conflicted. She had no doubt she was personally as intelligent, strong-minded, and rational as any man, perhaps more so. She was hard-pressed to think of many men who could go toe-to-toe with her and win. Perhaps that was why she liked the new Earl of Pembroke so much; she suspected he could and would, if necessary.

Was it that she thought she was set apart from the rest of her sex? Did she believe she could handle her affairs, manage her own money, and be relied upon for a rational opinion about who should run the country, but other women could not? Perhaps. But she wouldn't place much faith in most men she knew either. However, she had faith in Tabitha if she was really honest. She wouldn't have said so during the girl's marriage to Jonathan, but she had shown herself to be a singular woman since his death.

And this brought the dowager to the note before her. Since her husband's death, the dowager had made as much of her life as a widowed woman of her status and financial independence could. Nevertheless, it was a tiresomely prescribed life, hemmed in by boring supper parties, dreary afternoon visits, and long periods with not much else to do but embroider. But over the past few months, the new Earl of Pembroke had brought excitement and intrigue into her life. As much as she was genuinely pained by Manning's arrest and heartbroken by Melody's abduction, she had never felt as alive as she did now, thanks to her involvement in the investigation. Now, she had an invitation to become even more involved before her. But there was a quid pro quo implicit in the invitation.

The dowager wasn't sure Pembroke or even Tabitha realised what would be implied by her acceptance of the invitation to join them at the embassy ball. But she did. When Jonathan died, the dowager blamed and spurned Tabitha. Society had followed her lead, as it so often did. While she had seen Tabitha privately since then, she had not publicly acknowledged her. In fact, when Tabitha had so disgracefully attended the Duke of Kensington's recent ball, the dowager had given her the cut direct and every other attendee, who'd known what was good for them, had followed suit.

But if she were to attend this embassy ball on the Duke of Somerset's arm, at the request of the Earl of Pembroke, for the explicit purpose of helping Tabitha and him with the investigation, she would have to acknowledge the girl. And once she did, society would again follow suit. Was she ready to publicly forgive the girl and lubricate her re-entry into good society? Even if her natural inclination was to let the chit of a girl cool her heels for a few more months, was the petty satisfaction she derived from such power worth forsaking a pivotal role in the investigative action?

As the dowager reflected on it, she realised she cared far less about punishing Tabitha than she had not long ago. She had come to feel a modicum of respect for the girl, who had shown more backbone than the dowager had credited her with. However, there was the delicate matter of Tabitha's continued residence at Chesterton House. What would it say about the Dowager Countess of Pembroke if she were seen, in any way, to bestow, if not her blessing, at least her acceptance, on that unholy arrangement?

Of course, the dowager thought, could she blame Tabitha? She might be inclined to set her cap for the new earl if she were a few decades younger. He was a fine figure of a man, unlike so many of the dandies who swarmed society events these days. She saw how he looked at Tabitha and could sense something was between them, even if they hadn't acted on it yet. Their current living situation might be forgivable if either had been plain or aged. But two young, very attractive, single people whose relationship to each other was familial in the most distant of ways, well, that was asking for trouble.

Not for the first time, the dowager thought how nice it might be to have someone she could discuss such things with. But who? She trusted her lady's maid. But there were things one could not discuss with the staff, no matter how loyal they might be. The closest the dowager had ever come to a real female friend was Catherine Rowley, the Dowager Duchess of Somerset, Anthony's grandmother. Their daughters had been friends as children, and the then countess and duchess had shared confidences. But they had lost touch over the years. Perhaps that was something she ought to rectify. Certainly, Catherine had experienced her share of troubles recently. Tabitha and Wolf had helped resolve those troubles, even if the exact details had not been shared with the dowager.

The dowager glanced at the charming regency-era clock on the mantlepiece; it was still early. There was still time if she was inclined to make an afternoon call. As it was, she would have to deliver her answer to the duke. Why not deliver it in person?

If memory served her correctly, and it normally did, today was the Somerset women's at-home afternoon. She was not normally given to paying afternoon calls, preferring to have society wait on her rather than the other way around. However, having made the decision, the dowager wasted no time changing her outfit from her day dress and ordering her carriage.

Less than two hours later, she was announced and escorted into the magnificent drawing room at Rowley House. Recently redecorated, as far as she remembered, the drawing room had a light, modern air, pastel colours and a delicate floral pattern repeated throughout the furnishings. The room displayed its owners' wealth but in an understated manner, thoroughly approved of by the dowager. She was happy to find the two duchesses alone. Their faces expressed their evident surprise at seeing who their guest was.

"Lady Pembroke, Julia, what a delightful surprise," Catherine, the Dowager Duchess of Somerset, exclaimed.

"Yes, I'm sure it is," the dowager countess replied. "I fear becoming somewhat of a recluse in my old age."

"Pff, old? You? Never? After all, if you're old, so am I. And I refuse to accept that gracefully," Catherine firmly stated. She had been considered a great beauty during her season, and it had surprised no one when she caught the eye of a duke. Even now, she was a fine-looking woman who had aged surprisingly well given the family situation she had lived with, first with a husband no kinder than the dowager countess's own and then with a son who was a monster and corrupted his sister.

The dowager countess settled, and with tea and cake laid out on the low table in front of them, the women engaged in idle gossip and chitchat for a few minutes. But finally, realising that her allotted time for a social call would be up soon, the dowager countess, Lady Pembroke, broached the topic on her mind. "Catherine, we have known each other for many years, and while we have not seen as much of each other recently, I do consider you one of my dearest friends."

The dowager duchess nodded her assent, unsure where this conversation was leading. Her guest continued, "I know that my erstwhile daughter-in-law, Tabitha, and the new Earl of

Pembroke have been of service to your family recently. Even if they have not shared all the details," she added pointedly. Unsure how much their visitor had been told, the two other women again nodded in a non-committal way.

The dowager countess sipped tea while she considered how to continue. Not normally at a loss for words on any topic, she found herself suddenly unsure how to phrase her concerns. "As you probably know, society has shunned Tabitha since Jonathan's death." She paused, took another fortifying sip of tea, and added, "I may have had a part to play in that shunning." The other women exchanged glances but wisely kept to themselves whatever they knew or thought about their guest's role in her daughter-in-law's social banishment. "I now find myself at somewhat of a crossroads. Tabitha and Pembroke are involved in helping prove my butler innocent of this preposterous murder charge. As part of this investigation, they have invited me to attend a ball with them this evening, on the Duke of Somerset's arm, as it happens."

"Yes, Anthony had mentioned something of this to us," Cassandra interjected. "I'm assuming you've called to tell him you've accepted the invitation?"

"I can see why you might assume that," the dowager countess continued carefully. "However, I am not entirely sure it is appropriate for me to attend."

"Why on earth not, Julia?" Catherine, the dowager duchess, said impatiently. "Because all those holier-than-thou harpies are shunning Tabitha?" Of course, the unspoken fact hovered in the air that the dowager countess was herself chief among those so-called harpies. "Tabitha and Lord Pembroke are aiding you. And they have asked you to join them to facilitate that investigation. I cannot imagine what legitimate concerns you might have about accepting that invitation. After all, you are the setter of fashion, not a follower, right?"

The dowager duchess knew she was pandering to her old friend's vanity, but she also spoke the truth. Once the Dowager Countess of Pembroke was seen to have forgiven Tabitha, the rest of society would follow suit. Catherine suspected this power sat at the heart of her friend's dilemma; she wasn't sure she wished to be the vehicle by which the younger Lady Pembroke was welcomed back into society's fold.

Hearing this said out loud by an old and trusted friend, the dowager countess sighed, accepting what she must do. "Thank you, Catherine, dear. I knew I could rely on you for wise counsel. I won't take any more of your time, but please tell your grandson I will welcome his company this evening and be ready for his carriage at eight o'clock sharp." Julia, Lady Pembroke rose and bade her gracious hostesses goodbye.

As the drawing-room door shut behind her, the Duchess of Somerset raised her eyebrows and said to her mother-in-law, "Well, that was interesting."

CHAPTER 21

T abitha remembered her excitement and the delicious anticipation of her first ball when she came out. There had been much discussion about what she should wear. Her mother firmly believed that eighteen-year-old girls should advertise their virginal virtues by wearing white. Tabitha's next older sister, Samantha, who had managed to snag a marquess, albeit one from the wilds of the north, had weighed in that pastels helped set a debutante apart. Of course, her mother had won, and Tabitha had been presented to the marriage mart as a demure, pliable, untouched prize.

Was that only four years ago? How was that possible? What seemed like a lifetime later, Tabitha sat in front of her mirror while Ginny performed her magic on her richly coloured, thick chestnut hair. The fact that she should still be in mourning aside, Tabitha's status as a widow allowed her to dress far less modestly than even the married matrons; she had no husband to disapprove.

The dress Tabitha had chosen was very flattering. The fabric had a luminescence that seemed to make her alabaster skin almost glow. The amethyst jewellery sparkled, nestled in her rather daring decolletage. After applying subtle makeup and weaving pearls into the elaborate hairstyle, Ginny stood back and admired her handiwork. "You look beautiful, m'lady. I'm sure his lordship will be struck dumb."

Tabitha blushed, if only because her maid had articulated Tabitha's own thoughts; what would Wolf think? She admonished herself for such flights of fancy. Why did it matter what Wolf thought? But she remembered their last ball and how walking in with such a man felt. How exciting it had been to be taken in his arms and twirled around the dance floor. Wolf had surprised her; he was a remarkably good dancer. Being that close to him had heightened all her senses. And for a few moments, he had looked into her eyes, and she had believed he might be similarly carried away by her presence.

Maybe she was being as silly as a girl barely out of the schoolroom. Still, all the self-scolding in the world couldn't shake Tabitha's excitement at the prospect of again seeing naked appreciation in her housemate's eyes. Even in their marriage's first days and nights, Jonathan had never looked at her as Wolf had when he had first seen her dressed for the previous ball.

That evening, she had taken her first tentative steps towards finding her sense of style, dressing by her own standards and not her husband's or society's. Not many weeks later, she felt she was coming out all over again, this time as an independent woman in her prime rather than as barely more than a child, put on display for matrimonial selection. The previous ball had been a masked affair, and Tabitha had appreciated the relative anonymity provided. But now, she would hold her head high, stare down the gossip, ignore the pointed stares and whispers, and take in her stride whatever scandal might be generated by her presence there, on Wolf's arm.

Tabitha continued to look at the woman staring back at her in the mirror. How was this the same woman who had allowed herself to become a punching bag for her husband? How was this the same woman who had been so cowed by fear that she had gone from a young girl so rambunctious that her mother labelled her 'challenging' to a timid mouse of a wife whose only desire was to get through each day without drawing her husband's attention and ire?

Looking at her reflection, Tabitha had a realisation that shook her to her core; she would never remarry. She would never risk returning to the woman she had been. And how could she possibly know for sure what kind of man she was marrying? After all, Jonathan had been the picture of gentlemanly decorum and solicitation during their brief courtship. There had been nothing in his gentle, chaste handling of his fiancé to suggest the ugly, violent ravaging of her body and soul that was to come after the wedding night. She had walked innocently into a union full of nothing but emotional and physical pain and was not confident that she would choose more wisely a second time.

She tried to shake off such dark memories and instead looked forward to the night ahead. Tabitha was also fully mindful of the importance of the evening to their investigation. It was possible they were going to the building Melody was being held in, hosted by the people responsible for Claire Murphy's murder. Such serious considerations wiped away all thoughts of the pleasures of dancing with Wolf.

Wolf had also dressed with care. Normally, he considered the obsessive following of fashion by the men in society to be pointless at best and foppish at worst. He knew his cousin Jonathan had been such a man, and this knowledge only added to Wolf's desire to do otherwise. Wolf's life as a thief-taker had been one where fine clothes and good grooming, even if he'd been able to afford them, would only have drawn unwanted attention. His previous career had been one he'd pursued in the shadows, and he'd dressed accordingly.

But Wolf knew there was a time and a place for presenting a polished, well-turned-out facade to the world, and a high-society ball held at the embassy of one of the world's major powers certainly counted as such an occasion. Beyond even society's expectations of how the Earl of Pembroke should look, Wolf found he wanted to look his best for Tabitha. He had no doubt she would be nothing less than radiant, and he wanted to be the man worthy of escorting her. To that end, he'd even allowed Bear to trim his hair. It was hardly short enough for current fashions, but along with a close shave, he felt he looked acceptable, at the very least.

"You'll do," Bear announced gruffly.

"You know," Wolf pointed out tartly, "normally, when a master isn't turned out to perfection, it's seen as a poor reflection on his valet! Don't forget that."

Bear laughed, "It'll be a cold day in hell when my self-worth comes from how well-tied your cravat is. You can go out wearing sackcloth and ashes as far as I'm concerned."

"In all seriousness, if I keep going to these society affairs, I may have to consider hiring an actual valet. We'll find something else for you to do, assuming you want something. You know you're welcome to live here regardless, as far as I'm concerned."

Bear made a sound in his throat that could have meant anything. But Wolf had known the man long enough to know he was touched. Initially, it had made sense to call Bear his valet to explain the man's existence in the household. But Bear was now firmly ensconced and quite the staff favourite - being the only person tall enough to reach certain things without a ladder helped. Wolf knew Bear no longer had to justify his presence in the house. Talbot discreetly took care of most of the duties a valet would normally do and it wasn't a secret that Bear wasn't fulfilling the role. Wolf made a mental note to talk with Talbot about hiring an actual valet.

Finally dressed as well as he was likely to be, Wolf went downstairs to wait for Tabitha. He had enjoyed seeing her find her personal style over the last few months. When they first met, Tabitha had been buttoned up, literally. She was too young, beautiful, and vibrant a woman to dress as she had when he first arrived at Chesterton House. But now, she was becoming more daring in her choice of colours and styles. Her hairstyle was not the plain, severe chignon it used to be, and the overall effect was youthful but stylish sophistication. Given this, Wolf eagerly anticipated her outfit that evening. He was not disappointed.

When Tabitha began experimenting more with her outfits, she felt awkward and uncomfortable. Jonathan had so browbeaten her during their marriage, demanding the conservative austerity he felt befitted his wife, that finding her way back out of that mindset was hard. But this evening, she felt at ease, even proud, of how well she knew she looked. Seeing confirmation of this reflected in Wolf's eyes merely gave an additional boost to her confidence.

Wolf came towards her and, much as he had the night of the dowager's dinner, took her hand and kissed it. But this time, his hold lingered, and his gaze swept over her admiringly, "You have never looked more beautiful," he told her truthfully. "I will be considered the luckiest man at the ball."

Tabitha blushed prettily. Certainly, her husband had never spoken such words to her. He had been gallant enough during their courtship but always stiff and formal. The words Wolf spoke were said with passion and sincerity. He meant every word.

The evening was unseasonably warm, and Tabitha needed nothing more than a light shawl to leave the house. Ginny was already sitting up next to Madison, ready for her part in the evening's investigation. Wolf escorted Tabitha to the carriage and handed her in. Normally, he sat opposite Tabitha when they rode together. But tonight, Wolf found himself drawn to sit beside her. Wolf wasn't sure what he was doing, but had taken her hand before he knew it. "I meant every word; you are beautiful, and never more so than tonight."

Tabitha wasn't sure how to answer and was glad of the cover of darkness to hide her further blushes. Then, remembering her epiphany about remarrying, she abruptly withdrew her hand. She wasn't sure what Wolf might do next and didn't want to be caught up in an exchange she knew could never end well. Tabitha felt rather than saw Wolf's disappointment. She wanted to say something, but what? She couldn't deny that there was an attraction between them. More than that, there was a friendship. A friendship based on mutual respect and trust. That friendship meant so much more to her than any fleeting expression of passion. But how could she explain that? And so she said nothing.

CHAPTER 22

L uckily, the carriage ride was short. Wolf and Tabitha sat in silence, each contemplating the situation they had unexpectedly found themselves in. Wolf had not intended to create such discomfort between them. Now he wasn't sure how to return to their prior companionable ease. Tabitha could sense his uncertainty and was determined to fix the awkwardness she felt she had caused. She took him by the arm as they entered the embassy, squeezing it gently. Wolf looked at her, and she smiled. He had not offended her and was genuinely grateful for that. Ginny followed, and at a subtle nod from Tabitha, she disappeared into the servants' quarters.

The German embassy was a grand building, reflecting elements of the Teutonic architectural style. They entered the imposing vestibule with its white marble floors and the most enormous chandelier Tabitha had ever seen. The dowager and the Duke of Somerset had arrived just before them, and it was a matter of a moment for Tabitha and Wolf to join them so they might all enter the grand ballroom together.

The dowager saw the looks sent her way as Tabitha and Wolf joined her. This was the moment when she would be called upon to make clear whether her daughter-in-law was to remain a social pariah or would now be welcomed back into the fold. Looking at Tabitha in a beautiful but quite inappropriate dress for a new widow, the dowager was tempted to make a loud, cutting comment and prolong the younger woman's days wandering in the wilderness. However, Julia Chesterton, the Dowager Countess of Pembroke, was many things but not petty and vindictive. Well, perhaps a little vindictive. But not petty. She felt pettiness was unworthy of a woman of her status.

Tonight was about something much more important than her grievances against Tabitha. And so, she embraced her, saying loudly, "My dear, how well you look tonight. That colour so suits you."

As this scene played out, it felt like every eye was on the two women. Certainly, a hush had come over the place and seemed to extend back into the ballroom in a wave as the collective held its breath, waiting for what would come next. Tabitha understood entirely what part the dowager was playing and why and replied equally loudly, "Dear Mama, Your Grace, Lord Pembroke and I are so glad you are able to join us." With the embrace and kind words returned, the crowd's silence morphed into an echo chamber of gossip as the apparent rapprochement was whispered about eagerly.

Finally, with the possibility for interesting melodrama over, the ball's attendees turned their attention back to sipping champagne and silently, and sometimes not so silently, judging each other's outfits. The music started and added to the general buzz of conversation, providing cover for the foursome to strategise.

"How do you suggest we proceed?" the dowager asked Wolf.

"Carefully and subtly," he said pointedly. The dowager was not known for subtlety. "We're working on the assumption that these people have Melody and have used her abduction to swear us off the investigation. If that is true, our very presence here may ring alarm bells. However, we're also assuming, and hoping, that we have managed to convince them we are no longer investigating and that they have no idea we have identified this von Kletzer as being behind the murder and the spying.

"So, the first thing we must do is ensure there is no reason for them to believe we are at this ball for any other reason than dancing and socialising. We must do nothing to draw suspicion to our attendance tonight. To that end, what would you both normally do at such an occasion?" he said to Anthony and the dowager.

"I would find my friends and settle somewhere comfortably

with an excellent view of all the goings on," the dowager asserted. "My companion would then fetch me refreshments" She looked at Anthony as she said this. "As for the two of you," this was directed at Tabitha and Wolf, "I assume you would dance. At least, that is what you did at the last ball. Quite scandalously, if memory serves me correctly." She added, almost as an afterthought. As she was the main instigator of any perception of scandal at the time, Tabitha ignored this last comment. However, she realised the dowager's overall point was good; what would they do if they were there merely to enjoy a ball? Whatever it was, they had to spend a reasonable amount of time doing it and averting suspicion.

"Then Anthony, I will leave Mama in your capable hands, and Wolf, we should dance." With this, Tabitha put her hand lightly on Wolf's arm and let him lead her onto the dance floor.

Despite her earlier conclusions about the futility of any romance between them, as Wolf put his arm around her waist and took her hand in his, pulling her perhaps a little closer than was strictly necessary for a waltz, Tabitha's heart started pounding.

Wolf looked down at her face, turned up expectantly to his, and said, "We must put on a good show. If the gossips are having a field day at our expense, let us use the insinuation and muckraking to our advantage." He saw some doubt in Tabitha's eyes, "At some point, we may be able to sneak away and look for Melody. When we do so, it is to the advantage of the investigation if everyone assumes nothing more than a romantic rendezvous." As he said this, he considered the game they were playing, "I'm sorry if this puts your reputation at risk and exposes you to even greater gossip."

"Hah! Many of these people likely already consider me a fallen woman because of our living situation. And regardless, I have been welcomed back into society's good graces," Tabitha pointed out.

"You have?" Wolf asked, genuinely unaware of the highly choreographed scene that had played out on their entrance to the ball. Tabitha laughed lightly and explained how the dowager had signalled Tabitha's acceptance as the prodigal daughter-in-law. Wolf shook his head. Such social machinations were beyond his experience and comprehension. But he was glad if whatever had taken place meant Tabitha would now be welcome at social occasions. For her sake as well as his own.

They danced in companionable silence for the rest of the musical number. When the music ended, Wolf asked, "What would we normally do now?"

Tabitha considered the question. A brief glance showed the dowager happily ensconced among her cronies, with Antony patiently waiting at her shoulder. There was no doubt the dowager was more than capable of maintaining the illusion of doing nothing more than indulging in the usual gossip while surveilling the room and gathering relevant information. She had always treated social gatherings as battlefield excursions, and now she had a genuine role to play in covert intelligence; she would be in her element. So, the question was, what should Tabitha and Wolf do? What would they usually do?

"I think we should avail ourselves of the refreshments and learn more about our host, if possible," Tabitha decided. By this time, the ballroom was crowded with guests spilling into adjacent rooms. They decided to wander all the areas open to the guests to get the lay of the land. Tabitha and Ginny had agreed to meet back in the ladies' retiring room in an hour. Still, Tabitha was impatient to know what intelligence her maid might have gathered from the embassy servants.

They did a quick survey of all the reception rooms. If Melody were being held here, it would surely be somewhere away from anywhere guests might wander into. Tabitha just hoped it was a bedroom and not a less comfortable area of the house. She didn't even want to imagine what horrors the little girl might be subjected to by the kind of monstrous person who would kidnap her in the first place.

They entered the dining room with abundant refreshments covering the large table. Wolf left Tabitha sitting at a side table while he gathered food and drink. After waiting a few minutes, she was joined by Anthony. He sat beside her and said in a low voice, "I saw the new ambassador disappear into what seems to be a smoking room. I want to take Pembroke in to meet him. He is far better at judging people than I will ever be. I'm sorry, but it really would cause quite a stir if you accompanied us," he added apologetically.

"I understand. Look, Wolf is coming over now. Take him, and I'll wait here." Anthony was uncomfortable leaving her alone, but she assured him, "It's hardly the first time I've been left alone at a ball. Actually, it was quite informative last time. Perhaps it will prove to be again." Tabitha smiled mischievously. By this time, Wolf had joined them and placed a plate of dainty iced cakes and a glass of champagne in front of Tabitha. Anthony made his suggestion to Wolf, who glanced at Tabitha, obviously concerned she would feel left out or abandoned. She shook her head briefly to indicate she'd be fine and he shouldn't worry, and the two men left.

When they entered the smoking room, they saw the ambassador talking with the Marquis of Gantry, Anthony's godfather. Wolf and Anthony joined the men, and the marquis introduced them to Ambassador Peetz. Despite this being his first posting to Britain, the ambassador's English was perfect, but his conversation was dull. It seemed he was an avid birdwatcher and was most excited to explore Hyde Park, where he believed he might see some rare breed of bird. Wolf couldn't have said what breed because he stopped paying attention early in the conversation.

The introduction to the new German ambassador was quite underwhelming. The man was barely five feet high and almost as round as tall. His head was almost completely bald except for a few grey hairs by each ear that he had swept over his skull as if this would fool anyone into thinking he had a full head of hair. He wore a monocle and rested on an ornate gold-topped stick. There was something quite comical about the overall effect, and Wolf decided the man couldn't look less like a criminal mastermind. Of course, he wasn't sure what a criminal mastermind should look like, but he felt it should be someone who could be taken more seriously. Though, perhaps that was the cleverest disguise of all.

Certainly, the ambassador showed no recognition when he was introduced to the Earl of Pembroke. He was either an outstanding actor or had no idea he harboured a kidnapped child connected to Wolf. Of course, he might have had no idea because Melody wasn't there. That was a possibility they would have to entertain.

Just as he had run out of patience for even pretending to be listening to the raptures of bird watching as a hobby, he and Anthony were saved by an aide who appeared at the ambassador's elbow and whispered something in the man's ear that caused him to make his apologies and leave the room.

CHAPTER 23

The last time Tabitha had been left alone at a ball, she'd been accosted by Anthony's natural father, Lord Langley. This time, while she saw Langley from the corner of her eye and was sure he had noticed her, he did not attempt to join her. Tabitha was grateful for this small mercy; she was already on edge that evening and did not need to add to her tension by engaging in a battle of wits with the man.

Tabitha ate a cake or two and sipped on her champagne. She was beginning to wonder what was keeping Wolf and Anthony when she sensed someone approaching the table. Looking up, she saw a striking-looking man approaching. He was tall and slim, with thickly lashed green eyes, high cheekbones, and a chiselled jaw. But the most immediate thing Tabitha noticed about him was a prominent white streak in his dark hair. This must be Count von Kletzer.

Tabitha tried to calm her nerves and not show any recognition of who he was. That might be fatal for Melody. The man came to attention before her and clicked his heels together in almost a caricature of Germanic formality. "Guten Abend, Gräfin Pembroke. I hope you will forgive the presumption of me introducing myself," the count said.

Realising she wasn't supposed to know who he was, Tabitha answered, "I'm sorry, sir. You seem to have me at a disadvantage."

"Please excuse me. I am Count Dieter von Kletzer. At your service."

"And might I ask how you came to know my name?" Tabitha asked, aiming for a slightly flirtatious coyness to her question.

"I must admit, I saw you enter with your friends, and I made enquiries. I was told the gentleman accompanying you is Lord Pembroke, and you are Lady Pembroke, and yet you are not husband and wife." His satisfaction with this intelligence was evident.

"Indeed, your information is correct," Tabitha said. "Lord Pembroke is my deceased husband's heir. He was good enough to accompany me tonight along with the Dowager Countess of Pembroke, and an old and dear friend, the Duke of Somerset." The count's only reaction was a wolfish smile when she mentioned her deceased husband. "Would you care to join me?" Tabitha said, indicating the chair next to her.

"I would be delighted, your ladyship," the man answered. Under normal circumstances, Tabitha would not have entertained a man who leered at her so suggestively. But this opportunity was too good to pass up. She considered the approach she might take. She had never been a flirt. As a debutante, her mother would have never approved, and as a wife, she would have paid dearly for even the slightest suggestion of attention towards another man. But Tabitha had witnessed enough flirtation over the years to have a general sense of how to act.

Lowering her chin slightly and observing the man through her lashes, she slowly licked her lower lip. Tabitha was quite bemused by von Kletzer's reaction; he picked up her hand, turned it over and slowly kissed the soft skin of her wrist.

Wolf had returned to the dining room, leaving Anthony to talk to his godfather. As soon as he entered, he could see Tabitha wasn't alone. A second glance at the infamous, white-streaked hair told him who her companion was. Tabitha's back was to him, but the look on the count's face as he talked to her incensed Wolf. He rushed back to the table just in time to hear the other man say, "I will be sure to claim that dance and perhaps more." The count had risen and left before Wolf could ask what that statement meant.

Wolf sat in the vacated chair and asked, "What on earth was that all about?"

Tabitha raised her eyebrows at his tone and said, "As you witnessed, I have met our main antagonist. The man has a certain oily charm and seemed quite taken with me."

"I'm sure he was! And you plan to dance with him? What was that final comment, 'perhaps more'?" We came here to investigate the man, not so he could bed you!" Wolf was now in high dudgeon but couldn't have explained why.

Doing her best to ignore his outrageous insinuations, Tabitha replied, "How better to discover what he is up to than under the cover of flirtation?"

"How better? I can think of many better ways. And when do you intend to have this dance? Before or after we sneak around the building?" Wolf could hear the petulance in his voice but somehow couldn't stop.

"I was to be included in the sneaking?" Tabitha asked, not trying to hide the sneer in her tone. She had no illusions that Wolf had planned for her active participation.

The guilty look on his face told Tabitha all she needed to know about the accuracy of her statement, "Well, no, but you can't possibly think a ballgown is an ideal outfit for stealthy reconnaissance," he stuttered.

"Regardless, you never intended to include me, so I might as well make myself useful by ensuring our primary suspect is suitably distracted." Wolf had no answer; he knew Tabitha was right. But he hated the idea of that oily, lecherous Hun holding her as close as he had recently. Wolf knew he had no claim on Tabitha beyond friendship. But when he held her in his arms to dance, it felt so intimate and special. The idea of another man sharing that intimacy with her was sickening.

Tabitha must have seen some of this play out on his face and took pity on him. She put her hand on his and said, "It's just a dance, Wolf. Not all dances are as special as others." Looking into his eyes, Tabitha knew she had voluntarily taken them back to dangerous territory. But, somehow, she couldn't help it.

Wolf waved down a footman and took two fresh glasses of champagne. Taking a large gulp of his, he composed himself and asked, "So what is the plan? You'll keep von Kletzer busy, but what about the rest of the household?"

Smiling at her small victory, Tabitha thought for a moment. They needed a distraction and had brought their secret weapon with them. She quickly and quietly told Wolf her plan. As they spoke, Anthony returned to the dining room and joined them, and Tabitha told him the part he was to play.

The first part of the plan was for Tabitha to locate Ginny and see if the maid had any intelligence about Melody's whereabouts. The embassy was a large building, and it would be best if Wolf could be more targeted in his search. She headed to the ladies' retiring room, where she and Ginny had agreed to meet. Anthony was instructed to inform the dowager of her part but not to begin until he had a sign from Tabitha. Wolf was to wait until all the players were in place.

Tabitha found the retiring room easily and was happy to see her maid waiting. A large, gilded mirror was at the side of the room where the maids could fix hair or touch-up makeup. Under the guise of needing some minor hair restyling, Tabitha took a seat in front of the mirror, and Ginny joined her, fiddling with hair that didn't need to be fixed. But styling her hair was a good cover for Ginny to whisper into Tabitha's ear.

"Did you manage to find anything out?" Tabitha asked anxiously. Lady Hartley, a known gossip, had just entered the room, and Tabitha wanted to keep her conversation well away from those sharp ears and tongue.

"As you can imagine, m'lady, the staff is run ragged, so it was difficult to find anyone with time to talk about anything. But I tried to make myself useful in the kitchen plating food, and the kitchen maid was grateful for the help. It wasn't the easiest topic to weave into the conversation, but I did ask whether the ambassador lives here or uses it for formal occasions. She said he lives here. Then I asked if he was the only person living here, and she said his wife and five children also live in the residence. I asked the age and gender of the children, thinking maybe they're hiding Miss Melody in plain sight, surrounded by the ambassador's children. But no, five boys, all over the age of six."

Tabitha could see where this conversation was headed, and her fears were confirmed when Ginny said, "I'm sorry to say, m'lady, but if Melody is in this house somewhere, I don't believe the servants have any knowledge of her."

Finishing Ginny's thought, Tabitha said sadly, "So either they've locked Melody up somewhere even the servants don't enter, or she's not here."

"Yes, I think that's true. I did manage to ask about attics and cellars. There is a wine cellar, and the butler has the only key to it. Or the only key as far as the servants know. So that might be a place for m'lord to look. It's possible the butler knows about Melody and is keeping the information from the other staff. There's also an attic that isn't locked, but the servants' rooms are directly below that. I think if anyone were up there, the staff would have heard something. It's not like Miss Melody is a quiet one."

Unless the child was gagged, Tabitha thought. But then she shook her head at such thoughts. Ginny was right; it was hard to imagine a child being kept for days, even bound and gagged, with no one hearing anything. But she would tell Wolf to check the cellar. They couldn't afford to leave any stone unturned.

With the pretence of fixing her hair at an end, Tabitha returned to the ballroom. Entering the large, now overly warm room, Tabitha caught Anthony's eye. He stood behind the dowager's chair as she held court to her coterie of titled ladies of a certain age. Wolf was across the room, towards the main door, lounging against the doorframe with an impressive air of insouciance. Tabitha quickly approached him, relayed the information Ginny had gleaned, and then moved away and back into the crowd.

It took Tabitha a few moments to locate von Kletzer. But once she made eye contact with him, he wasted no time moving towards her. There was a brief lull in the music while partners were shuffled, and during this time, the count crossed the space between them and grasped her hand, kissing it as he bowed.

Tabitha didn't dare make eye contact with Wolf during this pantomime.

"Lady Pembroke, I hope you will allow me to claim this dance," the count said in a tone so lascivious that Tabitha felt the heat rising to her face. She wanted to stay in control of this situation and tried to calm her nerves.

"But of course," Tabitha smiled, though anyone who knew her could see it didn't reach her eyes.

Still holding her hand, the count moved closer and said, "I hope you will call me Dieter, and I might call you Tabitha."

Under normal circumstances, Tabitha would have been appalled at such intimacy from a virtual stranger, but tonight, she had a fly to catch and needed all the honey at her disposal. "Of course, dear Dieter," and she batted her eyelashes for good measure.

The count then led her onto the dance floor. She nodded at Anthony and set the rest of the plan in motion. Count von Kletzer held her far closer than was proper. Tabitha was appalled at the man's gall but said nothing. One thing Tabitha did want to establish was whether von Kletzer was in residence at the embassy. She considered how to phrase such a question so it wouldn't seem suggestive. Finally, deciding this man would likely find a way to interpret it suggestively regardless, she just asked.

"Why Tabitha, what a forward question to ask," the count leered, confirming Tabitha's worst fears. "Do you wish to make an illicit visit to my chamber this evening?" Tabitha didn't answer, assuming the man would continue to make whatever assumptions he wanted. "I hate to inform you, but I don't reside in the embassy. My services for Emperor Wilhelm are, let's say, less formal than Ambassador Peetz's. However, I have taken a charming house in Kensington. I do hope you will come and visit." With this, he pulled her into him even more closely. Tabitha resisted the urge to stomp on his foot and storm off.

As he whirled her around the room, the count took advantage of the waltz's intimacy to whisper sweet nothings into her ear, most of which she tried to ignore. Luckily, he didn't seem to need much encouragement or a reply. This left Tabitha free to observe her co-conspirators spring into action.

The first thing she saw was Anthony offering the dowager his arm as she rose to make her way to the dining room. The plan was to cause as big a distraction as possible. She had just started to walk away when, to all appearances, she swooned and was caught by Antony. Luckily, the dowager's cronies could be counted upon to be as dramatic as possible, and there were several very vocal screams of distress. Anthony made a lot of noise about needing a chair and a doctor. The music stopped, and everyone turned to witness the scene playing out. Every eye was on the dowager, which was the intention. Tabitha dared to look at the now empty doorway where Wolf had stood.

As the closest thing to a relative, Tabitha immediately rushed over, pulling the count with her. The dowager had come out of her 'faint' and was now fanning herself with a lavish lace fan. "My heart, oh my heart," she was heard to wail.

"Really," Tabitha thought, "the woman could have had a very successful career on the stage." Even knowing it was staged, Tabitha found herself drawn into the drama that the dowager was in great distress.

It seemed word had reached the ambassador, and he quickly pushed through the crowd, rushing to the dowager's side and bending over the seemingly prostrate woman.

"My dear madam," he said, "not knowing the dowager's rank, "how may I be of assistance?"

Anthony answered for the dowager, who was so caught up in her performance that even she was starting to believe she was dying, "Is there a doctor to be had?"

"Jawohl, my personal physician, Doktor Meyer, is here somewhere." Clapping his hands to summon a nearby footman, the ambassador said, "Find Doktor Meyer and tell him to meet us in my private sitting room." He continued to Anthony, "There is what you call a fainting couch in there, and I believe it would be a more comfortable and private place for this dear lady to be examined." As he said this, he gestured towards two very tall, well-formed footmen and indicated they should carry the dowager into the sitting room on the chair she was currently on.

The music started back up as the dowager was carried out of the ballroom. Tabitha was sure the count would have happily continued the dance, but instead, she said to him, "The lady who fainted was the Dowager Countess of Pembroke. I must follow her and assure myself that she is well. Would you please accompany me, dear count?" His facial expression made it clear he would rather hold her close, whispering flirtatious nothings into her ear, but the count was enough of a gentleman to realise he could not refuse a lady in distress.

A procession made its way out of the ballroom. First, the two very muscular footmen carried the dowager on her chair, preserving her dignity as much as possible. The dowager herself had decided to make the most of her moment in the spotlight and had taken up a most pitiful wailing. Next was Anthony, close behind the footmen, then the ambassador, and finally Tabitha on the arm of Count von Kletzer. Along the way, they picked up a maid who had been sent for a jug of water and the doctor who had been tracked down just as he was about to lose a game of billiards. The entourage made its way to the sitting room. The dowager was gently laid on the appropriately named fainting couch, and now, as far as Tabitha could see, she had decided to enact a death scene worthy of Shakespeare.

As the crowd filled the sitting room, Tabitha could sense von Kletzer trying to pull his arm away, presumably so he could flee the scene. Tabitha kept a tight hold of it and whispered in his ear, "Thank goodness you are here, dear Dieter. I would be so frightened otherwise." She had done her best to imbue these words with the kind of feminine delicacy embued with just a tinge of flirtation she felt would most appeal to a man such as the count.

Her act seemed to work well; she felt his arm relax beneath her hand, and he whispered back, "It is my pleasure to be of assistance to such a delightful companion. I hope you will allow me to be of even more personal assistance at some other time." Tabitha didn't want to consider what that more personal assistance might be and merely inclined her head.

CHAPTER 24

Based on what Ginny had deduced, Wolf decided to try the cellar first. He hoped the butler had brought up all the wine for the ball earlier and would have no reason to return. He made his way to what he assumed was the cellar door. It was locked. In anticipation of their activities that evening, Wolf had come prepared. He had his lock-picking kit with him as well as a revolver hidden in his boot.

The cellar lock was child's play to pick, and having opened it, Wolf quickly closed the door behind him. He was grateful to find the cellar equipped with electric lights and turned them on, hoping no light would spill out under the heavy oak door.

Descending the steep wooden stairs, he found himself in a cellar resembling his own. There was a large room lined with shelves holding bottles of wine. There were also some barrels on their sides. He saw a doorway and went through it, finding himself in a smaller version of the first room. He explored both rooms and found nothing to indicate hidden doorways or passages. Finally, satisfied he had scoured the place, he returned the way he came locking the cellar door behind him.

Wolf moved quickly back into the vestibule, where he could hear the dowager's plaintive wailing and see a crowd still gathered outside the sitting room, clearly enjoying every moment of the impromptu theatrics. Sure that the dowager's performance firmly held everyone's attention, Wolf quickly climbed the large marble staircase. He had already decided to claim to be lost and looking for a water closet if he ran into a servant or even a family member.

At the top of the stairs, Wolf found himself in a long, dimly lit hallway. He couldn't hear any sound coming from behind the closed doors. He decided the safest thing was to knock on each door gently. If there were an answer, he would use his water closet excuse.

He went down the hallway knocking on each door. With no answer, Wolf opened all the doors; none were locked. He found the normal collection of study, library, and drawing room. A brief glance in each led him to believe he would not find Melody there.

With the rooms in that hallway all explored, Wolf made his way up another staircase to, what he imagined, were the family bedrooms. He again made his way down the hallway and discovered only empty rooms. On the floor above, he could hear childish voices coming from what he assumed was the nursery. Mindful of Ginny's observation that the servants seemed unaware of any little girl mixed in with the ambassador's sons, he gave the nursery a wide berth. The large room next to the nursery was the school room, and again, a cursory exploration turned up nothing more than a very vocal large ginger cat.

Remembering Ginny's observation about the attic, Wolf didn't bother trying to find it and returned to the marble staircase as quickly as possible. Glancing down into the vestibule, it seemed that, once it was clear the dowager wouldn't die, or at least not that evening, the crowd had dispersed. Wolf glanced around for servants or stray guests, but the coast was clear. He quickly slipped down to the ground floor.

The ambassador's sitting room door was open, and Wolf peeked in. The dowager was still lying in state on the fainting couch. She had the back of one hand on her forehead and seemed to be giving a performance worthy of the West End stage. Hovering around her was the ambassador, who looked as if he'd rather be anywhere else, Anthony, who looked as if he were struggling to keep a straight face, and nearest to the door, Tabitha on the arm of von Kletzer. From what Wolf could see, Tabitha was less on his arm than forcibly holding him in place.

All eyes turned to Wolf as he entered the room. A quick shake of his head spoke of his failure to find Melody. "Dear Jeremy, where have you been?" the dowager said as if with her dying breath.

"Lady Pembroke, whatever has happened? I stepped away for a few minutes to talk to an old acquaintance, and when I returned to the ballroom, it was all aquiver with talk of your collapse."

"Yes, I was overcome," the dowager said in a shaky voice, holding a hand towards Wolf. "I needed you, Jeremy. Ambassador Peetz kindly had his doctor attend to me, but the stupid man said it was nothing more than the heat of the room and an excess of champagne. But I know it is my heart. I fear I may not have long, dear Jeremy."

At this point, it was all Tabitha could do not to roll her eyes. The dowager was definitely getting far too into character. It was time for them all to leave. "Mama, now that Pembroke is here, we should get you home to your own bed. And in the morning, we can call your personal physician, who I'm sure will have no trouble correctly diagnosing what ails you." Tabitha attempted to keep all sarcasm out of her voice, but a glance at Wolf showed him trying not to let his lips twitch in amusement.

"Perhaps that is for the best," the dowager said wanly. She had now struck a pose and a tone of voice that spoke of great fortitude in the face of enormous suffering. Taking her hand off her forehead, she reached out and grasped the ambassador's hand in both of hers. "Dear Ambassador Peetz, your kindness to a frail old woman will never be forgotten." Just as he was about to withdraw his hand in the hope he could withdraw entirely, the dowager held his hand tighter and added, "And do let me know whenever you require a proper English doctor."

With that last statement, the dowager let go of his hands, and the ambassador rose quickly before she could take hold of him again. Mumbling his wishes for her speedy recovery, he exited the room. Count von Kletzer looked longingly after him, and Tabitha decided there was nothing to be gained in keeping the man by her side any longer. She released her iron grip on his arm and turned to Wolf, saying, "Lord Pembroke, perhaps it is time to call for our carriages and to escort Mama home."

The dowager wasn't quite ready to end her performance; she was enjoying the attention far too much, "Jeremy dear, I'm not sure I can walk to the carriage. You may need to carry me." At this, Tabitha did roll her eyes and then hoped the count hadn't seen. Luckily, he was too busy backing out of the room.

"I fear I must leave you," he said, clicking his heels together again. "Lady Pembroke, it was a delight. We will meet again soon, I'm sure." And with that, the man was gone.

Now that there were just the four of them in the room. Tabitha said briskly, "Okay, let's go. Wolf, I'm assuming you found nothing?"

"Nothing. So, unless you feel anything else can be learned, I agree we should call for the carriage," he answered.

"Jeremy, dear, you may need to carry me out to bolster our story," the dowager said with a twinkle in her eye.

"Mama, I believe the narrative will hold up if you take Anthony's arm and he walks you to his carriage. Anthony," she said, "given that it is still early, why don't we all congregate at Chesterton House for a brandy?" She said this pointedly, and everyone nodded their agreement.

The dowager was quite disappointed to be denied a grand exit in the arms of a strong young man, but she accepted her fate and instead was determined to make the most of her final scene. She let Anthony help her off the couch and said, "I hope this is not a preview of how you will all react at my actual deathbed! Let me put you on notice that you all failed the rehearsal abysmally. Don't think I didn't see that eye-rolling, Tabitha."

Finally, they managed to exit the embassy and settle into their carriages. The dowager travelled with the Duke of Somerset, leaving Tabitha and Wolf some time to talk before arriving back at Chesterton House.

"Was Ginny right?" Tabitha asked anxiously.

"I'm afraid she was," Wolf answered, knowing how disappointed Tabitha must be with the results of their evening's adventure.

"And you looked everywhere?"

"I didn't want to spend too long, but I believe I checked all the likely places, including the cellar," he added. "There was no sign of Melody. They must be holding her somewhere else."

"I did discover that von Kletzer has a house in Kensington. Melody must be there," Tabitha said. She added, "He has expressed a wish for me to visit."

Even in the dark carriage, Tabitha could see Wolf's scowl at this comment, "I'm sure he has, but that will not be happening," he said with more force than he intended.

"Won't it?" Tabitha asked. "Let me remind you, again, you have no say over my actions. You are neither husband, father, nor brother. If Melody is being held there, this may be the perfect opportunity for me to gain entry to the house."

"And do what? You hardly think von Kletzer will introduce you to his charming abductee over tea?"

"I'm not a naive fool, Wolf," Tabitha said angrily. "But, at the very least, I may be able to glean some information about the house's layout."

"The layout of the house? How do you plan to investigate the upper floors while keeping your honour intact? Because if you ask to see the bedrooms, I can assure you that lizard of a man will make only one interpretation of the request." Wolf could tell this argument was getting them nowhere. He only hoped that in the light of day, after a good night's sleep, Tabitha would see sense in his concerns. They rode the rest of the short journey in stony silence.

Anthony's carriage had arrived just a few moments ahead of theirs, and they all entered Chesterton House together. Without thinking, Tabitha headed for the comfy parlour. On the few occasions of the dowager's visits recently, she had been received in the drawing room.

Entering the parlour, the dowager couldn't help but immediately notice the makeshift board covered in notecards. "What is this?" she asked, walking up to it.

Wolf crossed the room and stood beside her. "We started using this for our last investigation. Every fact and every open question has its own notecard, and they are grouped together as appropriate. The yarn connects the different groupings. It proved very helpful, and so we are using it again."

The dowager patted his arm, "How ingenious of you, dear Jeremy."

"Actually," Wolf admitted, "full credit for the idea and execution lies with Tabitha."

"Hrmph," the dowager said, indicating with a wave of her hand that suddenly, it seemed a less ingenious idea.

When they were all seated with brandy poured for Wolf and Anthony and sherry for the ladies, they compared notes from the evening. With a look in Wolf's direction, Tabitha repeated her discovery about von Kletzer's residence.

"I did not like how that man was dancing with you, Tabitha. That harpy, Lady Willis, made a rather crude comment, the like of which I do not care to have associated with the Pembroke name," the dowager said imperiously.

"Trust me when I say, Mama, I did not enjoy it either. But it seemed vital to let the man believe his attentions were welcome. If nothing else, to keep him close while Wolf investigated the house." Tabitha eyed Wolf as she said this and could see by the hard line of his mouth that he was not happy.

Absurd, man, Tabitha said to herself. What else would he expect? Wasn't the plan for me to keep von Kletzer occupied? How did he think I was going to accomplish that? By challenging him to a game of cribbage?

For his part, Wolf knew he was being childish. Irrational even. They had formed a plan, and Tabitha had done nothing more than execute it perfectly. Yet somehow, the memory of the suave but oily German with Tabitha in his arms, whispering sweet nothings into her ear and anticipating a future rendezvous, incensed him.

Tabitha then walked the dowager and Anthony through all their notecards, explaining all their suppositions about Claire Murphy. While they had each heard bits and pieces throughout the investigation, they had not heard the entire narrative from start to finish.

"Fenians helping German spies who are using courtesans to discover British military secrets. That all seems quite melodramatic, Tabitha. Are you sure you're not being a little fanciful?" the dowager asked, her voice dripping with scepticism.

Tabitha was saved from having to defend their theory by Anthony, "Lady Pembroke, I can assure you, the Fenian-German connection is a genuine one that Her Majesty's government is well aware of."

"But why?" the dowager questioned. "We are not at war with the Germans."

Anthony explained, "We may not be at war with them, but that does not mean there is not great tension between our two countries. Germany is a rapidly growing industrial power with a great desire to expand its influence beyond its borders. Britain is one of its main rivals. There is no doubt they covet our empire and our navy."

"How on earth do you know so much about these things, Anthony?" the dowager demanded. Tabitha and Wolf were equally interested to hear the answer.

The Duke of Somerset seemed to be debating how candid to be. Finally, he looked up and admitted, "I have some informal ties to the Naval Intelligence Department." He continued, "I was approached when I was at Cambridge. It seems I had been recommended as someone with the right aptitude to be useful."

"Useful how?" Tabitha asked, intrigued to hear more about her friend's secret life.

Anthony felt very caught suddenly; he probably shouldn't have admitted what he had, but he had felt very conflicted during this investigation. He had been withholding information, perhaps key information, from his friends. Very aware of the debt he owed Wolf and Tabitha in the matter of his father's many indiscretions, the duke nevertheless balanced this against his loyalty to the Crown. Weighing up his options, he finally decided that with a child's safety in the balance, it would be unconscionable not to reveal all he knew. Particularly to people he had every reason to trust.

"Oxford and Cambridge are both hotbeds for all sorts of clandestine activities. They're crucibles of youthful idealism and political activism. Given some of the great scientific discoveries being incubated at those institutions, there are many opportunities for political espionage. I was asked to keep an eye out and report back on what I saw and heard."

"So, you spied on your fellow students?" Wolf asked.

Anthony looked uncomfortable at such a description of his activities but admitted, "Well, I suppose, yes. And not just fellow students. There were plenty of professors involved in dubious activities. After congregation, I was asked to keep up my informal observations of my ex-classmates and others."

"How exciting," the dowager clapped her hands together. "Anthony, I wouldn't have thought you had it in you!" The young Duke of Somerset wasn't sure how to take such a comment. He was certainly used to being underestimated. Indeed, this was one of the reasons he had been identified as a perfect spy; no one would expect it from such a gentle, almost feminine young man.

Wolf considered Anthony's revelations, "Have you reported back our theory about Sir Desmond Chambers?"

Anthony looked even more uncomfortable but admitted, "Yes, I reported our findings."

"And what was the response?" Tabitha asked.

"That was the odd thing," the duke said. "They seemed very unconcerned."

Talbot had entered the room with some light refreshments, which were very welcome. Tabitha switched from sherry to tea and served herself some finger sandwiches. Satiating her immediate hunger, she asked, "What context did you give for your discoveries about Sir Desmond? And did you mention us?"

Anthony had helped himself to one of Angie's biscuits and finished chewing before answering, "All I said was that there was a missing child, and I was helping friends find her. During our inquiries, we stumbled upon some evidence that led me to believe Sir Desmond might be compromised."

Tabitha put down her plate and stood up. She walked to the board and immersed herself in its details for a few minutes, contemplating how they stood up in light of Anthony's information.

The dowager was quite the avid audience, totally caught up in the tale of international intrigue. Her eyes shone brightly, and any memory of her pretend infirmity was long forgotten. Watching the older Lady Pembroke's evident enthusiasm, Tabitha was nervous about how much they had involved her. "What is our next move?" the dowager demanded, confirming Tabitha's worst fears.

Wolf visibly winced at her use of the word "our." Tabitha did her best not to laugh. It was obvious he hadn't realised that the dowager would not be used when it suited them and then happily left out of the rest of the investigation. At least Tabitha knew the deal with the devil they had made when they sought the older woman's help.

CHAPTER 25

Their post-ball gathering had broken up quite soon after Anthony's dramatic revelations. Even so, by the time Tabitha had retired for the night and then managed to fall asleep, it was past one o'clock in the morning. Exhausted, Tabitha didn't wake until past ten. She called for Ginny and bathed and dressed quite sluggishly. Finally, the promise of coffee lured her downstairs, where she encountered a surprisingly chaotic scene.

There were workers busy in her hallway. An unusually flustered Talbot hovered over them. Tabitha descended to the hallway and demanded, "What on earth is going on, Talbot?"

He turned to her and said apologetically, "I did not want to disturb you, milady. And his lordship went out early this morning. I was unsure what to do."

"Who are they, and what are they doing?"

Talbot handed her a letter, "Perhaps this will explain," he suggested.

Tabitha read the note.

"Dear Jeremy, now that I am a vital part of your investigative team, I feel we need a more efficient method of communication. Jonathan was rabidly against the telephone. I have no idea why. He refused to install one and forbade me from putting one in my home. However, I recently found out that Lady Willis has had one installed, and I refuse to let that woman claim to be more forward-looking than I am. There is no point in having a telephone if I have no one to call, so I have sent workers to install one for you as well. While I can't be quite as demanding of the Duke of Somerset's household, I have sent him a note suggesting he also take full advantage of this technological innovation."

Tabitha read the note twice and turned to Talbot, "Did you read this?"

"Yes, milady. It was delivered with instructions for me to read it before delivering it to you."

Tabitha massaged her temples, feeling a headache coming on, "Talbot, I'm going to the breakfast room, where I will need a lot of coffee. Lord help me, I may need a swig of brandy at this rate. Let me know when his lordship returns."

Ensconced in the peace of the breakfast room with a steaming cup of coffee in front of her, Tabitha began to feel more able to take on the day. But what did that mean? What were they to do next? She hadn't realised until last night how much hope she had invested in the notion of Melody being held at the embassy. Looking through their notecards the night before with the dowager, Tabitha felt they had gathered much information and even drawn some significant conclusions. Yet, they were no closer to finding Melody or clearing Manning's name.

Flicking through the morning papers, she saw that the inquest into Claire Murphy's death had been held the day before. It was surprising that the inquest had taken as long as it had. But Tabitha was grateful for the time it bought them, even if they hadn't achieved all they'd hoped.

The article, which Tabitha noted was written by Wolf's contact Andrews, reported that the inquest findings would be forwarded to the Crown Prosecution Service, which would then review the evidence and decide whether to proceed with a criminal trial. The reporter editorialised that it was hard to imagine a more open and shut case and had every expectation it would go to trial. But he also noted a backlog of cases and the possibility that they could further delay the scheduling of a trial. It seemed Dr Blackwell's autopsy report had not been enough to save Manning.

Tabitha wasn't sure how long such a delay might be, and the reporter didn't mention a length of time, but it was clear the investigation had a ticking clock on it. There was no doubt, at least in the reporter's mind, that the punishment for such a violent crime would be capital punishment. Tabitha wished she hadn't started reading the newspaper. She could feel the headache coming back.

Unsure how long she dawdled at the breakfast table, Tabitha was unwilling to confront the chaos of the workers in her home, depressed by what she had read and paralysed by uncertainty as to what their next moves were. Her increasingly depressing thoughts were interrupted by Talbot. He carried a salver with a notecard on it. He also shared that the workers would be finished in a few minutes, and the foreman had offered to give him instructions on how to use the new and unexpected piece of technology now gracing her hallway.

"Thank you, Talbot. I supposed you might as well take him up on that offer. Though, for once, I must agree with the late earl and wonder why this progress is necessary." As befit an experienced butler, the ever-inscrutable Talbot merely inclined his head, which could have meant almost anything.

Tabitha took the notecard. It was sealed with a crest she didn't recognise. At least that meant it wasn't the dowager with yet another demand. Although Tabitha reflected, from now on, the dowager was likely to call them on their newly installed telephone rather than send a note. It was hard to believe that wouldn't be even more intrusive. She opened the seal and glanced down at the signature, Count Dieter von Kletzer. Oh my!

The note wasn't long, but it was to the point, "My dear Tabitha, how charmed I was to make your acquaintance last night. It is rare to meet a woman who combines so many physical charms with such sophistication about the ways of the world." Tabitha didn't want to consider too deeply what such a sentence was implying and continued reading, "I must admit to being quite disarmed by the coquettishness you combined with a delightfully brazen admission of desire." Tabitha was quite alarmed by now. She knew she had flirted and taken the flirtation further than was her natural inclination, but what on earth had this man read into it that he felt comfortable sending such a note? Perhaps Wolf's anger hadn't been misplaced the prior night.

Finally, the note got to its point, "My darling, daring Tabitha, I barely slept all night thinking of your luscious charms as I held you close to my manhood." At this last line, Tabitha found herself quite flushed. She had never been spoken to in such a manner and by a man she barely knew. What had she done to seem not merely open to such words but eagerly receptive? Finally, von Kletzer ended with, "I cannot wait a moment longer. You must come to me. I cannot wait for the evening, though I hope we may continue for that long. Join me for luncheon. Yours in delirious anticipation."

Well, it was lucky Wolf wasn't present because if he'd seen that note, there was little doubt he would have stormed over to Kensington and challenged the German to a duel, as rare and illegal as such conflict resolution was. She might even have encouraged him to do so. But Wolf wasn't there; Tabitha had no idea where he had gone or when he might return. It was now well past eleven o'clock, and she had a decision to make.

This was an opportunity to get into von Kletzer's house and determine if Melody was being held there. It was too good a chance to ignore. But there was little doubt what this opportunity might cost her. Tabitha was not a virginal young maid, and if this was the price of returning Melody home safely, it was one she was willing to pay. But she had to consider if there was any other way. And she didn't have long to come up with a plan.

Tabitha was startled out of her reverie by a loud, ringing noise. It almost sounded like a fire bell, and Tabitha jumped out of her chair and ran into the hallway, where she found Talbot holding the earpiece for their new telephone.

"Milady, the Dowager Countess of Pembroke, is on the telephone." Talbot announced this as if he had been handling telephone calls for his entire career. Tabitha wished she could feel a similar comfort level with this new device. She tentatively took the earpiece being held out for her. While she had seen people occasionally use a telephone, she had never felt the need to use such a device.

The telephone, an exquisite piece of craftsmanship, stood proudly on their intricately carved mahogany hall table, its gleaming brass components catching the light. Tabitha gingerly held the device to her ear, unsure of the correct protocol. Did one say something or wait to be addressed? Luckily, the decision was taken out of her hands.

"Tabitha? Tabitha, can you hear me?" A familiar voice boomed out of the earpiece. Tabitha was so shocked that she almost dropped the contraption.

Taking a deep breath, Tabitha mustered the courage to speak her first words into the receiver, "Hello? Can you hear me?"

A moment of silence hung in the air, filled with anticipation and uncertainty. Then, she heard the dowager's voice loudly in her ear. "Isn't this wonderful, Tabitha? I can't wait to call everyone I know. Of course, I don't know many people with such a device. I may have to call Lady Willis and listen to whatever poison that harpy is spouting now. But it may be worth it."

Tabitha was often at a loss for how to reply to the dowager, but this new mode of communication left her without any response. She suddenly realised that the dowager might call to speak to them daily, perhaps even more frequently. Tabitha could see that the household would quickly need to establish some protocol around receiving telephone calls. This was the last thing she felt she could cope with at the moment.

However, it dawned on Tabitha that the dowager might be the perfect person to help her with the dilemma the count's note created. Well, if not the perfect person, the most readily available at that moment. And as the dowager had proven the evening before, few people were more willing and able to create a scene.

"Mama, I find myself in need of some advice," Tabitha began. It never hurt to flatter the woman's vanity and certainty that she was now of an age where her great wisdom was in demand. Unsure how to paraphrase the note to do it justice, Tabitha read it over the telephone. She could feel herself blushing again and was grateful Talbot had discreetly taken himself back to the servants' hall.

When she had finished reading, there was a long pause. Tabitha wasn't sure how to check if the telephone was still working. She was just about to call for Talbot in the hope that the foreman had conveyed some helpful information when the dowager spoke, "Well, the nerve of that man. Typical of those continentals. No Englishman would dare speak in such a way to a lady. Even a lady who had led him on with such blatant flirtation," she found she had to add.

Tabitha sighed and replied, "Mama, I believe we have already discussed my behaviour. As you did, I played out a scene last evening as a distraction. However, I did not anticipate a response as blatant and outrageous as this. What should I do?" It was really a mark of her desperation that Tabitha would even ask the dowager such a question. What was her life coming to if this was where she found herself?

The dowager asked, "What does Jeremy say?" She quickly added, "Though I can imagine the dear boy is having quite a conniption if his mood towards the German last night was any indication."

"Well, that's just it. He's not here, and I'm not sure when he will be back. And this invitation is for lunch. If I am to accept or decline, I must do so soon. This may be our only chance to get into that house and discover if Melody is being held there. I feel I cannot miss the opportunity. But, well," she wasn't sure how to phrase her concerns delicately. "Well, it's just..." but the words failed her.

The dowager finished her sentence for her, "It's just that the man clearly has dishonourable intentions. Quite dishonourable, in fact."

"Indeed," was all Tabitha could answer. "Yet, I feel I must go."

"Of course, we must all make whatever sacrifices are necessary to save that dear child. And Manning, of course. However, one hardly thinks this particular sacrifice is called for. I have an idea."

Tabitha listened in increasing wonder at the dowager's plan. It was bold, audacious, and potentially dangerous. It relied heavily on the fear and awe the dowager tended to strike into the hearts of men. But would such a strategy work with a man such as the count? A man they had every reason to believe was not above using deadly force. On the other hand, they seemed to have no choice.

The plan was certainly better than the alternative; Tabitha entering the lion's den alone and unprotected. Worried about the wisdom of what she agreed to but fully realising that it was better than no plan, Tabitha consented to all the dowager's suggestions.

Hanging up the telephone, she stared at the contraption for a few minutes. Was this machine at least partly responsible for her impulsive acceptance of the dowager's suggestion? Tabitha felt sure that if the conversation had occurred face-to-face, she might have been more inclined to debate its wisdom. But something about the telephone lent itself to a brief, action-oriented discussion, quite unlike a more leisurely, measured dialogue over tea and cake.

CHAPTER 26

T abitha thought long and hard about how to dress for her luncheon. If the dowager's plan were to work, Tabitha would have to spur the man quite quickly to action. However, she did worry about that action coming so soon that there was no time for stage two of the plan.

Ultimately, Tabitha decided to reuse the outfit from her Lady Chalmers disguise. During their last investigation, Tabitha and Wolf had cause to visit a brothel. Tabitha had assumed the persona of a wealthy widow searching for her runaway daughter. Ginny had altered an old dark plum-coloured, silk walking dress of Tabitha's to be significantly more plunging in the neckline than Tabitha would ever usually wear. Unbeknownst to Tabitha, Wolf still had dreams about her in that outfit. While she didn't know how much Wolf continued to think of her in the dress, she had seen enough in his eyes when he first saw her in it to know it was precisely the right level of daring to spur a man such as the count to action.

As with her Lady Chalmers costume, Tabitha accessorised the dress with an ornate, if old-fashioned, necklace inherited from her grandmother. It contained large sapphires set in a heavy, gold setting and hung rather suggestively between her well-displayed cleavage. As she dressed, Tabitha explained the dowager's plan to an increasingly concerned Ginny. "I must come with you, m'lady," the maid said anxiously. "His lordship would never forgive me if anything happened to you."

"Ginny, I share your concerns; I really do. But, from what I know of such assignations, albeit not a lot, I believe it is not customary to arrive chaperoned, even by one's lady's maid. I must go alone. The dowager has a plan, and I hope it will work. And if it doesn't..." Tabitha wasn't sure how to end that sentence, so she left her words hanging.

Despite her concerns, which she continued to mutter under her breath, Ginny did a fine job with Tabitha's hair and makeup. She left some stray curls hanging over Tabitha's shoulders in a rather provocative manner, and the makeup, while simple, was more than Tabitha would usually ever consider wearing. It was even a little more than she had worn as Lady Chalmers. Looking at herself in the mirror, Tabitha felt like quite the fallen woman. There was no doubt that if the point were to dangle herself as bait, her outfit would likely be very successful. She just hoped it wouldn't be too successful.

Tabitha wasn't sure what the protocol was for such a visit, but she was sure she didn't want the Earl of Pembroke's carriage standing outside a single gentleman's home for the world to see. She had Talbot hail her a cab. Obviously, her butler had his own thoughts about her outfit and upcoming adventure. While he didn't know the details, Tabitha had the forethought to tell him that if the earl were to return before she did, he was not to worry and that she and the dowager had a plan. Tabitha didn't want to mention that she was visiting von Kletzer in his lair, fearing that Wolf would rush over and ruin everything.

The cab let her off outside a pleasant, non-descript townhouse in Kensington. Tabitha tentatively knocked on the door and was relieved to have it answered by a butler. At least there would be servants in the house. She only hoped they wouldn't turn a blind eye to a lady in distress if it came to that.

The butler led her into a large, bright drawing room. On entering the room, she saw von Kletzer waiting for her on a large, plush, fainting couch. He stood and approached her as the butler discreetly faded from the room. Tabitha heard the door close as the German took her hand and, turning it, pressed a long, lingering kiss on her wrist. Before lifting his lips, she felt him poke out his tongue and give her skin a brief lick. It took all her self-control not to shudder in disgust. But Tabitha knew she would have to put up with worse than that, even in the day's best-case scenario. She couldn't fail at the first hurdle.

"Oh, Tabitha," the count whispered in an oily voice, making no attempt to hide his lecherous assessment of her outfit, "you have exceeded my every expectation. Let me assure you, I have fantasised all morning about how you might appear before me. But I never dared hope you would offer yourself to me quite so brazenly."

At his words, Tabitha second-guessed her outfit and wondered if she had been wrong not to bring Ginny. However, in for a penny, in for a pound, she stiffened her spine, raised her chin and leaned in to whisper in the count's ear, "I am gratified to find you approve of my outfit." She felt sick just saying these words, but she could see they had the desired effect.

The count led her to the couch and pulled her down beside him. "Oh, you naughty, naughty girl, you will find out soon enough just how much I approve." And with those words, he began to kiss her neck, edging downwards at an alarming speed. Tabitha felt him slip the shoulder of her dress and realised this was all going much faster than anticipated. She had to slow him down but wasn't sure how to manage this. Such things were well beyond any experience of her twenty-two sheltered years.

Gently pushing the man away, she said, "Dieter, while your impatience is gratifying, I rushed out of my house on receiving your note and didn't even eat breakfast. And I'm sure some champagne will only heighten our eventual pleasure." Tabitha didn't know where her words came from, but they did seem to do the trick. She just had to ensure she drank very little without making it evident to her over-eager host.

The count stood up and smoothed his trousers, "Of course, you are, right, my darling Tabitha. Do forgive my over-eager ardour. Let it not be said I'm not a gentleman and a consummate host." Tabitha was quite sure he was no gentleman, but she was happy to win the point. He held out a hand to help her to her feet. While he lingered, staring lasciviously at the low neckline of Tabitha's dress, he made no further attempts to molest her. Feeling more in control of the situation, Tabitha pulled her sleeve back up and attempted to fix whatever else his manhandling had done to her outfit. She had no desire to appear in front of servants in a state of dishabille.

Count von Kletzer led her from the drawing room and across the hallway to a well-appointed dining room with a large crystal chandelier hanging over a table that could easily sit thirty. Two place settings had been set side-by-side. Her host settled himself at the head of the table, leaving her a seat that was too close by as far as Tabitha was concerned.

Even von Kletzer could show some discretion in front of servants, and their first two courses were unremarkable, at least as far as his attentions towards her went. Tabitha sipped her champagne slowly. Even so, she felt the alcohol's effect and resolved not to allow her inhibitions to be lowered further. The count drank liberally, and not knowing the man, Tabitha wasn't sure whether this would make him more or less controllable. However, it did seem to loosen his lips to her advantage.

"Dear Dieter, are you unmarried?" she asked.

"Liebling, are you worried about competition?" the man asked in a tone that made clear he would enjoy her jealousy.

"Not at all. It is just hard to believe such a man has managed to steer clear of the clutches of a woman," Tabitha answered. She would need to take a long bath and scrub her skin clean once this day was over.

"Ha! I have no desire to steer clear of women's clutches, just their matrimonial intentions."

Tabitha felt the conversation was leading to the questions she had to pose, "And so you live here alone?"

"Mein kleiner, Vogel, do not worry yourself. We will have all the privacy we need for as long as we need it. There is no one in this house except the servants, and I can send them away if that is your preference." That was not her preference, and she shook her head, perhaps more vehemently than she meant.

"And what of your Lord Pembroke? You share a home, do you not? Do you share a bed?" He snaked a hand towards her, but Tabitha was too quick and took up her fork to spear a piece of fish.

"Lord Pembroke is my late husband's cousin, nothing more. I have stayed on at Chesterton House to help the earl and the staff transition. I will be moving into my own establishment soon."

"I see the way the earl looks at you, though. I know desire when I see it in a man's eyes."

Tabitha wasn't sure how to answer such a blatant statement, "The earl has always been a perfect gentleman, and I'm sure he thinks of me merely as a cousin-in-law, nothing more."

The count chuckled, "I am sure he thinks of you as something much more, but no matter. If the man has not found his way into your bed by now, then more fool him. I would have never allowed such a delicious peach to bloom in my hothouse without plucking it and enjoying every moment of its sweet juices."

Her mother had given Tabitha very little information before her wedding night, and two years of congress with Jonathan hadn't added much to her awareness of relations between men and women beyond something harsh and brief. But even she understood the count's allusions and blushed deeply.

"My my, have I shocked you, mein liebchen?"

Tabitha wasn't sure how to get back to the topic of other possible occupants of the house. "Do you not desire children at some point?" she asked in something of a non sequitur to the prior conversation.

"Kinder? Nein. I have no time for the little brats," he said with such vehemence that Tabitha suddenly couldn't imagine him tolerating a four-year-old girl, even as a visitor. But she had to be certain.

"Really? I could imagine nothing more delightful than having a little girl. My husband and I were never lucky enough to be blessed with children, but it has always been my dearest wish."

"My brother has three daughters, terrors all of them. I steer clear of the entire pack when I am home in Munchen. I find little girls even more ferocious than boys." All flirtation had gone from his voice. Quickly recovering himself, the count said, "And yet, somehow, little girls often grow up to be the most luscious young women. And then, I have all the time in the world for them." Tabitha could see from the look in the man's eyes that she would only be able to hold him off for so long. He continued, "Surely your appetite is satiated now, my love. Perhaps we can return to the drawing room and pick up where we left off?"

This was said with so little effort to disguise his lust that Tabitha was determined to string the meal out for as long as possible. "Dieter, what is the hurry? I like to take my time over a meal, as I do over all things," Tabitha tried to say this as flirtatiously as possible. She needed to walk a fine line between keeping the man interested and keeping him at bay for as long as possible. She glanced at the grandfather clock standing in the corner of the room and realised she'd already been in the house for an hour. What was holding up the dowager? Surely she hadn't gotten cold feet?

Tabitha had no sooner thought that than she heard a great commotion outside the dining room. The sounds increased. One male voice, probably the butler, was trying to be heard over a much louder, more strident voice that Tabitha had never thought she'd be so grateful to hear.

The door opened, and the dowager burst in with the discombobulated butler following in her wake. Despite her anxiety over the situation she found herself in, Tabitha was nevertheless amused to see the outfit the dowager had chosen. Dressed in a forest green riding habit with epaulettes that gave it a distinct military air, the dowager carried a riding crop, which she brandished as if it were a sword, and she was leading the battle charge. The diminutive older woman stormed into the dining room, brandishing her weapon as brashly as any young hussar riding into battle.

The dowager strode to the end of the table where von Kletzer sat with a stunned look on his face. She came to a standstill, barely an arm's length before him. He stood and attempted a bow, but the dowager took her riding crop and poked him in the chest with it, "What on earth do you think you're doing with my daughter-in-law?" she demanded.

The count looked utterly flummoxed and glanced at Tabitha, a pleading look in his eyes that she found so amusing that it was all she could do not to laugh out loud.

"Liebe Frau," he stammered, clearly thinking to use his charm on the fiery old woman bearing down on him.

"How dare you call me a frau!" the dowager said with all the indignation one might expect if he had called her a harlot, "I am the Dowager Countess of Pembroke and will be addressed as nothing less. I would have thought a so-called count, even a continental one, would know better. Are you Germans nothing more than a bunch of savages?"

The count didn't know how to answer and began to realise his celebrated charm was unlikely to serve him well with his latest guest. "Excuse me, your ladyship," he pointed at a chair opposite Tabitha, "Would you care to join us? As you can see, Lady Pembroke and I were engaged in nothing more than a pleasant luncheon."

"Poppycock!" the dowager exclaimed, again poking him with her riding crop. "I went to Chesterton House and was shown the highly indecent note you sent around earlier. Luckily, the butler had been so alarmed by the outfit he saw his mistress leaving in that he took the liberty of retrieving it and alerting me to her outing. And thank goodness he did. I would say that I can't imagine what I have prevented, but given her dress and your reputation, I believe I know all too well."

Feeling caught on the back foot but now recovering his composure, the count adopted a more flirtatious tone. He had never met a woman he couldn't beguile, and he doubted this strange little old English woman dressed in her odd outfit was any more immune to his Teutonic charms. "Lady Pembroke, you wound me to my heart. " At this, he theatrically placed both hands over his heart and adopted what he imagined was an irresistible pose and facial expression. He had no idea who he was dealing with. And then, he made his fateful move; he grabbed the dowager's free hand and bowed his head to kiss it. At this, the dowager raised her riding crop and struck him.

"How dare you! I can only imagine the liberties other women, including my daughter-in-law, are prepared to allow you to take. But I assure you, I will not tolerate such licentious attacks on my person from a man, certainly not a continental one. I understand you may do things differently in Germany, but this is England, and you would do well to remember that."

The count was so stunned by her physical assault that he sat down in his chair with his mouth hanging open as if he had thought to counter the insults rained down on him and then reconsidered.

"Tabitha, I have never been so appalled, and that is saying something where you're concerned." It was only to be expected that, even though playing a part, the dowager could not help throwing some low blows at Tabitha. "You will leave with me immediately."

Truly, thought Tabitha admiringly, this was the moment the dowager had been born for. Armed and bestriding the enemy on the battlefield, taking no prisoners. The dowager cocked an eyebrow at Tabitha, asking if she'd had any success. Unsure of what she had found out, Tabitha discreetly shrugged her shoulders.

And that was when the dowager's offensive was ratcheted up to a level Wellington would have been proud of. "In fact," she announced, pacing the dining room floor and gesticulating wildly with her riding crop while the count cowered in his chair, "I am now worried that you may have other English maidens entrapped in this den of inequity."

Tabitha held her breath. Where was the dowager going with this? And then she found out.

"I will be conducting an inspection of every room in this house to assure myself, and Her Majesty," she added for good effect, "that this assault on our sovereign soil has no further tentacles. I need to be able to report that this audacious attempt to gain a strategic advantage over our great land of Albion by the corruption of the fairest of our gentle sex has been nipped in the bud."

It was unclear if the count thought the dowager was truly mad or might believe she had some direct line to the queen reporting on the ravishing of British noblewomen by Germans to gain some military advantage. Tabitha suspected the dowager's full-frontal assault didn't allow the man to ponder her words' logic. Instead, he was swept along by her militant rhetoric. Whatever the reason, he saw a way out of the adversarial turn his planned seduction had taken. Jumping out of his chair, he declared, "Lady Pembroke, I can assure you the mighty, majestic Vaterland would not stoop to such tactics. It is now a matter of patriotic honour for me to personally conduct you through this house to assure you that the only woman intended for ravishing today was the younger Lady Pembroke!"

As he said these words, the count turned an amusing shade of red and quickly almost puce. He turned to Tabitha, who had to bite her lip to contain her amusement, and then back to the dowager just in time to receive another strike of her riding crop on his side. "So, you admit it, foul demon!" she shouted. Tabitha was worried she would get too carried away by her Boudicca routine and not take advantage of the offer to search the house she had somehow been offered up on a platter. Luckily, the count himself saved the situation. Eager to move out of striking distance of the dowager, he began heading to the door.

Tabitha indicated with a nod of her head to the dowager that they follow him. For the next thirty minutes, they searched every room in the house, including the cellar and the attics. The dowager even insisted they enter the servants' quarters, absurdly claiming he might have some young maids tied to their beds as if they were all in the middle of some Thomas Hardy novel full of wicked seducers of young women. Such was the frenzied state that she had thrown the count into, he not only insisted on personally conducting them into every room but made a grand, almost comical, show of throwing open cupboards, looking under beds and ensuring they had thoroughly searched every square inch of the house.

Finally, there was nowhere left to look, and it was clear that

Melody was nowhere in that house. Disheartened by their failure to find the child but grateful to the dowager for appearing in the nick of time and ensuring they were able to do a thorough search, Tabitha said, "Mama, I believe you can now give assurances to Her Majesty that you have personally, and thoroughly scrutinised every part of Count von Kletzer's home and have found no indication of a German plot to overthrow Britain by the mass seduction of its young women. I think we may leave now."

There was a moment's hesitation, and it was clear the dowager was enjoying herself far too much. If she could have thought of a reason to prolong her performance, she would have. But a hard stare from Tabitha warned her they would only have so much time. If they pushed their luck too far, the count might start questioning the absurd tale the dowager had spun.

A great general knows when to attack and retreat, and the dowager proclaimed, "Indeed! I shall be reporting back to Her Majesty. But consider yourself put on notice, young man. Your villainous activities are now being watched, and I suggest you confine your amorous endeavours to other continentals. I hear that French women are easily corrupted. Or perhaps the Italians?"

With that, she swept out of the house, Tabitha following quickly in her wake. They left so fast that there were no formalities of farewell. But Tabitha considered that probably for the best. Even the British penchant for exhibiting a stiff upper lip in the face of any and all situations was hardly sufficient to provide her with a graceful way to end such a luncheon.

The door safely closed behind them, the dowager and Tabitha stood on the steps outside the count's house. "Thank goodness you came when you did!" Tabitha said, sincerely grateful.

"Well, perhaps if you had dressed a little less...Well, let's be polite and say gaudily, then perhaps you wouldn't have had such an urgent need for rescuing," the dowager said. As she spoke, she pointed her riding crop at Tabitha's exposed cleavage for emphasis. Tabitha didn't entirely disagree, so she let the dowager win the point.

"Your performance was impressive and manipulating him to help us search his house was inspired." Tabitha wasn't even trying to butter the dowager up. She was genuinely impressed by the woman's performance, nerve and ingenuity.

"I have my carriage here," the dowager answered. "I'm hoping you had the good sense not to drive here in a Pembroke carriage."

"I took a cab, so I would be grateful for a ride home."

Beyond Michael, the footman standing in for the dowager's butler Manning while he was incarcerated, Tabitha was unfamiliar with the rest of the dowager's staff. The dowager was so busy continuing to berate Tabitha that she took no notice of the footman who helped her into the carriage. Entering first, the dowager sank back against the cushions, only to see a man sitting in front of her pointing a pistol, his other hand held in front of his lips to indicate the need for her silence. Even if she could have reacted quickly, Tabitha had entered and sat beside her almost immediately.

The door closed behind them. Tabitha looked at their armed assailant and gasped, "Lord Langley, what on earth do you think you're doing?" she exclaimed. Langley banged on the carriage roof, and it began to move.

"Did you bribe my footman and coachman?" the dowager exclaimed, her more immediate worries being staff disloyalty rather than the gun pointing in her direction.

"Not at all, your ladyship. Never fear. Your people are being detained while we talk. They are unharmed."

"What on earth do you want, Langley, and why are you pointing a gun at me? I remember when you were a snotnosed, bucktoothed runt of a lad, and now you presume to hijack me. Whatever is society coming to? Wait until I tell your mother!" the dowager said as if speaking to a ten-year-old boy caught stealing apples.

As it happened, Langley visibly paled at the threat, which, given the circumstances, Tabitha found quite amusing. However, he pulled himself together and said, "I'm sorry to have to resort to such tactics, but I received information today that forced my hand."

"Langley, I have no idea what you're talking about, nor do I care to know. Please take me home. I've had an arduous afternoon, and I am in need of a strong cup of tea to fortify me," the dowager demanded.

Even though he held the gun, Tabitha could see Langley was uncomfortable under the dowager's withering glances and authoritativeness. The hand not holding the weapon tapped nervously on his knee, and he glowed with a sheen of perspiration, even though the day was not overly warm. "Lady Pembroke, I am sorry I cannot immediately comply with that request. However, I can offer you a cup of tea at Langley House."

"You're abducting us and stashing us in a hideaway house?" the dowager asked melodramatically, holding her hand against her forehead as if in imminent danger of fainting. Something Tabitha was sure was not an actual danger. She was surprised the woman didn't just attack Langley with her riding crop. As if reading Tabitha's mind, the dowager brandished it and announced, "I, too, am armed, you know." Lord Langley ignored that for the empty threat, it clearly was, so the dowager continued, "What do you want from us that you resort to such despicable behaviour?"

"All in due time, Lady Pembroke. We are almost at our destination, and I would rather have our discussion over a cup of tea for you and a large brandy for me," their abductor said with every indication that he was not joking about his need for a stiff drink. Whatever he had imagined when he hijacked the coach, it was not how the scene played out.

Within a few minutes, the carriage came to a standstill. The faux footman opened the door and helped the two women out. Langley's voice came from inside the carriage, "My man is also armed. Please don't attempt anything rash." He exited and encouraged the two women to climb the steps.

The door was opened by Langley's butler, a first cousin to Tabitha's own butler and also called Talbot. The two men so resembled each other that the dowager was initially quite confused and said, "Talbot, what are you doing here? Do you know your mistress has been kidnapped? You weren't part of this nefarious plan, were you?"

Langley's voice came from behind them, "This is my butler, also Talbot. Cousin to Lady Pembroke's man. Please go in, and Talbot, my Talbot, will escort you into the drawing room."

While not as grand as Chesterton House, Langley's home was impressive. But it was clear there was no mistress of the house. The entire residence had dark, old-fashioned furnishings and needed some fresh decorations. The dowager looked around her and sniffed, "And when I speak to your mother, I will suggest she also take charge of this house. What is she doing hiding away in Devon, or Dorset, or somewhere down west that starts with a d?"

"Delabole," Lord Langley answered. "Our family estate is near Delabole in Cornwall. Mother has always preferred the country, having no time for London society." He hadn't spoken intending to offend, but his face showed his awareness of what he had said immediately after he said the words.

It was received much as he feared, "No time for London society? What on earth do you mean by such a statement?" the dowager exclaimed furiously, gesticulating with her riding crop for emphasis. "Are you suggesting that Lady Langley believes herself to be better than those of us who choose to remain in London? Is that what you're saying, Langley?"

Tabitha couldn't help but roll her eyes at the spectacle of her mother-in-law in high dudgeon at a perceived social slight from a man otherwise threatening her life. She saw Lord Langley had seen her eye-rolling and was almost tempted to give him a conspiratorial smile, except the man was holding a gun at her.

"Why don't we all have a seat?" Langley suggested. "Talbot, please bring tea for the ladies unless you prefer something stronger. And see if Cook has any of those wonderful teacakes left. I will have a brandy." He glanced at the dowager and added, "A large brandy."

"I will not be fobbed off with tea and cake," the dowager said indignantly, "This is not an afternoon call. We were forced here against our will, and I will not pretend otherwise."

"I will also have a brandy," Tabitha replied. Whatever stance the dowager chose to take, she needed a drink to calm her nerves.

The dowager glared at her but then sat down and said, "If you are willing to break bread with our captor as if this were just any other social visit, then I suppose there is no reason to deny myself sustenance. You at least ate lunch with that appalling German."

Langley saw his opening, "Indeed. Count von Kletzer, the very man I wanted to talk with you about and why I felt I had no choice but to insist on meeting with you today."

CHAPTER 27

Wolf had tossed and turned all night, a thought nagging at the edge of his dreams. Finally waking and realising he was unlikely to fall back to sleep, even though the sun had not risen, he got out of bed, threw on his robe, and descended to the kitchen. Unlike other peers, Wolf had fended for himself long enough that he knew how to make coffee and even cook some rudimentary dishes. But at that moment, it was coffee he desired. He sat at the large kitchen table, sipping his beverage. He had glanced at the clock on his way through the hall; it was four o'clock. Too early for even the maids to be up and about.

Wolf had another cup of coffee and managed to find some bread which he cut into thick wedges and ate slathered in butter. He ate far better as an earl than he ever had as a thief-taker. But sometimes, he missed the simpler meals he had enjoyed in his previous life; thick slices of bread with lashings of butter were one of them. The bread served at breakfast was pre-cut into thin, elegant slices. Somehow, it just didn't taste the same.

By the time he had finished eating, it was past five in the morning, and he started hearing the house come alive as some servants began going downstairs. Early morning chores included lighting fires, cleaning and tidying rooms, preparing breakfast, setting tables, and opening curtains.

Wolf still felt uncomfortable having servants minister to his every need. His father's household had servants when he was a child, but money was always tight, and their staff was minimal. Then Wolf went away to Eton, followed by Oxford. After a fight about his future profession led to Wolf's banishment from his father's house, he learned to make do for himself.

He had met Bear during those early years. Bear had lived a far tougher life than Wolf ever had. While he hadn't grown up on the streets like Rat, Bear's mother, Mrs Caruthers, had worked hard to keep a roof over the heads of Bear and his siblings after their father died. Many a meal was nothing more than watered-down soup with barely a vegetable or scrap of meat. Bear grew up scrappy and able to fend for himself. He taught Wolf everything he needed to know about survival in even the most dangerous areas of London.

Wolf had become used to living quite a hardscrabble existence when he had to. Sometimes he and Bear were flush with coin and enjoyed soft beds and decent claret. But other times were tough, and they slept where they could and ate pies filled with animal parts they didn't want to know too much about. But this life, which had fallen into his lap due to nothing more than the fate of his birth and his cousin's lack of offspring, was filled with so much luxury, such pampering and ease, that Wolf wasn't sure he would ever get used to it.

These days, he wanted for nothing. The merest whisper from him of a food preference, and suddenly Cook was serving it regularly. He had now learned to be careful how much he praised dishes he didn't care for. They would be in regular rotation at his table before he knew it. He discarded clothes at the end of the day, and somehow, they were whisked away to be returned, cleaned and mended. Not by Bear, of course, even though these were the normal duties of a valet. Another reason he needed to deal with that situation sooner rather than later. It wasn't fair to burden Talbot with additional duties merely because Wolf wanted a suitable cover to keep his old friend nearby.

During his occasional visits with his grandfather, the old earl, Wolf had seen how the upper ranks of society tended to talk to and treat those who worked for them. His grandfather had never been able to keep the maids' names straight and so hadn't tried, calling each one, "You girl." And that was far from the worst behaviour he had witnessed. Even as a child, Wolf felt ashamed of this treatment of the people who worked long, hard hours to ensure his family's comfort.

Now he had inherited the earldom and made sure to put no more burden on his staff than could be helped. If he needed something, he would search for it himself, often causing consternation amongst the servants who, at least early on, thought they had done something wrong and were about to be fired. By now, they had become used to their new master's odd ways, at least for the most part. It still sent the kitchen staff aflutter when he insisted on coming downstairs to get his coffee and biscuits most afternoons. But at least now they were prepared and had it waiting for him.

Such was his concern about not placing any additional burden on his staff that the last thing he wanted was for them to rise at such an early hour, find him downstairs and then feel the need to tend to his needs in addition to their duties. So, Wolf slipped back upstairs to his room. He sat in an armchair beside the hearth, too distracted to start a fire. He sat there for what felt like hours until Nancy, the under maid, entered his room to set the fire. Shocked to see her master up at such a time and sitting in a chilly room, she began backing out, but Wolf held up a hand to stop her, "I'm sorry to have surprised you, Nancy. Please go about your duties."

The fire set and the room warming, it was still far too early to go back downstairs for breakfast. Wolf sat staring into the fire and thinking. They were missing something; he knew they were. They'd accumulated many facts, yet nothing was adding up. There was a piece of the puzzle they hadn't found yet, and he had no idea where they should be looking. He reflected on some of the past crimes he and Bear had solved as thief-takers. Had any been as convoluted and frustrating as this one? He felt some had been. How had they gone about solving those?

As he reflected, he wondered, had he become soft in this new life? Had he lost the instincts and intuitions that were necessitated by his old life? Certainly, he and Bear had always needed to have their wits about them. They had been responsible for putting a lot of criminals behind bars over the years, and there were always old and new foes ready for vengeance. This kept them sharp, alert and ready.

But now, he was beyond the reach of the petty criminals who might come for him. Few people from his old life knew about his new rank, and he intended to keep it that way. When he moved into Chesterton House, Wolf ensured that word got around that he was leaving London. Even though he had made the occasional reappearance in Whitechapel, for the most part, he believed he was out of sight, out of mind. Had this safety and security come at an unexpected price?

Wolf realised that if his life as a pampered aristocrat had lost him some of his hard edges, then the only way to get them back was to take off his well-tailored clothes and handstitched, soft, supple boots and step back into his thief-taker life, if only for a few hours. Hopefully, returning to that persona would help him get a new perspective on this investigation. And if it were to do that, he needed his trusted ally, his best friend and confidant by his side. Wolf dug out his old thief-taker clothes, laundered and neatly pressed but still at hand, and shrugged off the Earl of Pembroke and was once again, Wolf, thief-taker.

When he was ready, he went looking for Bear. There was a bell in his room he could have rung. That was how his valet was supposed to be summoned, after all. But it had never felt right to call his friend to his side in such a way. Dressed in his old clothes, it felt even more inappropriate. Luckily, Bear had always been an early riser, and Wolf quickly found him in the kitchen, sitting at the same table where Wolf had drunk his coffee earlier.

Seeing his friend and putative master's outfit, Bear raised his eyebrows in query. Wolf said nothing but sat beside him, drinking coffee. If the servants wondered why their master was sitting amongst them dressed as someone they would turn away from the backdoor under normal circumstances, they kept their counsel.

"Do you think I have become soft?" Wolf asked his friend, staring into the dark depths of the coffee.

Bear paused before answering. He was not a man given to

platitudes under normal circumstances, and he certainly was always plain-speaking and straightforward with Wolf. Despite his friend's best efforts, the dynamic between the two of them had inevitably shifted. They might both know Bear's role as valet was a sham, and the rest of the servants might know that. Yet, even so, one of them was a peer of the realm with vast estates and wealth at his disposal, while the other was nominally employed at his pleasure.

When Wolf first learned of his inheritance, there had been no discussion about whether Bear would join him in his new life. Over the weeks, now months since coming to Chesterton House, there had been an unspoken agreement between them that Bear would stay by his side. And yet, sometimes, Bear did wonder about this life he was now living. More importantly, he wondered if he would lose his edge and if the longer he stayed by Wolf's side, the harder it might be to return to his old life if the need arose. And so, the question Wolf posed did not feel theoretical to Bear but rather pierced the soft underbelly of his insecurities.

"Perhaps we both have," Bear answered. "It was inevitable, to some extent. We no longer look over our shoulders constantly. We don't hustle for work, wondering where the next meal will come from. How could such a change not affect us in some way? This is a good life, an easy life. While not without its own cares, they are of a different kind. You carry the burden of the welfare of many other people now. You have estates and businesses in your custody to manage for the benefit of your tenants and the legacy of the title. I'm sure this weighs on your shoulders and brings its own worries. But those worries are very different than those we used to carry and share."

Wolf didn't answer immediately. He knew his old friend spoke the truth, as he always had and would. Finally, he said, "I need to walk, to slip back into my old skin, if only for a few hours. To try to see this investigation as I might have before all this," he gestured around him to the house and the servants. "And I'd appreciate your company if you're willing."

"Let me change, and I'll meet you here in ten minutes. I assume we're slipping out through the back?" Bear asked.

"In these clothes, of course. We don't need to give Lady Davenport any more fodder for her gossiping about this household," Wolf replied, mentioning their notoriously nosy next-door neighbour.

Bear was back even sooner than promised. Wolf was so invigorated by stepping back into his old persona, even if only for the morning, that he forgot to leave word with Talbot for Tabitha. When he realised this oversight, he and Bear were halfway to Whitechapel. Wolf shrugged it off; she'd likely sleep late after their evening out, and he might even be home for lunch.

They hadn't consciously agreed to walk to Whitechapel. They'd started walking towards Covent Garden, and their feet automatically took them towards their old stomping ground. By the time they realised which way they were headed, Wolf laughed and said, "Let's go and see Angie. I only had some bread and butter much earlier this morning. I could do with some of her baked goods."

They didn't talk about the investigation as they walked. They didn't talk of much, in fact. Bear had always been taciturn, inclined to listen more than speak. When he did speak, his words were normally measured. This was one of the many things Wolf cherished about the man. Their friendship was such that long periods of silence were not uncomfortable or awkward. That morning, Wolf was grateful for the silence; he wanted to think. He had always found that walking had helped him sort out his thoughts. The replacement of his own two feet by a grand carriage as his main mode of transportation had definitely been a loss in this way.

They had been walking for more than an hour. The hustle and bustle of London provided a background hum to their companionable silence. They were almost in Whitechapel when Wolf said, "What are we missing, Bear? Something is off. I know everything points to von Kletzer killing Claire Murphy, and maybe he did. But did he take Melody? The man is as slippery as an eel, there's no denying that, but my gut is telling me someone else is trying to warn us off this case. But I have no idea who."

Bear had worked and lived side by side with Wolf for many years and greatly respected the man's gut instincts, "Why do you feel it's someone else?"

Wolf thought momentarily before answering, "Last night after the Duke of Somerset and Lady Pembroke left, Tabitha and I stayed downstairs talking for a while. I had her convey all her interactions with von Kletzer, what he said, and how he said it. As far as Tabitha was concerned, nothing gave her any sense of concealment or guilt. Unless he is a very good actor, it seemed like nothing more than a rather weaselly man acting inappropriately with a lady. As she reflected on the evening, Tabitha agreed.

"If he was involved in abducting Melody to warn us off investigating Claire Murphy's murder, you might think there would be something in the man's manner that would feel threatening somehow. Don't get me wrong, his behaviour was lecherous in the extreme, but it never caused Tabitha to feel any undercurrent to their conversation."

Wolf thought about the night before. There was a detail he had not told the others. Now he realised this nugget was at the heart of his disturbed sleep. As he had been leaving the smoking room and returning to the dining room to find Tabitha, he suddenly found his path blocked by Lord Maxwell Langley. The man put a hand out to halt Wolf's progress and said in a voice quite as cold and chilling as he had used at White's, "Pembroke, mind the waters you muddy. You may find yourself sucked into quicksand before you know it."

"I have no time for riddles, Langley. If you have something to say, then say it," Wolf had growled, brushing the man's hand away. He found the man personally repellant and these vague threats irritating.

"Then let me make my point more plainly. Stop meddling, " Langley said threateningly. And with that, the other man had turned and walked away.

Wolf had shaken off the words then, but now, he wondered what they meant. He thought back to Langley's comments about Melody's disappearance days before. How had he known about that?

Wolf stopped and slapped his hand against his head, "Langley! Last night he made some rather vague but dark insinuations about what might happen if we continue this investigation. I was so consumed with our search for Melody that I brushed off his words. And the other day, at White's, he came right out and mentioned Melody's abduction.

"I wondered how he knew about it, but we were so focused on Germans, spies, and scotch whisky that I put it down to nothing more than the man's usual unpleasantness. But what if it wasn't? Bear, we have to find a hackney cab. I need to get back to Mayfair as quickly as possible."

They hailed a cab and climbed in. Wolf gave the driver the Duke of Somerset's address in Mayfair. Bear raised his eyebrows questioningly. "I have to talk to Somerset," Wolf explained. "He told us something last night, and I need some clarification." During the ride, Wolf told the story Anthony had recounted about his recruitment as an informal spy for Naval Intelligence.

There was a lot of traffic on the roads, and Wolf was often tempted to jump out of the cab and walk. But eventually, they arrived back in Mayfair and pulled up outside of Rowley House. They got out, and Wolf bounded up the steps. It was a good thing Wolf had visited multiple times before. It was unlikely he would have been admitted otherwise dressed as he was.

Wolf had been so eager to talk to Anthony that it never occurred to him that the man might not be home. Luckily, the duke had not yet left for his appointment with his tailor. They were shown into the drawing room, where the duke met them a few minutes later.

As soon as Anthony entered the room, Wolf jumped up, too impatient to wait another moment, "Somerset, that story you told us last night about being recommended as someone with the right aptitude to gather intelligence, do you know who the person was who suggested you?"

Anthony sat down and encouraged his overly excited guest to retake his seat, "Actually, I do know. I didn't at the time, but I subsequently found out that my father had recommended me." He saw their surprised reaction and added, "My natural father, Lord Langley, that is."

Wolf thought carefully about how best to phrase his next question, "And why was it that Langley was in a position to recommend you for such a role?"

There was an awkward silence, and it was clear Wolf had asked a question Anthony was uncomfortable answering. Finally, he decided and replied, "Because he was recruited to a similar role at Cambridge and also continues in some sort of intelligence role to this day."

"I knew it!" Wolf exclaimed.

"What do you know?" The Duke of Somerset asked, at a complete loss for why they were having this discussion.

"I knew Langley was involved in all of this. I think he has Melody," he exclaimed.

"No. Surely not. I know you don't like the man much, and I understand why. But to think he would sink to abducting little girls, well, that's a bit much, old fellow. I must say."

Wolf continued ignoring the other man's protestations of his father's innocence, "It all makes sense. Let me ask you, in the abstract, is it possible that the intelligence services might know about attempts to steal British secrets and decide not to do anything about it? You did admit last night the higher-ups seemed surprisingly unconcerned about Sir Desmond."

"Why would they ignore you?" Bear added.

"Well, there will always be spies. Our enemies, even our so-called friends, spy on us, and we spy on them. It's the way of the world. If we take down one spy ring, another will eventually spring up. But we may not know about that one so quickly. So yes, Wolf, to answer your question, I believe it is possible they would do nothing to break up a known spy ring."

Wolf continued, his thoughts almost speeding too fast for him to form coherent sentences, "So, perhaps the intelligence services discovered Sir Desmond was feeding information to the Germans, however unintentionally. Rather than intervening, they began using him to feed false information." Wolf stopped, second-guessing what he was saying, and asked, "Wouldn't the Germans realise, at some point, that they had false information?"

By this point, Anthony feared so much had been guessed or given away that there was no point in denying anything, "Probably. But they might waste a lot of time and money recreating false plans by the time that became evident. And, after all, it would make much more sense to continue to feed false information through Sir Desmond rather than take him out of the equation and have the Germans pivot to an unknown source. This way, the government can control what gets leaked and when. If you're right about Sir Desmond, I'm sure they occasionally gave him some accurate but unimportant information to leak for credibility."

"So, if I'm right, do you think the Germans have no idea?" Wolf asked.

"Probably not," Anthony admitted.

Wolf continued rushing to make connections between this new information, "If all this is true, then presumably, the intelligence services would not be happy to have the spy ring exposed? Even if a murder had been committed." Anthony reluctantly agreed that this was possible.

"And what might they do, or might someone in their employ do to dissuade some over-enthusiastic investigators from pursuing their inquiries?"

While he didn't want to admit his natural father might stoop to kidnapping little children, it was hard to refute when it was plainly laid out in front of him. Anthony's services to the Crown had been informal and occasional enough that he was unsure how far the intelligence services might be prepared to go.

Wolf jumped to his feet, "We must go and confront Langley.

Somerset," he said apologetically, "I fear you must come with us. The man will deny everything. But he will know he has been exposed if you are with us." The duke looked incredibly uncomfortable at such a plan, but he was too honourable a man to do otherwise than agree to join them.

CHAPTER 28

Talbot, the other Talbot, had brought in the refreshments and served the dowager tea. "Could you please track down my guest and send her in?" Langley said to his butler. Tabitha was curious to meet this guest. Was she somehow connected to why Lord Langley was holding them at gunpoint? Though, to be fair, he was no longer pointing the weapon at them. It was hard to drink brandy and eat cake while brandishing a firearm.

Tabitha was unsure what the etiquette was for taking afternoon tea with a peer of the realm who had abducted you at gunpoint. Did one engage in the usual social chit-chat? Gossip about common acquaintances?

Luckily, she didn't need to wonder about this for long because the dowager took charge of the conversation in a way only she could. "Maxwell, I demand to know why you have taken us by force. It is quite an ungentlemanly thing to do. I would have thought your mother had raised you better. Something else to take up with her if she ever again deigns to grace us benighted souls in London."

The dowager stopped momentarily, considered her next move, and added, "Actually, perhaps I should write to her. I can't imagine the Fiona I knew as a debutante and then as a young wife and mother would countenance such behaviour from her only living son. I realise you were not raised for the earldom and, as the third son, were not even raised as the spare. Still, nevertheless, this is the most shocking social breach, and Lady Langley should know about it immediately."

The dowager paused again. Then, with a sly smile, she added, "I wouldn't be surprised if she weren't on the first train to

London as soon as she receives my missive. Certainly, it is what I will suggest to her in the strongest possible terms."

Tabitha was highly amused to see the always-pale Lord Langley blanch to an even more extreme skin pigment. He was the one with the gun, but it seemed the dowager was wielding the more dangerous weapon; the man was afraid of his mother. How delicious. There were times when Tabitha gave thanks for the older Lady Pembroke. There were also definitely times when she didn't, but even so.

Luckily, Lord Langley was saved from having to answer the dowager by the sound of the door opening. From where Tabitha and the dowager sat, they couldn't see who the mysterious guest was. But Langley was sitting in her line of sight and a small, high and excited voice called out, "Uncle Maxi, guess what? I helped bake a cake. I stirred it all myself, and Mrs Smith says I'm her special helper now."

Tabitha looked up in shock. She knew that voice. It was the voice so absent from her own home these many days. It was Melody. The little girl ran into the room, right up to Langley, and hugged his legs. It took a moment for her to register Tabitha and the dowager's presence in the room. "Melly," Tabitha cried out. It was clear the little girl was surprised to see the two women, but that surprise didn't seem to hold any particular relief at being rescued.

Melody ran up to Tabitha and hugged her eagerly, "Thank you, Tabby Cat, for sending me for a holiday with Uncle Maxi. It was so much fun when we played hide and seek with Mary in the park that first day. And then he told me all the lovely things we would do, and it's been even better than he said. Do you know," the child added conspiratorially, in a rather loud stage whisper, "that Uncle Maxi is far better at the tickle game than Wolfie is? And he plays it with me a lot more.

"And I've gotten so good with my letters. We work on them every day. And I can count to a hundred now, and I know some multification. And we play with Dodo in the garden every afternoon." Tabitha was so overwhelmed by the little girl's narrative that she didn't even question who Dodo might be

Five minutes ago, Langley was a gun-toting kidnapper of old ladies. Now it turned out he was Melody's abductor but apparently had been acting more like a beloved, indulgent family friend. She looked over at the man himself, and he gave a little shrug of his shoulders and made a face that indicated a certain embarrassment at having his evil villain persona so quickly and easily pierced.

Melody continued, excited to share all the wonderful things she had been doing with Uncle Maxi. Her litany of fun and learning was so long and told with such enthusiasm that Tabitha felt guilty; perhaps she hadn't provided a sufficiently stimulating environment for the child. The thought that Langley, Melody's kidnapper and a middle-aged single, childless man, was somehow better able to entertain and educate the child was sobering.

"Do I not get a kiss, Melody?" the dowager said. The little girl ran over to the older woman, who bent down to receive a kiss on the cheek.

"I've had so much fun, Granny. Is it time to come home?" The child said this with such wistfulness that it caused Tabitha paroxysms of even more parental self-doubt. Melody then added, "But I did miss all of you. I miss Rat, Wolfie, Mary, and you most of all, Tabby Cat."

Langley had smiled the first time Melody used this nickname, and this second time he commented, "The child has a wonderful imagination and has also given everyone in my household nicknames. She immediately noticed the similarity between my butler and yours. He is now known as Little Talbot after he informed her that he is a year younger than his cousin."

Lord Langley then leaned forward, rested his arms on his knees, and said in an avuncular tone, full of pride but also concern, "She is a very intelligent child, you know. I hope she is being educated at a high enough level at Chesterton House. She has shown signs of being quite gifted in several areas. Do you know she can now read? She knew most of her letters when she first arrived here, but we've been working daily on reading books, and she has picked it up at impressive speed."

Tabitha didn't know how to answer. Was she being criticised for her parenting skills by the man who had kidnapped a child from her nursemaid's care? Even worse, Tabitha worried he had a point. She answered more defensively than she intended, "I have engaged a tutor to work with Melody, and her nursemaid practices her letters with her every day."

"Her nursemaid! That slip of a girl who was with her in the park? Well, that explains it, then. And I question her tutor's teaching skills if I could teach her to read in just a few days."

Again, his words hit a nerve. While Tabitha had engaged a tutor, Mr James, he now taught various members of her household staff every day. Did he have enough time to devote to Melody? Was it possible Langley had a point?

"I'd like to suggest, well request really, that Melody come to me, perhaps even every day, and I will continue to study with her," Langley said with a certain hesitation. Even he realised the audaciousness of his proposal. He was unsure if Tabitha would allow him to leap from abductor to godfather.

Before Tabitha could answer this outrageous request, Melody ran back to Langley, climbed on his lap and said to Tabitha, "Please, Tabby Cat. Please let me come back every day to Uncle Maxi. I will miss him so much when I go home." Then she added in a heart-breakingly wise little voice, "And he will miss me. He lived here all alone before I came. He told me I bring the sunlight into his house."

The little girl then turned to Langley and said plaintively, "Who will sing Milly Dilly Philly to me before I go to bed every night?"

"Perhaps, I can teach Tabby Cat Milly Dilly Philly, and she can sing it to you. Or perhaps even Wolfie," Langley answered with a wicked grin aimed at Tabitha. Clearly, the idea of Wolf singing bedtime songs to a four-year-old girl struck him as absurd. As far as Tabitha was concerned, it was not as absurd as the idea that Langley had been doing so for almost two weeks.

Tabitha realised she had been put in an impossible situation. They still didn't know why Langley had taken Melody. She looked over at the dowager for guidance. Heavens help her. Is this what it had come to?

For once, the dowager seemed quite lost for words. Making eye contact with Tabitha and seeing the mixed emotions play out on the younger woman's face, she said, "This one unfortunate incident aside, that I would hope is a minor aberration that will both be explained and apologised for forthwith, I have known Lord Langley his entire life. The child has clearly been well cared for and even flourished while in his care. I see no harm in allowing her to continue to visit." The dowager paused and added, "Of course, her regular cadence of visits with me will take precedence, Langley."

He bowed his head, "I would expect nothing less, your ladyship."

Tabitha listened to the Dowager Countess of Pembroke and the Earl of Langley haggle over visitation rights for a child who, a few months ago, was living on the streets unwanted. Tabitha felt she might have fallen through writer Lewis Carroll's looking glass. She half expected to look up from her brandy and see Alice having tea with Tweedledum and Tweedledee. Barely an hour before, she had been scared about defending her honour against a possible German spy. Then she had been kidnapped at gunpoint, and now she was discussing which highly placed member of the beau monde would take priority with a four-year-old orphaned girl.

Just as she felt that day could not get any more surreal, Wolf, Bear and the Duke of Somerset burst into the drawing room. After Wolf's epiphany, they had rushed over to Langley's residence and as good as forced their way into the house. "Where is your master?" Wolf had demanded. The butler, noting Bear's size, pointed towards the drawing room.

Wolf wasn't sure what he expected to find. In the short time it had taken to get there from Rowley House, he had begun to envision Langley with a medieval torture chamber setup in his reception rooms. He didn't expect to find Tabitha and the dowager calmly taking afternoon refreshments and Melody sitting happily on Langley's lap. The tableau brought him up short. Such was the abrupt change in pace that Anthony and Bear almost ran into his back.

Wolf took in the scene, and its participants took in the sight of the Duke of Somerset and the Earl of Pembroke rushing into the room. It seems everyone was at a loss for words. Langley was the first to recover his composure, saying, "Tea or something stronger, gentlemen?"

Tabitha held her glass aloft and said, "I must warn you that after the day I've had, I opted for brandy. I suggest you do the same. Whatever caused you to storm in here, I can guarantee this tale will not be all you expect."

Gathering his composure, Wolf gestured to Melody, happily ensconced on the lap of her abductor, and replied, "That much is clear."

Bear stayed by the door and Wolf and Anthony moved further into the room and sat in armchairs. Both indicated their need for something stronger than tea and Talbot, who had followed them into the room, obliged.

Then they all sat there, looking at each other; no one quite sure what to say. Finally, after a few sips of brandy, Wolf turned to Tabitha and asked, "How did you come to be here?"

Now there was a question. Tabitha took a deep breath and said, "Well, I went to luncheon with Count von Kletzer."

She got no further when Wolf stood up and demanded, "You did what? What on earth were you thinking?"

"I couldn't agree more, Pembroke," Lord Langley agreed. "What on earth were you thinking, Lady Pembroke?"

Tabitha wasn't sure which of them to glare at first or most. Finally, she landed upon the one who had kidnapped her at gunpoint, "I was thinking to investigate whether or not he had abducted Melody. I wouldn't have bothered if I had known she was having a lovely little holiday just around the corner from home."

At this point, they seemed to make a collective decision that the conversation was headed in a direction not for little, sharp ears, and Tabitha said, "Melly, dear. Perhaps you can go play for a little before we go home."

"Yes, sweetheart," Lord Langley said.

Sweetheart? Tabitha thought.

Langley continued, "Perhaps you can go and play with Dodo and round up her toys."

As much as Tabitha hated to digress from their conversation, she had to ask, "Who exactly is Dodo?"

Melody jumped off Langley's lap and clapped her hands in glee, "Uncle Maxi gave me a puppy."

The man had taken her at gunpoint, abducted her ward, and who knows what else, but as far as Tabitha was concerned, this was the straw that broke the camel's back. "You gave the child a dog without consulting me? What on earth were you thinking, Langley?" she asked angrily.

To be fair, the man did look rather shamefaced. "Well, I felt Melody needed company during her visit. I can't be home all day, after all. And Talbot is not really a child person. So, I thought a puppy would keep her company."

It was clear from the look on all his visitors' faces that they had a lot to say on the subject, but everyone realised it was best to keep such thoughts to themselves until the little girl had left the room. As soon as she did, the dowager said in the same voice she likely used on him when Lord Langley was ten years old, "Maxwell, what on earth were you thinking? I'm unsure where to start in my missive to your dear mama."

Eager to share his discovery, Wolf jumped in, "Let's start with the fact that Langley is a spy for British Intelligence, and he kidnapped Melody to try to stop us from investigating Claire Murphy's murder. He didn't want us to expose the Fenian-German spy ring because Naval Intelligence was already aware and feeding it false information." On pronouncing his final reveal, he sat down and crossed one leg over the other triumphantly.

"Is it true, Maxwell? Is that what this absurd charade today has been about? Is this why you abducted Melody?" the dowager demanded.

Lord Langley shifted uncomfortably in his seat. What had he expected to achieve by kidnapping a small child? It seemed like a good idea at the time. He knew Wolf and Tabitha had been sniffing around and felt they were getting too close to the truth. He had hoped, even assumed, that they would be quickly and easily put off by the threat to the child's safety. He certainly hadn't expected that to spur them on even more fervently.

If he was honest with himself, it had been clear days ago that they hadn't stopped their investigations. When he spotted Somerset and Pembroke talking with Sir Desmond at White's, he knew how close they were getting. That would have been the right time to pivot and return Melody. But he'd grown fond of her and was enjoying her company. So, he had rationalised his continued holding on to the child to himself and his higher-ups. Only now did he realise he had only upped the ante in the investigation by taking the child.

Perhaps the hardest part of this entire situation was the disappointment he saw in his son's eyes. Lord Langley and the Duke of Somerset had maintained a cordial, arms-length relationship for some time. Since the old duke's death, Langley had held out hope he and his natural son might begin to forge a closer relationship. When the appropriate mourning period was over, and Langley could openly court and marry Anthony's mother, Cassandra, perhaps they might even arrive at something like a genuine father-son bond. Looking at his son's face now, Langley realised how much damage he had done to that dream, perhaps irreparably.

Given how much the group before him already knew, or at least guessed, it was clear that there was nothing to be gained by further subterfuge. However, it was also clear some eating of crow was needed first. "You are right, Lady Pembroke, as always. What was I thinking? Taking Melody was neither my finest moment nor my sagest decision. My only defence is that these

Fenian-German spies imperil the security of this great nation. It was felt, by people far higher than I am, to be imperative that the operation we have set up not be exposed."

"Are you saying Her Majesty's government knowingly harboured a leaker of sensitive information?" the dowager asked incredulously.

"It is not unheard of for those acting on behalf of Her Majesty's government to not act under such circumstance and instead feed false information to someone they believe has been compromised," Langley admitted.

"Ha!" cried the dowager. The dowager might not understand the machinery of government. Still, she understood the battlefield operations of aristocratic society. She knew a thing or two about harbouring a viper in one's bosom with ulterior motives.

"This spying business has far more in common with the machinations of society than I realised. Why, when I want to circulate a particularly salacious piece of gossip, true or otherwise, but don't wish it attributed to me, I always let it slip to Lady Hartley. The woman is a shrew and the worst gossip there is. She cannot keep a secret for love or money. Ideally, I don't even tell her the gossip directly. Instead, I ensure she overhears it. She loves nothing more than being the first person in society to know something titillating and supposedly private. You are saying Sir Desmond is a Lady Hartley?"

While the two situations weren't entirely analogous, Langley could see the futility in trying to persuade the dowager that government espionage was any different from society tittle-tattle, so he agreed.

Tabitha had to ask, "But who killed Claire Murphy?"

Realising he needed to explain fully, Langley said, "Count von Kletzer visited Claire on Sunday evenings, and she delivered whatever information she had discovered from Sir Desmond. We believe the butler is a Fenian. But it seems the rest of the staff were quite innocent of the spying going on in the house and needed to be kept out of the way.

"As I think you may know from your visit to Dr Blackwell, Claire Murphy was pregnant. Having met von Kletzer, I'm sure you can appreciate he is the kind of man to take advantage of a beautiful young woman. We believe she was carrying von Kletzer's child and had begun to make demands on him, becoming a liability. The most likely scenario is that von Kletzer killed her, and the butler helped stage the discovery of Manning at the scene," he added.

"So, you know Manning is innocent and yet have left me managing with the inferior services of a footman for weeks now instead of my butler?" the dowager said with great indignation. "Whatever was the government thinking? I shall complain personally to the Home Secretary," she threatened. "Do you know, Lady Browning visited the other day, and we almost had a tea-spilling incident? Good gracious man, this is unforgivable!"

Tabitha looked at Langley's face and realised that as absurd as the dowager's complaints were, she had somehow struck real terror into the man's heart. Tabitha had to wonder just how much childhood trauma the dowager had managed to cause Maxwell Sandworth, Earl of Langley, that she could reduce him to such a puddle of self-doubt now? Given this, it was amazing that the man had somehow summoned the nerve to kidnap the dowager. Though now she thought about it, he may not have realised she and Tabitha would be a packaged deal. By the time it was evident which Chesterton carriage he had hijacked, the die had already been cast. Thinking about the discomfort such knowledge must have caused him made Tabitha smile.

However, the dowager's complaints about her household staff aside, she had made one valid point, "So, what was the plan?" Tabitha asked. "Were you going to let an innocent man hang for a crime you, and the government, knew he didn't commit?"

By this point, Langley was squirming on his chair like a boy being called out in class by his teacher. "Well, erm, well, we certainly wouldn't have let it get that far?" he claimed.

"How far would you have let it go? An innocent man is awaiting trial in prison, with a likely death sentence hanging over his head. At what point would there have been an intervention?" Wolf chimed in.

Langley realised he had no good answer for this and tried to move away from hypotheticals about what miscarriage of justice the intelligence services may or may not have been willing to allow. Instead, he said, "I will ensure Mr Manning is released today. The official word, leaked to the newspapers, will be that new evidence has come to light that he is innocent but that the actual culprit remains unknown."

The dowager said tartly, "About time, too. I have to wonder if and when you would have seen to this if I hadn't imposed myself on you today."

This complete rewriting of the day's events was so outrageous that no one had any comment to make. However, Langley, trying to take back control of the conversation, said in a severe voice, "However, I must have the assurance of everyone that any investigation into this death or the spy ring will cease immediately. And that none of you will speak of this matter nor what you have learned about the roles Somerset and I have in the intelligence services."

Tabitha, Wolf, Bear and the dowager glanced at each other. With the promise of Manning's freedom, absolution, and Melody's return, they had no reason to continue investigating. Wolf spoke for all of them when he said, "You have our word, Langley."

CHAPTER 29

Before they left Lord Langley's house, the man had awkwardly returned the dowager's coachman and footman, who were unharmed but rather shamefaced. "Maxwell, don't think this won't all go in my letter to your dear mama. I expect and hope she will be appropriately appalled at today's shenanigans."

Langley sighed. Beyond national security, he had to handle this situation carefully for his own sake. "Lady Pembroke, while I offer my sincerest apology to you and your staff for the inconvenience caused today, you just gave your word to remain silent about what you have learned today."

Rarely at a loss for words, the dowager stood and stared at him, "Well, it goes without saying I will not be discussing the investigation, but your shameful behaviour today is surely a separate matter?"

"It is not, your ladyship. Everything I did was for the cause of national security and on behalf of Her Majesty's government. You cannot talk about any of it." Lord Langley could see the wheels turning in the woman's head as she attempted to devise a rationalisation for a carved-out exception to the promise she had just made. He had known the dowager his entire life and understood her all too well. While she claimed Lady Hartley was a terrible gossip, in reality, the dowager was the one who loved being the first person to know society's secrets. She adored being able to drip such information out as she saw fit. Being denied such a role would pain the woman deeply.

"So, what can I write to Lady Langley?" she demanded.

It was clear he would have to throw her a bone if only to get his home back any time that afternoon. He just wasn't sure what that might be. He said, "You cannot mention Melody's stay here, anything to do with the Claire Murphy murder or anything that alludes to my intelligence role. Or, indeed, Somerset's. I'm assuming it goes without saying that the unfortunate need to detain you this afternoon also must not be mentioned. "

"I'm assuming it will not threaten national security if I mention that I was here for tea this afternoon and that the house is in an alarming state. It needs to be redecorated and refurnished immediately. Quite disgraceful," she countered.

Lord Langley did not entertain guests. Ever. He enjoyed his own company, and he found his house to be homey. The fact that it was essentially unchanged since his childhood felt comfortable. However, it was not lost on him that if he wished to woo and win Cassandra, the Duchess of Somerset, he might need to freshen up the house he hoped she might one day call hers. Because he didn't understand women, it never occurred to him that if he and the duchess were to marry, she would likely redecorate the house, no matter how recently it had already been done.

Langley had no time, patience, or interest in overseeing a redecoration. His mother coming to town to take charge wasn't the worst outcome. He conceded the point to the dowager, "I see no reason why that particular horror might not be shared with my mother. I'm sure she will be as appalled as you anticipate."

Maxwell Langley resigned himself to the likely outcome of such a communication. He wasn't sure his mother would care about the state of the house. She never came to London, and it was unlikely to surprise her to hear her bachelor son had made no effort with its upkeep. However, hearing this criticism from the dowager, a friend, at least in the sense of the word women of the aristocracy understood it to mean, would surely spur his mother to abandon her pastoral peace and rush to London. If nothing else, she could never countenance the idea of the Dowager Countess of Pembroke whispering all over town that Lady Langley knowingly allowed the family's London home to become derelict.

With that problem dealt with, there was nothing more to be done other than to corral Melody and send his guests on their way.

"What about the dog?" Tabitha asked. Tabitha's mother hated animals. So, except for some hunting hounds her father had kept at the estate, dogs had not been a part of her childhood. Tabitha was happy to maintain that status quo. "Perhaps, Dodo should stay here and be Melody's pet at Uncle Maxi's." She couldn't help the sarcasm that leeched into her tone. It would be a while before she could be comfortable with Uncle Maxi's new role in her ward's life.

As Tabitha said this, Melody came down the stairs holding her new puppy. While Tabitha didn't know one breed from another, Langley informed her the dog was a Cavalier King Charles Spaniel. That meant nothing to Tabitha. However, even she could admire the tiny dog. The puppy had an expressive face with large, dark and soulful eyes. Its coat was a rich chestnut colour and was medium-length, silky, and beautifully feathered.

"My mother has always had Spaniels," Langley explained. "They are wonderful dogs and make particularly delightful companions for children.

Tabitha looked at the man saying pointedly, "And one day, Lord Langley, if and when you have children of your own, you can surround them with as many of these delightful creatures as you wish. In your home!" How was she going to get out of this dilemma? It was clear from the look on Melody's face that the child was utterly delighted with her new pet. Tabitha could hardly bear to break the little girl's heart, particularly given the situation of the last couple of weeks.

If Tabitha was honest with herself, a little part of her worried Melody might not want to return to Chesterton House and would instead want to stay with Uncle Maxi. Tabitha had no real claim on the orphaned child, after all. If Tabitha insisted on leaving the puppy behind, would Melody still go home willingly with Tabitha? As Melody descended the last stair, Tabitha approached her and looked at the puppy happily nestled in

Melody's embrace.

Tabitha looked into those huge liquid chocolate eyes and put her hand out to stroke the soft, silky ears. And then the dog licked her hand. It had a soft little pink tongue that administered eager little licks. It wasn't as unpleasant a sensation as Tabitha had imagined.

In a voice that indicated she knew she had already lost the battle, she said weakly, "I know nothing about training dogs."

"But I do," Wolf surprised her by saying. "We always had dogs in the house when I was a boy. Honestly, I've missed having some around. I think Dodo will be a great addition to the household." Tabitha realised Chesterton House was Wolf's home, not her's anymore. It was only right he had the final say.

"As you can imagine, my household was unequipped for a child's extended stay, so I bought some clothes, books and toys for Melody. I will keep most of the books and some toys here for when she visits," Langley explained rather sheepishly.

Tabitha could only nod in acknowledgement.

Wolf and Anthony had come in the Somerset carriage. With the dowager's coachman and footman still quite discombobulated from their afternoon's trauma, the duke suggested that Tabitha, Wolf, Melody, and Dodo return to Chesterton House with him. Bear offered to walk the short way home.

The trip was quite chaotic. As the carriage began to move, Dodo became overly excited, perhaps even scared. Tabitha was concerned the puppy might throw up or worse.

The ride was blessedly short. Within a few minutes, they had pulled up outside of Chesterton House. As Talbot opened the door to greet them, Melody rushed into the house and hugged his legs. "Talbot, Talbot, you'll never guess who I'm friends with now? Your cousin, Little Talbot."

The normally inscrutable butler looked at his master and mistress and raised his eyebrows just a fraction in question.

"It's a long story, Talbot. But suffice it to say that Miss Melody has had a delightful little holiday at Lord Langley's,"

Wolf answered the man's unspoken question. He and Tabitha hadn't had time to consider what story they might tell their household staff. Everyone knew Melody had been kidnapped. Her continued absence from the house had caused every servant to be downcast, and Mary was still inconsolable every time Melody's name came up.

It was inconceivable that the child could reappear in the house without some explanation. It was likely Melody would talk about her time with Uncle Maxi. Better to get ahead of any staff speculation. But how? Luckily, Tabitha had considered this very concern since the moment Melody ran into Lord Langley's drawing room, "Talbot, it was all a huge misunderstanding. While it seemed to Mary, Lord Pembroke, and me as if Melody had been abducted, Lord Langley meant it all as a silly prank." Even as she said these words, Tabitha realised how absurdly unbelievable they were. But she hoped that whatever Talbot might think, the rest of the staff would take this story at face value and not ask questions.

The butler's disbelief at her story was clear when he raised his eyebrows again, but higher, at this statement, "Yes, not the best prank, I agree," Tabitha continued a little too hurriedly. "And trust me, Lord Pembroke and I have had strong words with his lordship about the distress he has caused this entire household, not the least Mary. However, Miss Melody had a delightful time and has even returned home with a pet."

At this, the butler looked down at the puppy Melody had now placed on the floor. The tall, quite imposing, and normally entirely decorous butler got down on his impeccably dressed haunches and put out a hand. The spaniel ran over to him, and the man began to stroke the silky ears.

"What a delightful puppy, Miss Melody. What is her name?" he asked.

"Dodo," the little girl said proudly. "From Alice in Wonderland. Remember, Talbot, when you read that to me?"

"I do indeed, Miss Melody. What a marvellous name."

"And, Talbot, I can read now. All by myself. Uncle Maxi taught me," the little girl said excitedly.

By this time, word of her return had spread to the servants' quarters, and all the staff rushed in to greet the beloved child, including Rat who rushed to hug his little sister, relief shining in his eyes at her safe return.

Mary, who had been at quite a loose end with the absence of her charge, and spent her time moping in the nursery, was the last person in the house to hear that Melody had come home. But now, she ran down the stairs and threw all etiquette to the wind, sweeping the child up in her arms and, with tears streaming down her face, hugging her as if she would never let her go.

"Mary, I missed you. Wait until you see my new doll from Uncle Maxi and hear how good my reading and numbers are. Oh, and I have a new dotty dress that is so pretty. Uncle Maxi said I look like a princess in it." The little girl continued her stream of consciousness.

Every servant took their turn greeting Melody, though Mary was unwilling to let the girl out of her arms. Finally, calm was restored. Melody went to the nursery with Mary, and Dodo went to the kitchen so Mrs Jenkins could find something suitable for the dog to eat and ensure a bowl of fresh water.

They had been in the house for more than fifteen minutes, but it was only now, when they were finally alone in the vestibule, that Wolf spotted the new telephone and said, "What on earth is that contraption doing here?"

"The dowager had it installed this morning," Tabitha said as if that explanation were sufficient. "She feels she needs a quicker, more efficient way to communicate with us for future investigations. In which she believes she will be a key player," she added with an edge to her voice. "There was an explanatory note if you wish to see it."

Wolf ran his hands through his hair, "I've never had cause to use one of these things. I don't even know how it works."

"Well, you speak into it and the person on the other end answers. Talbot has been instructed on how to place a call, and it doesn't seem unduly difficult. Of course," she pointed out, leading the way into the parlour, "I fear the greatest challenge will not be the operation of the technology but an increased frequency of dialogue with the dowager countess." Tabitha had just sat down in her favourite chair as she said this when the telephone's discordant bells rang out.

Wolf started, "What on earth is that noise?"

"That is the telephone," Tabitha replied. "Given only one person is aware we now have such a communications device, I fear my previous words have been quite prescient; it must be the dowager calling."

"And what do we do now? How do we stop the noise?" Wolf asked.

"Well, apparently, the correct telephone etiquette is that Talbot will answer and either relay a message or call for one of us."

No sooner had she said this than Talbot entered the room and said sonorously, "The Dowager Countess of Pembroke is calling, milord."

"She wants to speak to me?" Wolf asked incredulously. "You talk to her, Tabitha. I don't want to use that machine."

"Oh no!" Tabitha grinned and said, "If she wants to talk with you, you might as well get it over and done with. You know she will not be put off."

Grumbling under his breath, Wolf went to take his first telephone call. He wasn't sure how far away from his ear to hold the headpiece, but when he said a tentative hello into the mouthpiece, and a loud voice boomed into his ear, he decided a little further away was best. "Jeremy dear, I wanted to let you know I returned home safely," the booming voice said.

Given that the dowager lived no more than a five-minute ride from Lord Langley's house, the odds of some calamity befalling her were low. However, Wolf considered that the older woman had been held up at gunpoint earlier that day, so perhaps she was allowed some consideration. For now, at least.

The dowager continued, "And I want to remind you that, while I understand Melody will need a few days to acclimate back to Chesterton House, I expect our regular cadence of visits to resume on Saturday." She paused and added, "The dog is not invited."

"Of course, Lady Pembroke. Melody will see you on Saturday."

Wolf hoped this would be the end of the conversation, but he was to be disappointed. "And Jeremy dear, while I realise the child has inexplicably formed an attachment to Lord Langley, and as beyond belief as it may be, it seems reciprocated, I hope it is fully understood that any time she spends with him will not be coming out of my allotment."

Wolf assured her it was fully understood by all involved and was hopeful this new technological experience could now come to an end. But the dowager, realising she now had a whole new way to ensure a captive audience, rattled on for at least another five minutes about nothing in particular. She might have kept talking for longer if not for the fact that Talbot, correctly assessing his master's distress, said very loudly, "Milord, your steward is here and must see you." Giving the man a grateful smile, Wolf told the dowager he must go and put the receiver back before she could give any rebuttal.

Over the next couple of weeks, life fell back into old rhythms. Wolf began meeting regularly with his man of business and steward, and Tabitha visited the Dulwich house. But life at Chesterton House had some new routines as well. While Melody continued to visit with the dowager on Tuesdays, Thursdays, and Saturdays, Mondays, Wednesdays, and Fridays became her time with Uncle Maxi. She would study with her tutor for an hour or two in the morning, have lunch, often joined in the nursery by Rat and sometimes by Tabitha, and then, accompanied by a still wary Mary, travel the short distance to spend the afternoon with Lord Langley.

Despite her initial wariness about allowing the child to spend time with the man who had kidnapped her, Tabitha had to admit Melody's education had really come along. One day, the child came home and announced that Uncle Maxi had taught her chess. The normally taciturn, one might even say socially

241

awkward lord, seemed to delight in the four-year-old's company and opening her mind to new ideas and learning. Despite her animosity towards the man, Tabitha found it hard not to appreciate his effort with Melody.

The other regular occurrences were phone calls. It started with the dowager calling daily and asking for Tabitha or Wolf. She rarely had anything of substance to say and merely wanted to gossip. Neither Tabitha nor Wolf had the patience for this. It was one thing to be held captive in the woman's drawing room, confined by the rules of etiquette to stay seated and smile politely. Feeling compelled to do so in one's own home was another thing. And so, Talbot was instructed to make excuses for why neither could come to the phone.

Whether she believed the excuses or not, the dowager seemed not to care who she spoke with, as long as it was someone. Consequently, she began bending the poor butler's ear. Until after a few days. a miracle happened. It was so simple and obvious that they all wondered why they had not considered it before. One day the phone rang, and Melody answered it. She had watched them all pick up the earpiece and speak into the mouthpiece and apparently knew what to do. Tabitha then watched in amazement as the child spoke to Granny for fifteen minutes, at least. Hearing only Melody's side of the conversation, she wasn't entirely sure what they talked about. There was a lot about Dodo, then long periods of silence on Melody's part, then some stuff about her favourite doll.

The next day, hearing the phone ring loudly throughout the house, Melody rushed down from the nursery, worried someone else would get to the phone before her; she need not have been concerned. Realising a saviour when he saw one, Wolf instructed Talbot to move the phone to a lower table and put a small chair beside it.

After a week, Tabitha realised the dowager's calls were disrupting Melody's schedule. She took the phone before the end of the next conversation and suggested to the dowager that she call at ten o'clock each morning, just before Melody's tutor came.

This settled, the phone's ringing was no longer a source of panic for Tabitha, Wolf, or Talbot.

EPILOGUE

It had been almost three weeks since Melody's return to Chesterton House, and everyone felt settled and relaxed finally. At ten on the dot that Monday morning, the telephone rang, and Tabitha, who was reading in the parlour, heard Melody rush to answer it. A minute or so later, the parlour door opened, and a little face appeared around it, "Tabby Cat, Granny wants to speak with you."

Tabitha felt an immediate tightness in her chest; she couldn't imagine what her mother-in-law might want with her now. Putting her book down, she left the parlour, picked up the telephone and said warily, "Mama, how lovely to talk with you. How can I help?

"Tabitha, I wanted to let you know I will be leaving town for a few weeks, maybe a month, maybe longer. We will have to pause Melody's visits but make sure Langley doesn't get any ideas about taking my slots permanently, even if he uses them while I'm gone."

Tabitha couldn't imagine where the dowager might be going for so long. The woman was notorious for her refusal to leave London. While many only came to town for the season, retreating to country estates immediately after, the dowager had always preferred to stay in her London house year-round.

"Where are you going, Mama?"

"Scotland," the woman said with little enthusiasm. "It's my eldest Jane, well, her daughter, to be precise. I don't know whether you remember Jane. She's the one Jonathan agreed to marry off to that Scottish heathen."

Tabitha didn't remember the exact details of the story. She did know the dowager's contention was that, with his father dead, the new young earl was happy to take the first offer made for his sister. Tabitha had known Jane had married a Scot and, from what she could remember, had a brood of children.

Luckily, the dowager was extremely comfortable holding one-sided conversations, in fact, she usually preferred it. She continued with no response needed from Tabitha, "Her girl is eighteen and ready to come out. Jane would like to ensure she makes a good marriage and has asked me to sponsor her for the season. But even Jane admits the girl needs some polish."

The dowager paused, then continued, "I'm sure polish hardly does justice to what the child will need having grown up amongst savages. The season will be upon us before we know it. Sponsoring some country bumpkin will reflect poorly on me, to say nothing of what will be said when people find out she's my granddaughter. I have no choice but to sacrifice my health and possibly my safety and make an expedition to the wilds of the north and see what miracle I can manage to pull off in a few weeks."

The woman paused briefly for breath, but Tabitha could think of no response to make. Luckily, it was but a moment before the dowager started up again, "At least they are not currently in residence at that crumbling pile of stone he calls a castle. Apparently, rather than coming to London like a normal person, her husband prefers to visit Edinburgh from time to time. I believe they have a townhouse there. One can only hope it has modern plumbing and other conveniences. As it is, I'm taking Manning with me. I don't know what language those forsaken Scottish servants might speak. I need to ensure my needs are appropriately met. Anyway, I must go and supervise the packing." And with that, she hung up the telephone.

When Wolf returned later that day, Tabitha informed him of the unexpected reprieve they seemed to have from any demands the dowager might see fit to make. Then, they thought nothing more of it.

A telegram was delivered three days later while Tabitha and Wolf ate breakfast. Talbot delivered it to Wolf, who opened and read it, then passed it to Tabitha.

With a sinking heart, she read, "Come at once. I am in great need of your expertise. Time is of the essence. I am depending on you."

"Edinburgh! She expects us to drop everything and run up to Scotland, and she doesn't even say why," Wolf said in exasperation.

"We could just refuse," Tabitha mused. "We could send a telegram and say we cannot spare the time."

Wolf looked at her. It was a look that said so much. It said, "Wouldn't it be wonderful if we could do that? But if we did, we would pay for such insubordination for the rest of our lives." And then, finally, the look morphed into resignation, and he said, "I'll ask Talbot to pack for me. Should we bring Bear with us?" What was Tabitha's wedding to Jonathan really like?

❊ ❊ ❊

What was Tabitha's wedding to Jonathan really like? Discover exclusive short stories about your favourite characters, and more, by signing up for my newsletter.

AFTERWORD

Thank you for reading **A Singular Woman**. I hope you enjoyed it. If you'd like to see what's coming next for Tabitha & Wolf, here are some ways to stay in touch:

SarahFNoel.com
Facebook
@sarahfNoelAuthor - Twitter
Instagram

Coming in February Book 5 of the Tabitha & Wolf Mystery series - **An Audacious Woman**

The Dowager Countess of Pembroke is missing!

While Wolf is contemplating whether or not he wishes to continue taking on investigations, it seems that the dowager has taken the matter into her own hands and is investigating a case independently. But why has she gone missing from her home for two nights and what mischief has she got herself into? Tracking down the elderly woman takes Tabitha and Wolf into some of the darkest, most dangerous corners of the city.

What on earth is the exasperating dowager caught up in that she seems to have become entangled with London's prostitutes?

ABOUT THE AUTHOR

Sarah F. Noel

Originally from London, Sarah F. Noel now spends most of her time in Grenada in the Caribbean. Sarah loves reading historical mysteries with strong female characters. The Tabitha & Wolf Mystery Series is exactly the kind of book she would love to curl up with on a lazy Sunday.

THE TABITHA & WOLF HISTORICAL MYSTERY SERIES

Tabitha, Lady Chesterton, the Countess of Pembroke, is newly widowed at 22. Her childless marriage to Jonathan, the deceased Earl of Pembroke, was unhappy and abusive. Jonathan's heir, Jeremy Wolfson Chesterton, known as Wolf, is a very different man from his predecessor. Before his unexpected elevation to an earldom, Wolf worked as a thief-taker, spending time in the least salubrious London neighbourhoods.

Now Tabitha finds herself sharing a house with the new earl, a handsome, charming, but, unlike her husband, also a kind man. And despite Wolf's desire to leave his thief-taking days behind him, it's harder than he had hoped, and he keeps getting dragged into cases of theft and murder. To his initial dismay, Tabitha insists on being involved in the cases.

Can a very proper Victorian countess not only find a place in some very sordid criminal cases but even become an indispensable part of the investigations? This new historical mystery series from writer Sarah F. Noel follows this unlikely but delightful investigative pairing.

A Proud Woman

Tabitha was used to being a social pariah. Could her standing in society get any worse?

Tabitha, Lady Chesterton, the Countess of Pembroke, is newly widowed at only 22 years of age. With no son to inherit the title, it falls to a dashing, distant cousin of her husband's, Jeremy Chesterton, known as Wolf. It quickly becomes apparent that Wolf had consorted with some of London's most dangerous citizens before inheriting the title. Can he leave this world behind, or will shadowy figures from his past follow him into his new aristocratic life in Mayfair? And can Tabitha avoid being caught up in Wolf's dubious activities?

It seems it's well and truly time for Tabitha to leave her gilded cage behind for good!

An Independent Woman

Summoned to Edinburgh by the Dowager Countess of Pembroke, Tabitha and Wolf reluctantly board a train and head north to Scotland.

The dowager's granddaughter, Lily, refuses to participate in the preparations for her first season unless Tabitha and Wolf investigate the disappearance of her friend, Peter. Initially sceptical of the need to investigate, Tabitha and Wolf quickly realise that the idealistic Peter may have stumbled upon dark secrets. How far would someone go to cover their tracks?

Tabitha is drawn into Edinburgh's seedy underbelly as she and Wolf try to solve the case while attempting to keep the dowager in the dark about Peter's true identity.

An Inexplicable Woman

Who is this mysterious woman from Wolf's past who can so easily summon him to her side?

When Lady Arlene Archibald tracks Wolf down and begs him for help, he plans to travel to Brighton alone to see her. What was he thinking? Instead, he finds himself with an unruly entourage of lords, ladies, servants, children, and even a dog. Can and will he help Arlene prove her friend's innocence? How will he manage Tabitha coming face-to-face with his first love? And how is he to dissuade the Dowager Countess of Pembroke from insinuating herself into the investigation?

Beneath its veneer of holiday, seaside fun, Brighton may be more sinister than it seems.

An Audacious Woman

The Dowager Countess of Pembroke is missing!

While Wolf is contemplating whether or not he wishes to continue taking on investigations, it seems that the dowager has taken the matter into her own hands and is investigating a case independently. But why has she gone missing from her home for two nights and what mischief has she got herself into? Tracking down the elderly woman takes Tabitha and Wolf into some of the darkest, most dangerous corners of the city.

What on earth is the exasperating dowager caught up in that she seems to have become entangled with London's prostitutes?